An evil presence in the shadows of Yellowstone

Amy scrambled back up the trunk. She screamed as the grizzly slammed into the tree with the force of a large truck. Shaken loose, she began to fall, but grabbed at branches and caught herself before she tumbled completely down.

Scrambling again, she pulled herself back up, but not before the grizzly had raked its claws down the back of her right leg.

The grizzly rose onto its hind legs. Its huge paws came up towards her. With a tremendous roar, the bear began stripping bark from the trunk, clawing it into fragments. . . .

THE QUIET

PATRICK BILLINGS

TOR
HORROR ®

A TOM DOHERTY ASSOCIATES BOOK
NEW YORK

THE QUIET

Cover art by Jim Thiesen

A Tor Book
Published by Tom Doherty Associates, Inc.
175 Fifth Avenue
New York, N.Y. 10010

Tor® is a registered trademark of Tom Doherty Associates, Inc.

ISBN: 0-812-52131-5

First edition: July 1994

Printed in the United States of America

0 9 8 7 6 5 4 3 2 1

To Sergeant John Rosenberg,
good friend and dedicated lawman.
Thanks for the help over the years.

I would like to extend grateful acknowledgement to Mr. Howard Teten, FBI, retired, for his generous sharing of time and experience in the profiling of serial killers; to Ms. Sandra Mays, Wyoming State Crime Lab, for her gracious assistance in detailing field and laboratory crime work, and to Mr. Kerry Gunther, Yellowstone National Park, who gave me an inside look at bear biology in our nation's last great wilderness.

Also, for their help and support, I would like to thank Mr. Don Despain, biologist, Yellowstone National Park; Mr. Pete Dunbar, FBI, retired; Mr. Ken Goddard, Director, National Fish and Wildlife Forensics Laboratory; Ms. Marsha Karle, Public Affairs Officer, Yellowstone National Park; and Mr. Michael R. Wright, FBI.

And a special thanks to my editor, Harriet P. McDougal, for her great depth of feeling and understanding, and for her ability to fine-tune a manuscript to its highest possible key. Nobody does it better.

The mind is a useful servant,
but a bad master.

—Paul Twitchell
The Spiritual Notebook

one

A MIDNIGHT moon shone brightly over Yellowstone Lake. In a secluded area near Bridge Bay Campground, the sounds of a private party echoed through the trees. Three kegs of beer and a live band had brought everyone to a dancing mood.

Along the shoreline, a massive grizzly bear, hidden in the shadows of tall pines, lumbered toward the music. A continuous low growl rumbled from its throat, and it stopped often to tear up small trees and rip holes in the forest floor.

No one at the party could hear the bear approaching. No one had any idea that eight hundred pounds of rage was just two hundred feet away.

Amy Ellerman ran her fingers through her shoulder-length blond hair and moved closer to the fire. The mid-July night had been pleasant, but a sudden breeze was stirring, bringing clouds across the lake.

Amy had been in Yellowstone Park since early June, studying forest burn areas. She was particularly interested in a small wild geranium that frequently grows on newly burned slopes and ridges. Her Ph.D. in plant ecology depended on finding and sampling the geranium, and comparing its numbers with other postfire plant species.

The raging flames of '88 had left scarred hillsides that were now forming new plant communities. Amy had been studying the plants for three years. She wanted to become the foremost authority on the revegetation of forest burn areas.

Beside her sat Allen Freeman, the featured actor in a major motion picture that had just completed shooting in and around the park. He had played the role of a smoke jumper in the 1930s who had saved a young woman and her family from a wall of flames.

Freeman, now in his midthirties, had become a major box office attraction. This latest film was destined to make him *the* major male star of Hollywood.

Amy listened to the band and watched the dancers as Freeman discussed the beauty of the area. He wanted to come back and look for land to buy.

Those words made Amy feel good. She had thought about spending her life in the area, if she could. She had known Freeman just three weeks but was convinced she cared about him deeply. She wanted their futures to merge and hoped to see tonight that he felt the same way.

"Good party," Amy commented. "Everyone really had a good time making the film, didn't they?"

"It was great," Freeman said. "I wish there could have been some *real* adventure, though. It would have been interesting to run into one of those mad bears they've been talking about."

"I don't think so," Amy said. "Mad bears can't be any fun."

Freeman was looking across the lake. "They never have figured out who the woman was that was killed in June, have they?"

"I don't think so," Amy said. "That was horrible."

"The park people didn't let the press get near her. She must have been mauled pretty bad."

"Don't talk about it, Allen," Amy pleaded. "You're giving me the creeps." She turned her face skyward as clouds slowly began to obscure the moon. "We should be inside somewhere. It's going to rain."

"Why now?" Allen Freeman complained. "Why does it have to rain tonight?"

"I told you this would happen," Amy said. "Didn't I?"

"What'd you want me to do?" Freeman asked. "They wanted to be outside, under the stars."

"Do you see any stars now? You should have made them listen to me. I've been up here awhile. I know the weather patterns."

"So, you're better than the weathermen. The sky is falling." Freeman laughed and tipped his beer.

Amy pulled a stem of grass from beside her and studied it in the firelight. *Calamagrostis rubescens.* Pine grass. She wondered if a botanist and a major film star could ever have a future together, or if they would argue over plants as well as the weather.

Amy turned, hearing something in the darkness behind her. There were but a few very large trees in their camp, but twenty feet back the lodgepole pine grew thick and tangled.

Something was shuffling around in the trees. There was a heavy growl. She could hear it plainly, even over the music.

"What was that?" she asked Freeman.

"What?" Freeman said.

"I heard something in the trees back there."

Freeman grinned and drank more beer. "Maybe it's a bear."

Amy got up. "That's not funny, Allen. Have you got one of your buddies back there playing a trick on me? You've done that before."

Freeman frowned. "No. . . . Really."

"Allen, tell me the truth."

"Sit down. You're just hearing things."

Amy studied him. She saw that he wasn't playing tricks on her. He was puzzled by her behavior.

"Would you please sit down and relax?" he said.

Amy sat down and drew her knees up. She wished she had pressed her argument to hold the party closer to Bridge Bay or another major campground. Everyone else had voted for privacy. They had wanted distance, to deter uninvited guests. Amy had suggested they rent a lodge and hire security.

No one had wanted to stay inside. They could do that anytime. This would be the only chance for many of them to have a wilderness experience and camp overnight on the lake shore.

Amy had argued that the forest wasn't safe. The woman who had been killed in June was still on the news periodically. A male grizzly had been shot, but authorities weren't willing to state that they had gotten the killer bear. The warning signs not to hike the Grizzly Lake Trail hadn't been taken down.

Allen Freeman got up and fetched two beers. He handed Amy one of them. "You still think you heard something?"

Amy took her beer and set it down. "I know I did, Allen. I wish we'd go. Look, it's starting to sprinkle."

"Maybe it'll blow over," Freeman said. "Besides, if a bear comes, he'll be looking down the bore of my forty-four."

"Allen, that pistol isn't any security. Not really. It's dark out here."

"Would you quit worrying?" Freeman insisted. "You're spoiling everything."

During filming, Freeman had wanted to find a grizzly, just to say he had seen one; preferably, a grizzly that had killed a human. He wanted to tell his friends in California that he had really known true wilderness. He had often gone out with field glasses on his days off.

Because of the June mauling, Amy had always gone into the back country under escort. Two rangers had accompanied her each time. The Park Service had initially told her that she couldn't finish her work. But they were getting pressure from environmental groups to prove that the fires hadn't caused permanent damage. Amy's study results were extremely valuable.

From the darkness outside of camp came another deep growl. This time closer.

Amy pointed to the trees. "Allen, there *is* something back there. Can't you hear it?"

Freeman got up. "Okay, okay." He left and rustled in his tent, returning with his .44 Magnum pistol, a recent purchase from an outdoor shop in Bozeman. He popped the cylinder open and began loading it.

"What do you want me to shoot?" he asked Amy.

"It's not funny, Allen! What's the matter with you?"

The sprinkles of rain increased. Suddenly a small terrier burst from the trees, barking loudly. The band stopped playing and everyone turned to look.

The dog ran to Marlene Mason, the female lead, and jumped into her arms. "Katie, what's the matter?" she asked.

Everyone laughed. Allen Freeman became annoyed.

"Is that your bear, Amy?" He stood with the pistol cocked.

"Listen, Allen, it wasn't Katie I heard. It was something much bigger. Uncock your gun, please."

Freeman struggled to release the hammer gently. Amy took a deep breath. She knew Freeman's gun experience was limited.

"Are you sure you can stop Katie with that forty-four, Allen?" one of the cast asked. "She's damn tough." More laughing.

Freeman turned to Amy. "Are you satisfied? You've made me into a huge fool." He stuck the pistol in his belt. "This is in case I have to draw fast, or something. You know, Wyatt Earp. That's me."

"Allen, this is serious." Amy said. "Can't you see that?"

"There's no need to make such a fuss about this, Amy. Try and relax, will you?"

Freeman sat down against the tree and slugged his beer. Amy looked into the darkness outside of camp, feeling her stomach tighten.

The highway was a hundred yards away, through scattered timber. Though the hour was late, there was brisk traffic, for Bridge Bay Campground was one of the most active in the park. There were rangers on patrol on the other side of the highway, where this party should be taking place.

But if something happened here, no one could help. No one could stop the bear that Amy knew was back in the trees. No one would know anything until it was much too late.

two

AMY WATCHED the trees outside of camp, listening, wondering. There had been no sound for a few minutes. She thought about going to look, then decided against it.

The terrier huddled in Marlene Mason's arms, growling, despite Marlene's whispers and petting. She finally carried the dog to her tent.

Allen Freeman filled a plate at a picnic table near the fire. The movie production crew had moved three tables in from Bridge Bay. Amy wished the rangers had caught them and stopped them.

They had pitched camp on a thousand square feet of nearly open space along the Yellowstone Lake shoreline. There were three large pines growing together near one end, just up from the shore. The tables were placed in a row, some twenty feet from the large trees, near the forest line.

The band had been hired from nearby Bozeman and had set up near one of the trees, at a right angle to the picnic tables, so that the partyers could dance down to the water line if they wished. The film crew had used set trucks to provide power and lights. The result was a first-rate night-club sound in a wilderness setting.

Amy followed Allen to the table. "Allen, take the gun out of your belt, please."

Freeman set the pistol on the table. "Feel better now?"

"Allen, why don't we suggest that all of us break camp? Let's go to the main campground. I don't feel good out here."

"Amy, let this go. They got the bear that killed that woman. I heard it on the news."

"No, you didn't hear that. They don't know for sure."

"Would you quit this crap? Please?"

"You don't care, do you, Allen?" She lifted the pistol and opened the cylinder. "Why did you just load three bul-lets?"

Freeman snatched the gun. "Because that's all I would have needed. Do you want something to eat?"

"No. I want to go, Allen. Now! You coming with me?"

"Where're you going to go? How're you going to get there? You came with me. Remember?"

Amy heard a deep, guttural growl. She turned toward the shadows. A heavy, musky odor invaded her nostrils.

She turned to Freeman. "Listen, I know that's a bear. We've *got* to go!"

Freeman seemed rooted where he stood, his eyes wide. "God, I think I see it."

Amy stared into the darkness and saw a huge shape with little eyes that caught the light of the fire. The rain began to fall harder. She ran to the bandstand and grabbed a microphone.

"Listen! Please, everyone listen! We've got to get out of here and back to the campground. There's a bear just out-side camp!"

"What?" someone asked. "A bear? Really?"

"Yeah," someone else said, "a little white, furry one, named Katie." Everyone laughed.

Freeman suddenly yelled. An immense blur exploded from the shadows into the firelight. Huge and dark, it rose from the ground into a towering form of long, shaggy hair and claws. The flames outlined a massive grizzly with eyes like gleaming black beads.

The screaming began. Amy fell backward over an amplifier. The band fled the stage and ran with the others, back along the shore of the lake toward Bridge Bay. The terrier emerged, yapping, from the tent and scrambled away with its mistress.

Amy came to her feet and started toward Allen Freeman, who was staring at the huge grizzly towering above him. Amy crawled under a picnic table and yelled for Freeman to come. Freeman stood frozen with fear, rain pelting his face.

The bear dropped to all fours and popped its jaws. A thick froth drooled down its front. It was now within feet of Freeman.

"Allen!" Amy screamed. "Fall down and cover up! Now!"

Freeman remained frozen, his eyes wide, his fingers trembling. The grizzly roared and lunged.

Amy screamed as the grizzly cuffed Freeman a glancing blow with a huge front paw, sending him over the picnic table. Bottles and cups and food exploded everywhere. The bear roared again and slammed a paw into the table, lifting it from the ground, stripping the seat boards from one end.

Amy rolled clear and scrambled toward a tree five feet away. She began climbing, her arms and legs churning from pure instinct, the bark burning her like fire, the branches tearing at her like long, jagged fingers. She came to rest twelve feet from the ground, clutching the limbs, gasping for breath.

Freeman tried to rise. Part of his scalp hung down over his face. The grizzly was on him again, cuffing him to the ground. Freeman curled into a ball.

The bear used its claws to peel the flesh from Freeman's back, then tried to get Freeman's head into its mouth, biting and chewing strips of scalp and neck tissue while

Freeman fought without effect against the monstrous weight on top of him.

Through the rain the scene was blurred and surreal. Amy wanted to think it was a bad dream and closed her eyes. It couldn't be happening. Freeman's primeval screams rose over the bear's growling, and Amy felt her stomach turn inside out.

While vomiting, she nearly fell. She regained control and looked down to where the pistol lay on the ground fifteen feet from the tree. Maybe she could save Allen Freeman, if she could only get the pistol.

Amy lowered herself down the trunk. Trembling, she reached the forest floor, fell, then rose again and started for the pistol.

Amy had no concerns about shooting. At one time she had been within two weeks of graduating from a law enforcement academy in Illinois. She could hit any spot she wanted on a target. But that was a target; a raging grizzly was far different.

Freeman's voice was now a high, continuous wailing. The grizzly clamped its teeth into his shoulder, picked him up, and shook him like a cloth doll.

Amy stumbled past bloody fragments of clothing on her way to the pistol. She did not notice the Park Service vehicles pulling off the highway, lights flashing, or the wild yelling as everyone tried to tell them what was happening. She heard nothing but the heavy drumming of blood within her head as she took the pistol.

Amy cocked the gun and took two halting steps toward the grizzly. Her training took control of her, and she pressed forward. The bear remained busy with Freeman, paying her no attention. She wiped her wet and muddy hands on her pants, then clamped them tightly around the pistol grip.

She fought to hold the weapon steady as she circled to get a broadside shot at the bear. Freeman was no longer screaming, but the bear was still tearing him apart.

Amy stopped and set herself. She cocked the gun and

pulled the trigger. The pistol jumped in her hands and a roaring blast echoed through the trees. She saw the grizzly turn and stare at her through the rain. Freeman's leg was in the bear's mouth, and his torn body hung upside down from its jaws like a tattered sack.

Amy fired again and heard the pin hit against an empty cylinder. The grizzly continued to stare at her, as if not understanding what she was about. A rumbling began from deep in its throat and a wild glare invaded the small black eyes.

Breathing in gasps, Amy once again forced the hammer back. The pistol bucked again and a flash of flame sped into the grizzly's shoulder. The bear slumped. Its jaws opened and Freeman's body fell in a limp pile.

The grizzly stared at Amy, as if she had played an ugly trick upon it. Then it turned to lunge at her.

For an instant, Amy thought she could fire again and stop the bear. But her instincts told her that would not happen. The grizzly was too close and too enraged to go down. It was coming after her.

Amy dropped the pistol. Her legs moving like pistons, she ran for the tree. The grizzly was right behind her, crashing through the ruins of the party, its breathing ragged with rage and pain.

Amy scrambled back up the trunk. She screamed as the grizzly slammed into the tree with the force of a large truck. Shaken loose, she began to fall, but grabbed at branches and caught herself before she had tumbled completely down.

Scrambling again, she pulled herself back up, but not before the grizzly had raked its claws down the back of her right leg.

Had there been large branches on the lower trunk, the grizzly would have climbed up to her immediately. As it was, the small limbs snapped like matchsticks under the bear's weight and the animal slid back to the ground.

It hammered against the trunk with huge paws and tried

to push the tree over. But the pine was too big and would not budge, even under the grizzly's incredible strength.

Then, like a clown, the bear sat back on its haunches and began to swing its head back and forth, bawling, spewing a bloody froth down its front. The froth was diluted by rainfall, and the bear coughed up more.

Amy stared down through the branches. The grizzly came to all fours and looked up at her. She could feel its rage. She held fast to the tree, hoping her trembling hands would not give way.

The grizzly rose onto its hind legs. Its huge paws came up toward her. With a tremendous roar, the bear began stripping bark from the trunk, clawing it into fragments.

Amy heard the shouts of park rangers. They were yelling, pointing through the darkness, gathering near Freeman.

The shooting began. The grizzly grunted and whoofed and roared while bullets tore through its body. It finally slumped over into a huge, ruffled lump and lay still.

Amy grew dizzy. Though she tried to catch herself, she slipped through the branches and toppled down onto the massive bulk of wet and bloody fur.

The shock caused Amy to scream. There were flashlights everywhere, the light blurry and scattered by the rain.

Hands helped her to lie down on the ground; voices tried to calm her. Nearby, other voices told onlookers to return to their camps and stay back away from the grizzly and the torn body.

One man near her broke into a laugh and said he doubted if she would sit by the fire on a bear rug after tonight. Another man, angered, told him to move away from the scene.

An ambulance came to a stop a few feet away. Amy moaned and tried to sit up, but hands and voices kept her down. The rain felt like ice against her face. An EMT began talking to her, examining her leg. She felt herself being lifted into the back of an ambulance.

"Where's Allen?" Amy asked. "I thought I saw him. . . ."

"You're fine," the EMT said. "You'll be just fine."

"Allen? Where's Allen?"

He continued to probe scratches and gouges along her leg. As the ambulance began to move, Amy brought her hands over her face and began to weep uncontrollably. Nothing in her life would ever be the same.

three

NATE JACKSON, assistant chief ranger, watched the ambulance leave. Paramedics had assured him that the woman would survive, if she didn't go into a deep state of shock.

Jackson had been in the middle of a late-night meeting at the Lake Ranger Station when the call came in: bear trouble near Bridge Bay Campground. He and a number of staff rangers had been discussing the grizzly trouble in the Lake District.

Jackson had been outlining steps on handling the backcountry hikers during a year when it seemed the grizzlies were unsettled. Tonight's meeting hadn't gone well. Now the rest of the night was going to be worse.

They still hadn't closed the case on the young woman found along the shore of Grizzly Lake during the first week of June. Now another grizzly mauling. This was going to cause *panic*.

As Jackson looked around the site, he wondered how a party could have taken place so far away from a developed area or regular campground. The discovery of the badly mutilated woman at Grizzly Lake should have been a clear warning to campers.

Jackson hurried to his Suburban and lifted his radio. If the press didn't know about this yet, they soon would. He called headquarters at Mammoth Hot Springs. His wording was careful.

"Listen, Jane, get the chief ranger out of bed. Tell him he's missing quite a party at Bridge Bay Campground. Tell him that I'll meet him in the lobby of the Lake Hotel in an hour."

Jackson left his vehicle, shouting orders to the rangers preserving the scene. It was important to hurry, to keep the rain from obliterating evidence. Everything had to be left intact, without any more unnecessary disturbance.

Jackson helped the rangers secure the perimeter, chasing curious tourists away, while others covered Freeman and the grizzly's remains with plastic. As Freeman had been partially dismembered, rangers were searching with flashlights, to be sure they hadn't left pieces of him uncovered.

Jackson had been assistant chief ranger for five years. Never had he seen anything like this, not in his worst nightmare.

He walked over to the ranger who had made the remark about the bear rug, trying to understand why someone would make such a remark, especially when a mauling victim was present.

Leland Beckle, head ranger for the Lake District, was seated in his vehicle, filling out forms with the aid of a flashlight. He had been on the job since late February, far too long in Jackson's estimation.

During the meeting, Beckle had argued about everything suggested by anyone but himself. He was solely responsible for the meeting having lasted so long. When the call had come in about the bear trouble, Beckle had insisted that he be the lead investigator. "It's my district," he had told Jackson. "I'm in charge."

Jackson had disregarded him, telling him he would follow procedure, like the rest of the rangers.

Beckle sat in his vehicle, the wipers going full speed. Jackson stepped up to the window.

"Beckle, I don't get it. Why would you say something like that? Especially in front of the woman?"

Beckle didn't look up from his writing. "Jackson, you just don't know a joke when you hear one."

"A joke?"

"Didn't you hear me laughing?" Beckle showed no expression. "I guess you colored folks have no sense of humor." He put the vehicle in gear.

Jackson watched Beckle leave. There was no use in writing him up; no one was able to discipline him.

Beckle had been hired under protest by Park Superintendent Bob Canby. The gossip was that Canby had been pressured from Washington to hire Beckle, the son of a nearby state senator with a lot of power.

Beckle had come to his job amid press headlines. He had taken a very important position, with a scant two years' experience in the national park system. He flaunted his power over everyone.

Canby had put up a real struggle before giving in. He had a stack of records on Beckle that should have kept him out of the position, but somehow, the senator had won.

During his brief tenure in Yellowstone, Beckle had already made more enemies than friends. He had been responsible for the removal of a grizzly into the Shoshone National Forest, just east of the park. The bear had immediately killed a crippled cow and had been shot by a rancher. "He had the bear dropped in an area filled with livestock," Jackson had complained. "What would you expect?"

Canby had immediately placed a letter in Beckle's file, admonishing him to coordinate better with state and regional officials in the future. Beckle had laughed it off.

Those concerned about the future of grizzlies were mortified. Though the bison issue had been making national news on a regular basis, grizzly bear management remained the most controversial subject within the greater Yellowstone ecosystem. Leland Beckle was single-handedly bringing a string of black eyes to the park's record.

Jackson watched Beckle's taillights disappear and joined Jim Clark, a young ranger who worked the Lake District under Beckle. He was scoping the area outside the perimeter with a flashlight.

Clark, in his midtwenties, had accepted a job in Yosemite National Park as a head ranger. He had three weeks left in Yellowstone.

Clark was good at law enforcement and natural resources. The rangers were calling him Saint Jim, for the way he seemed to accept Leland Beckle's continued harassment.

It was Jackson's hope that in a few years he might bring Clark back to Yellowstone, in the position now occupied by Beckle.

Clark turned off his flashlight as Jackson approached. "I don't think we missed anyone," he said. "We're ninety-nine percent sure the woman and Freeman were the only casualties."

"Who did you say it was?" Jackson asked.

"Didn't you hear? Allen Freeman, the number-one box office attraction in America, no longer recognizable, on screen or off."

"I had heard Allen Freeman was in the area," Jackson said, "but I had no idea he was out here tonight."

"Private party," Clark said. "They didn't want *anyone* to know." He walked with Jackson toward the fallen bear. "This is a real strange situation. This grizzly's got paint on him."

"Paint? You mean he got into a warehouse or something?"

"No," Clark said. "I mean he's been painted. Someone painted him up."

Jackson stopped. "Do you mean someone used a paintbrush on him?"

"That's the way it looks," Clark replied. "He's got what looks to be circles and stripes on him. A lot of it's gone, but there's enough in the fur next to the skin to see it clearly. Strangest thing."

Jackson and Clark walked to where three rangers were securing a plastic covering over the grizzly. Jackson knelt down and studied the bear with his flashlight.

"What the hell is this all about?" Jackson asked, noting remnants of circles around the eyes and lines coming out from the mouth along the throat.

"Somebody had to do that to him," one of the rangers said. "I've never seen anyone mark a bear like that."

Everyone agreed that they had never seen a bear painted in that manner. No one painted bears for study anymore.

"I'm going to have to call Sally Hays in Cheyenne," Jackson said. "There's definitely been human involvement outside of park personnel."

"Another thing that's confusing," Clark said. "This grizzly shouldn't even have been here. This one hasn't ever been seen close to a village or a campground. Not ever."

"How do you know that?" Jackson asked.

Clark knelt down and pointed into the grizzly's mouth. "The tongue's been tattooed," he said. "That's Barney, the grizzly still under observation by your game warden friend, John Tanner."

Jackson stared at the huge bear. "You sure about that?"

"Yeah, I'm sure." Clark reached into his pocket and handed Jackson a scrap of paper. "Check it out yourself. He's supposed to have a radio collar on him. We couldn't find it anywhere around here, though."

Jackson studied the numbers on the paper under his flashlight. With Clark's help, he opened the grizzly's mouth and pulled the tongue tight. Someone handed him a cloth and he wiped the tongue clean of blood.

"Yeah, it's Tanner's bear," Jackson said. "And you're right. No one's ever seen this grizzly near a campground before. In fact, Tanner tells me this bear has never been within a hundred yards of a human. But someone got close enough to paint him. What's going on here?"

"You think you can get Tanner to help us now?" Clark asked.

Jackson cleaned his hands. "I hope so. Lord knows I've tried already. But if anything will get him to change his mind, this will."

four

John Tanner awakened just after dawn to the sound of a vehicle churning its way up the twisting road to his cabin. The rain had ended and the sky in the east was a deep red.

As a game warden for Montana's Department of Fish, Wildlife and Parks, Tanner was responsible for enforcing fish and game laws across much of the area surrounding Yellowstone Park. He lived on a mountainside near the small community of Gardiner, at the north entrance to the park.

The day before, Tanner had helped Gallatin County authorities rescue a boy and his dog from an island in the Yellowstone River. This had followed a three-day search for a lost hiker in the Absaroka Wilderness. It had been an exhausting week, and he had hoped to get some of the needed sleep this morning.

Tanner eased out of bed and peered through his bedroom window. In the mountain fog he could see a Yellowstone Park vehicle.

He suspected it was his good friend Nate Jackson. But it seemed awfully early in the day for a social visit.

Tanner slipped into a pair of jeans and moved to the picture window in his living room. From here he could see into the cab of the Suburban. It was Nate Jackson.

Though trained as a biologist, John Tanner had also graduated from a law enforcement academy. He had become one of Montana's top game wardens, a specialist in backcountry crime, as well as an expert on grizzly bears and their behavior, having made a study of them throughout his professional career.

Before joining Montana Fish, Wildlife and Parks, Tanner had worked as a ranger in Yellowstone for three years, in charge of the Shoshone District. He was presently gathering continuing data on two bears: a black bear named Jack in the Absaroka Wilderness and a grizzly in Yellowstone Park named Barney. Jack had been a two-year project, while he had been studying Barney for six years.

Tanner turned on a radio and set water to heat for herb tea. The top-of-the-hour news had already begun. A grizzly had attacked a gathering of movie people near Lake Village in Yellowstone Park, killing one of the actors. The actor's name would be released pending notification of relatives.

A woman had also been attacked by the grizzly, a botanist named Amy Ellerman, who had been spending the summer researching within the park. She was in good condition at Lake Hospital.

The announcer added that this recent incident followed the death of a young woman killed by a grizzly just over a month earlier. Her body had been mauled beyond recognition. She had yet to be identified.

Park officials would say only that the deaths were uncharacteristic. Leland Beckle, ranger for the Lake District, was quoted as saying he could now personally ensure the safety of park visitors, for they had gotten the killer bear. But no other park officials would verify his statement.

The reporter echoed the thoughts of the masses: How many more bears would attack unsuspecting tourists? What was happening?"

So that was it, Tanner thought. Jackson was coming to ask him once more to work with park personnel in solving the problem. When Jackson had asked before, Tanner had politely declined.

John Tanner wanted nothing to do with the remains left behind by angry bears. His wife, Julie, had died at the jaws of a grizzly. He still blamed himself. He should have been watching better. He should have known the wind was wrong. They should have been wearing bells to announce themselves. It still haunted him.

Of course, this case was different. His wife had been mauled by a female protecting her cubs, not by a bear that had wandered into a group of campers.

According to Tanner's sources, the young woman killed in June had been found beside a backcountry lake. None of her remains had been buried, as bears usually did with their kills. The Wyoming State Crime Laboratory in Cheyenne was still working to identify her.

Tanner suspected that the actor had died at the hands of a wandering grizzly. From Fishing Bridge to Grant Village was grizzly country. Bear management areas surrounded two-thirds of the lake shoreline. Grizzlies could be anywhere at any time.

Tanner watched through the window as Jackson slammed the door to his vehicle and hurried to the door. Jackson was chewing gum, chomping it, actually, as he always did when under pressure.

"No doubt you already know what's going on," Jackson said as Tanner let him in. "It's been on every news broadcast there is."

Tanner nodded. "You came all the way up here to tell me?"

"Yeah," Jackson said, removing his coat, his mouth busy with the gum. "What are friends for?"

"Who got killed?" Tanner asked.

"Allen Freeman," Jackson replied. "America's favorite actor, torn to shreds." He headed for the kitchen table.

Tanner knew Allen Freeman. Three weeks before, he

had given Freeman a citation for fishing without a license. Freeman had been pleasant about the matter, saying he should have bought a license. But he had failed to appear on the charge or pay the fine.

"I can't imagine what kind of stir that's going to create," Tanner said. "I don't envy you, dealing with all that."

"I don't want to have to deal with it alone," Jackson said. "I'm much better as a team player, but with a good team. Know what I mean?"

Tanner brought cups to the table. "Care for some herb tea?"

"Got any coffee?"

"Your stomach's riled, Nate. Herb tea will settle you down a little."

"I've been up all night, John. I don't want to be settled down. I haven't got time." He stuffed a stick of Doublemint into his mouth. "So, what about the coffee?"

Tanner started for the cupboards. "I'll put some on. I'll bet you haven't had breakfast either."

"Skip that," Jackson said. "I can't handle your cooking on an empty stomach."

"I've got a new eggs and peppers dish I want to show you. I learned it from a Mexican friend who owns a restaurant up in Laurel."

"Not this morning, John. Another time." Jackson drummed his fingers on the table while he chewed and watched the fog lift from peaks in the distance.

Tanner and Jackson had become friends during their college days. They had both played football in the defensive backfield at Montana State University and had both majored in fish and wildlife management.

In his junior year, Tanner had left football to keep up his grades and Jackson had pulled out of fish and wildlife management to concentrate on football. But after college, he'd gone into law enforcement.

Tanner had always wondered why Jackson hadn't tried out for the Dolphins. He'd been drafted in the fourth round. "Can't leave the mountains," Jackson had told him.

"I grew up in the ghettos of Atlanta, but now I can't leave this high country."

Jackson's time with the Park Service had been good to him. He had spent a few years at the Grand Canyon, a few more in Yosemite, and had then come back to Yellowstone as assistant chief ranger. In his five years in that position he had gotten three awards for superior service.

Tanner poured Jackson a cup of coffee. He brought the trash can with him. "Want to dump that gum? You'll choke on it."

"I need it," Jackson said.

"You've got more," Tanner said. "I'd bet on it."

Jackson tossed his gum into the garbage and slurped coffee noisily. Tanner poured hot water into his cup. He took a pinch of home-grown herbs from a can and put them in a small cloth bag for steeping. He brought the cup over to the table and sat down.

"What do you think is happening?" he asked Jackson.

Jackson scowled. "Why do you think I'm here, John? I don't understand any of this. Something real crazy is going on. I've never seen people as dead as that woman and Allen Freeman. You couldn't even tell they were human."

Tanner took a deep breath. He closed his eyes as he saw Julie screaming, her mouth open wide. She was on the ground, trying to claw herself away from the grizzly. It had her by the leg, dragging her back into the woods.

Tanner jerked and knocked his cup over. Tea spilled everywhere.

"You okay?" Jackson asked.

Tanner got a dishcloth and cleaned up the mess. "You've got any number of bear experts who'll help with this," he said. "I'm no better than most of them."

"Yeah, we've talked to some guys, and they're all good," Jackson said. "But this case is different, in a lot of ways. We need you."

Tanner wouldn't budge. "I'm sorry, Nate. You've got guys who know bears, and you know the park as well as

I do. What do you really need me for?" He threw the cloth in the sink and refilled his cup.

As Tanner sat down, Jackson pulled a folded piece of paper from his pocket and tossed it across the table. "The grizzly we killed last night had a tongue tattoo. I'm afraid you know this bear real well."

Tanner opened the paper and read a series of numbers. His mouth dropped.

"I'm sorry, John," Jackson said. "I figured you would want to know."

Tanner was staring at the numbers, hoping he had seen one wrong. He had gotten to know Barney like a friendly neighbor. Somehow, he couldn't see Barney as dead. Certainly he couldn't see this grizzly as a mad killer.

In his master's thesis, Tanner had stated that Barney seemed to prefer rolling down a hill to fighting with other bears over leftovers at an elk or bison carcass. Barney had watched people, including Tanner, any number of times, but he had never come any closer than a couple of hundred yards, even when the other bears were moving in to investigate.

Over the years, Barney had never changed his behavior. The previous night was the first documented sighting of Barney anywhere near a settled area. And the bear died as a result.

Tanner tossed the paper back to Jackson. "That really hurts to hear about Barney. But I still don't want in on this. I don't need any more nightmares." He got up for more tea.

"Don't you think there are other people having nightmares?" Jackson asked. He stuffed more gum into his mouth.

"Yeah, so I should make mine worse?"

Jackson stared at him. "Maybe it will help you. Did you ever think of that?"

Tanner brought more coffee over for Jackson. He took a deep breath. Help him? Seeing mutilated bodies and remembering his wife's cries would help him?

"You've got to deal with it sometime, John," Jackson said. "I don't profess to be a therapist, but I do know that helping people who've survived car accidents made me realize I didn't survive the one I was in for nothing. I lost a brother. I watched him die on the ground next to me, and I couldn't even move to help him. And I'd been driving. You remember me telling you about that?"

"I remember," Tanner said. "You told me more than once."

"I tell people all the time not to blame themselves for tragedies," Jackson continued. "A lot of things happen that aren't anybody's fault."

Tanner sat down again. Barney was gone, along with another grizzly that had been killed shortly after the woman had been found. He knew Barney well, but nothing about the first bear.

"Who shot the other bear?" Tanner asked.

"Leland Beckle," Jackson said, disgust evident in his voice. "I can't understand why he shot that grizzly. There was no clear evidence that bear had attacked the woman. None. He said there was, but the lab couldn't find a trace of human remains anywhere inside or outside the carcass.

"And the paw prints don't match with those found at the scene. He just shot it because it was in the area, and hoped he'd gotten the right one. He wants to be John Wayne."

"I've heard Beckle is hard to deal with," Tanner said. "I don't like anyone who shoots bears without provocation, especially if they're trying for glory."

"I don't like Beckle at all," Jackson said. "I'd like to see him take a hike. But he's the head ranger in the Lake District, and I've got to put up with him." Jackson cleared his throat. "But the oddest thing about all of this so far is the paint all over Barney."

Tanner frowned. "Paint? What do you mean?"

"We found circles of black and yellow paint around Barney's eyes. There were other paint markings. You didn't do that, did you?"

"Of course not," Tanner said. "Has anyone else been studying Barney?"

"No. Just you."

Tanner gulped tea. "Where's Barney now?"

"At the scene, covered with a tarp. The movie people were partying outside the campgrounds. We're calling it the Freeman Site. That looks good on a map."

"Who's working the site with you?"

"Sally Hays is on her way from Cheyenne. We called her right after we found the paint." Jackson looked at his watch. "She should be here in about three hours. You could come with me to help evaluate the scene. We could talk to her together."

Tanner rubbed his face with his hands.

Jackson chewed his gum hard, staring at Tanner. "Help me, John. I need you on this one. Do it for Barney. He deserved better."

Tanner looked up. "What do you think I can do for you that no one else can?"

"Help me figure out what's going on," Jackson said. "You know there's something really wrong with all this. I need to know what's going on."

"What about my superiors? Can the state make a deal with the Park Service for my work time?"

"I already called your boss. He said it was up to you."

Tanner looked out the window. Light was spilling through the trees. Two people had been killed and would never see the mountains again. Barney, a docile grizzly who had never been in a campground before, had killed one of those people and was also dead. He had been painted in some fashion as well. None of it made sense.

Jackson leaned forward. "If you don't help me, John, you won't be able to sleep at night. You know that."

"That's nothing new," Tanner said. "I can't sleep as it is."

"You know what I mean, John. Something very strange is going on. No one wants any more dead people, or dead bears."

Tanner took a deep breath. "Okay, I'll help you. I need free rein in this, though. I don't want a bunch of red tape choking me."

"You've got all the freedom you want," Jackson promised. "I'll see to it."

Tanner got up from the table. "Let's go have a look at Barney."

five

THE UPPER Yellowstone River, as it passed from Yellowstone Park, worked its way through a deep gorge lined with rock and timber. The sun shone brightly on the wings of a golden eagle that soared with the wind.

Tanner rode with Jackson, staring out at the high peaks that rose on both side of Yankee Jim Canyon, named for an old frontiersman who had carved a wagon road out of rock and had then charged toll behind the barrel of a .50-caliber buffalo gun.

Local legend said that the railroad had run him out and that his ghost could still be seen shouting at the engineers, waving his rifle, his white hair and beard flying under a weatherbeaten hat.

It was the first time in two years that Tanner had ridden anywhere in Jackson's vehicle. At that time, Tanner had been working with Jackson and a game warden from Wyoming to stop a poaching ring that had been operating in and out of Yellowstone Park.

The three had surrounded four poachers hacking antlers, in velvet, from a six-point bull elk. Three of them had been killed in the resultant shootout, and the remaining one had been sentenced to prison for five years.

Tanner knew this case would be much more difficult than the poaching ring. Something unnatural had happened to Barney to cause his rogue behavior.

Jackson had mentioned that Barney had been painted in yellow and black. This was bothering Tanner considerably. He knew, from his own distant heritage, that Native Americans revered bears, especially grizzlies, and considered them sacred. Ceremonies and dances to honor the grizzly's spirit were common among all tribes.

Tanner knew that the colors red and black were commonly used in ceremonies, but he had never heard of yellow and black being used together.

Though diluted by two generations of white blood, Tanner was linked to the Indian past of the area through his great-grandfather who lived northeast of Yellowstone Park, in a small cabin deep in the Pryor Mountains of south-central Montana, on the edge of the Crow Indian Reservation.

The old man was a mixture of Scots-Irish and three Indian tribes. Tanner had always called him Grandfather. His Indian name, Bear Medicine Dreamer, had been given to him in childhood.

Tanner knew that his grandfather would know about the colors. In time, he would visit the old man and learn.

Jackson slowed for Gardiner, a little town on the edge of Yellowstone Park filled with trading posts and tourist shops. The north end was residential, nestled under steep mountain slopes. The south end touched a broad plain covered with grass and sagebrush, where elk, deer, and antelope browsed year-round.

The Yellowstone River divided the town in half, its waters rolling through a small gorge cut in the valley floor.

They eased through town, already stirring with eager tourists. No matter the event, tragic or otherwise, people would still come to the world's most fascinating natural wonder.

"Want to stop for anything?" Jackson asked.

Tanner shook his head, deep in thought, remembering his study of Barney, his notes on the grizzly's every move, watching him grow from a cub into adulthood. Twice he had sedated Barney with tranquilizers to put a tracking collar on him and to get growth measurements. The bear eventually became one of the biggest grizzlies ever seen in the greater Yellowstone ecosystem.

An inscription on the great stone arch at the park's north entrance reads: "For the Benefit and Enjoyment of the People." Tanner wondered if Allen Freeman's death wouldn't attract even more numbers. After all, how many people could say they'd been where Hollywood's number one star had been torn to pieces by a grizzly?

As they passed the toll booth at the park's northeast entrance, Tanner thought about the last time he had seen Barney. It had been a warm October day, the previous fall, deep in the backcountry of the park. Barney had stocked up on roots and rodents. He was as fat as an oil drum, his tan coat glistening. Shaggy and huge, he had lain quietly in sedation while Tanner and Martin Linders, the head of bear management, had taped him everywhere—length, width, head size, claw length, everything.

That time Tanner had watched the big beast get up and amble off. To see him now, his coat covered with blood, would be like seeing a good friend after a fatal car crash.

Mammoth Hot Springs, the site of park headquarters, was brimming with people from everywhere in the world. Large granitic stone structures three to four stories high, surrounded by lawn and tall shade trees, housed the Park Service and the U.S. Fish and Wildlife Service.

Rows of wooden apartments housed park employees, and small wooden cabins served to accommodate guests and seasonal help at the various concession businesses.

The road that led into the park passed the giant thermal feature that had given the town its name. Tourists roamed like ants along trails and board walkways that spread over a massive hill. There hot water spewed to the surface in trailing streams over a large terrace covered with calcium carbonate deposits, forming a sea of layered salt that rolled down the steep hillside like steaming, crusted snow. Scattered algae growth colored the salts in hues of yellow, orange, and red, shining brilliant in the morning sun.

Tanner watched a tourist aim his camera at a bull elk browsing under a pine at the edge of the terrace.

Jackson shifted his gum and said, "We've had too many grizzly problems this year. Something's really wrong. I know I've said that before, but I'm really wondering about all this."

"I want to know more about the woman who died earlier," Tanner said. "Was she a park employee?"

"That's what we think," Jackson replied. "But we can't be sure. A lot of women come and go in a season."

Tanner realized that trying to keep track of the many employees that worked in the park each year and where they went after leaving would be impossible. Only forensic evidence would bring a positive identification.

"Sally Hays did a facial reconstruction at the lab," Jackson continued. "She's sent pictures out everywhere, but no results so far."

Tanner had seen reconstructions before. When a body was unidentifiable and no dental records could be found, the skull was cleaned and clay applied to the bones to reform the head and face. Glass eyes were inserted and a wig placed over the skull.

It was a precise craft. Sally Hays, who had a special knack for this work, could almost bring a bleached white skull back to life.

"Was the woman killed at the site?" Tanner asked.

Jackson added another stick of gum to his wad. "No. It appears the bear dragged the body along Straight Creek to the Grizzly Lake shoreline, then turned around and went back into the water and disappeared. Strange. And, as I told you, there was no sign that any part of her had ever been buried."

"So the woman was torn up and carried around, then just dropped?" Tanner asked. "The bear didn't feed on her at all?"

"We think the bear fed on her," Jackson said. "Her abdomen and intestines were gone, and everything else inside of her. And her breasts were missing. Her face was torn beyond recognition, too. She was just ripped to shreds."

"A real angry bear," Tanner concluded.

"But the bear never buried her," Jackson continued. "I don't understand why he'd drag her around and not bury her. I mean, they always bury the remains to feed on later, don't they?"

"Most usually," Tanner said. "I suppose you can't say all of them *always* do. There's bound to be an exception to everything. But I would say it was rare that a grizzly wouldn't bury at least part of its kill."

Jackson pointed down the road. "We're coming up on the trailhead. The lake's not far back in and we've got some time. You want to have a look?"

"I don't know what I'll find," Tanner said. "It's been over a month. But let's stop."

Jackson pulled over at the Straight Creek Trailhead. The fires of '88 had raged through the area, leaving the lodgepole pines looking like ragged, black skeletons. The heat had split many, burning the branches back to twisted stumps that hung from the trees like broken arms.

However, beneath the dead trees new vegetative life had developed. Where the soils were shallow and rocky, the blues of penstemons and forget-me-nots flourished among the yellows of groundsels and stonecrop. The flat, white top of common yarrow showed itself in scattered clumps.

Tanner and Jackson followed the trail to where it broke into a sloping valley filled with grass and sedge. Straight Creek flowed shallow and clear, filled with minnows. A small herd of deer bolted from the grass that grew tall along the shore. They bounded up onto the hillside, working their way through the charred and naked pines.

Tanner and Jackson paused at the edge of Grizzly Lake, a long and narrow pool of still water, shrouded in dense stands of grass and sedge. A family of ducks hid themselves among drooping stalks of monkeyflower on the far shore.

Jackson walked slowly, searching the shoreline carefully. He stopped. "The remains were found here. At the time we found her, there were a lot of grizzly tracks around the body. The vegetation was trampled and blood-stained, and the ground was littered with fragments of cloth and flesh. It's all gone now."

Tanner looked around, uneasy, his mind racing. Something felt strange to him. It made his flesh crawl. He let his eyes scan the entire area, trees and ground.

Ever since his childhood, Tanner had been very sensitive. He had always been able to feel things and know the truth about them. People especially. He didn't know how it happened. It just happened. It was a gift that frightened him. As much as possible, he stayed away from it.

"What do you think?" Jackson asked. "Something odd about all this, wouldn't you say?"

"It feels really odd to me," Tanner said. "Really odd."

"This is touching your Indian blood, isn't it?" Jackson said.

"Yes, I guess it is," Tanner said. "This whole thing is getting to me on a deep level."

"Yeah," Jackson said, "and you haven't even seen Barney yet." He studied Tanner. "Maybe you should talk to your old grandfather about this."

"I've thought about it already," Tanner said. "He's my great-grandfather."

"I get confused," Jackson said. "You always call him Grandfather."

"That's the Indian way," Tanner said. "He says he's seen over a hundred winters. I believe him."

"Go see him," Jackson said. "He could be of help."

Tanner couldn't remember when he hadn't known the old man. As a child, Tanner would go with his grandmother to visit. The old man taught Tanner the ancient art of sign language and some Indian words.

Tanner still visited him once a month. The old man would laugh each time and invite Tanner to live with him. Tanner would politely decline.

"Too used to white ways," Grandfather would say in Indian and sign language. "You'll die young and soft in the middle."

Tanner roamed the shoreline, looking for clues and evidence that hadn't been lost to animals and weather.

He knelt to check a series of paw prints he had found in the mud. They had dried but were clearly visible.

"Have you got photographs of all this?" he asked Jackson.

"We took a lot of them," Jackson said. "I'll get them to you when we go back up. Do you think this was Barney, too?"

Tanner studied the paw prints. "Maybe."

"I hope so," Jackson said. "We could close this thing today."

They walked out, Tanner wondering why Barney would be so close to the road, dragging a dead woman around, leaving her remains by a lake where he'd never been before.

He thought about it as they drove on, past Obsidian Cliff and over rocky summits covered with burned lodgepole pines. Jackson said he hoped there was a connection between the two deaths. "This nightmare will be over," he kept saying. "Over, so I can get some sleep."

At Norris Geyser Basin, the hottest ground in Yellowstone, steam rose in thick columns from pits and holes filled with boiling mud and water. It was a pastel world of browns, yellows, and reds, lost in rising columns of sulfurous gas and steam.

Below lay Hayden Valley, moist and filled with heavy grass and sedge cover. Elk and bison grazed everywhere, many near the roadway. Jackson slowed often for the lines of parked cars, where tourists hurried from their vehicles for photographs.

"Elk jams, bison jams," Jackson said. "If the roads weren't jammed tight with cars, and people running everywhere with cameras, I wouldn't know how to act."

They reached Canyon Village, on the western edge of the Grand Canyon of the Yellowstone, a twenty-mile stretch where the river had carved itself down fifteen hundred feet through sheer rock.

The walls caught the early sunlight, reflecting yellow and red-gold along jagged outlines. The quiet morning air brought the sound of cascading water, where the river fell over two spectacular falls.

Tanner had often watched them with wonder, the Upper Falls of 109 feet and the Lower Falls, thundering down 308 feet into a foamy torrent.

Jackson stopped for a group of pedestrians. One ran up and asked, "Where are the grizzlies? I hear they're everywhere up here."

"If you see one, please stay in your car," Jackson said, and drove on, cursing and chomping gum. "That's all we need: some nitwit looking for bears who gets himself chewed in half. Why am I doing this? I ask myself, why do I need this?"

"Because you love it," Tanner said. "You're crazy about it."

Jackson looked over at Tanner. "You want to trade places for a week?"

"Not even for a day," Tanner said.

Yellowstone Lake came into view, a broad expanse of deep blue set within a huge volcanic cauldron. Glaciers from twelve thousand years past melted to form the headwaters of the Yellowstone River.

The lake stretched toward the south, farther than the eye could see, and spread west to the base of giant peaks. The road paralleled the eastern boundary, set against a tight forest of lodgepole pine.

The lake was dotted with sailboats, brilliant white against the cold blue water.

Jackson looked at his watch. "We've got at least an hour until Sally gets here. Do you want to talk to Amy Ellerman? Maybe she can tell us something that will help."

"We've got nothing to lose," Tanner said. "Nothing at all."

six

AMY ELLERMAN lay on her stomach. Two nurses and a park ranger named Molly were measuring the claw marks on her leg. The nurses measured and the ranger took notes: length, width between marks, width of marks.

Amy had been in the hospital close to ten hours, the longest period of time she had ever lived through—next to the less than five minutes it had taken the grizzly to kill Allen Freeman.

The incident now seemed as if it had happened a month earlier, maybe two or three. Maybe even a year or years. She didn't know. Time had lost any meaning.

Amy had been told by the doctor that two officials had come to talk to her about the night before but she didn't have to talk if she didn't feel up to it.

Amy hadn't hesitated in telling the doctor to show them in. She wanted to tell what had happened. It still seemed like some terrible nightmare that wouldn't allow her to wake up.

When Tanner and Jackson entered the room, Amy turned sideways, watching them intently. Especially John

Tanner. She remembered seeing him before. He had given Allen a ticket for fishing without a license.

Jackson formally introduced Tanner and himself. Tanner wore jeans and a beige shirt, with the Montana Fish, Wildlife and Parks symbol on it—the head of a grizzly bear within a circle. Jackson wore his Park Service uniform of green and gray. Both men looked intent.

Jackson cleared his throat. "We were hoping for some observations from you about last night. I mean, if you'd care to. We're not pressing."

"I'd like to talk," Amy said. "I need something to do besides lie around and have people measure me up and down."

The ranger and the nurses finished their work. Amy's wounds were dressed and she turned over on her back.

"I haven't been able to eat or sleep," Amy continued. "I close my eyes and all I can see is Allen and that grizzly. It seems like it happened a thousand years ago. It's way, way back in my mind. But here I am. I don't know how much help I can be."

"We just wanted to tell you that we're sorry," Tanner said, "and that we're glad you're not seriously injured. If you think talking to us will be too hard, we'll go."

"No," Amy said, "it's fresh in my mind now. I'd like to tell you what I saw, or at least what I think I saw."

Tanner took out a notepad. "We'd like to hear anything you can remember."

"I'll tell you right away, that bear acted crazy from the beginning," Amy said. "It didn't act right at all."

Tanner was writing. "What do you mean?"

"I'm not an expert on grizzlies, but I know that one wanted nothing to do with the food. It went right for Allen. It definitely wanted to kill. That has to mean something."

"It means a great deal," Tanner said. "Start from the beginning, if you would."

Amy described the evening with Allen Freeman and the cast, and talked about the rain and the noise in the trees.

."I told them all that we had to get out of there. But it was too late."

Amy took a deep breath and continued. She said the grizzly came at Allen Freeman as if it had been stalking him for years, as if it wanted revenge.

"It acted like it wasn't going to let Allen get away, not for anything. It was like a man, a crazy man who wanted to close in on one particular victim. I hope I never have to see anything like that again. Not forever." Tears ran down her cheeks. She covered her face with her hands.

"We don't have to continue," Jackson said.

Amy blew her nose into a tissue. "No, I'm fine. I want to help you with this."

"Did the bear go for you first?" Tanner asked. "Did Allen Freeman step between or something?"

"No, I told you, the bear came right at Allen, like no one else was there. It wouldn't have even known I was around if I hadn't shot it."

Amy described how Freeman had gotten a pistol from his tent and how she had ended up with it. "I shot the bear twice and it wouldn't go down. It was crazed, I tell you. My only chance was to climb a tree."

"You took good care of yourself," Jackson said. "It's lucky you'd had police training."

"Maybe that's what makes me want to understand this all the more," Amy said. She thought back on the end of her law enforcement training. She had been within two weeks of graduating when she and her fiancé had happened upon a robbery in progress.

Amy's fiancé had entered the convenience store just ahead of her. He had been shot and killed; a bullet had passed through her left thigh, missing the femoral artery by less than an inch.

During the funeral, Amy had decided she didn't want to continue in law enforcement. She still wanted a career that would help people, but dying the way her fiancé had wouldn't help anyone.

On the way out of the cemetery, she had happened upon

a small patch of field chickweed. The plants had been run over and stepped on several times, yet they still held their natural beauty. She had propped them back up and had sat looking at them for a ling time. That was when she had chosen to pursue botany.

Amy was beginning to wonder about her luck with men. First, her fiancé had died before her eyes. She was just getting to know Allen Freeman, and then the grizzly got him. What next?

"Miss Ellerman? You okay?" Tanner was leaning over her.

"Yes, thank you. I guess I drifted away for a moment."

"Are you getting tired?" Tanner asked. "Why don't we come back another time?"

Amy's eyes filled with tears. "I told them to have the party inside somewhere. I *told* them! Allen shouldn't have died."

Amy was sobbing when the doctor came in. He looked at Tanner.

"We were about to leave," Tanner said.

"No, don't go yet," Amy said. "I need to understand this."

"Maybe it's best if they come another time," the doctor suggested to her. "You've been under a lot of stress."

Jackson and Tanner thanked Amy for her time.

"I want you to come back day after tomorrow," Amy said. "Doctor Jones says I'll be up on crutches by then. Didn't you, Doctor?"

The doctor nodded. "If you get some rest, I don't see why not."

Amy turned to Tanner. "I want to go back to where Allen was killed. Maybe I'll remember something important that I can't think of right now."

"Are you sure?" Tanner asked.

"I'm certain," Amy said. "I need to know why this happened. I need to know in the worst way."

"I'll be back to see you, then," Tanner said.

The hospital halls were quiet. Tanner's boots made tiny

squeaks against the newly polished floor and Jackson chewed his gum loudly. They walked out the front, where the lake was sparkling in the sun.

"Everyone's pretty shook up," Jackson said. "Too many chewed-up bodies."

"What she saw must have been unreal," Tanner said.

Jackson popped fresh gum into his mouth. "This whole thing is unreal."

Tanner walked down to the lake and stood looking across the water. Jackson, who had followed, was writing notes to himself, so he wouldn't overlook any of the many forms he would have to face back in his office.

Tanner marveled at the clear, open morning. The air was still and the sun was warming the shoreline, where two avocets probed the rocks with their bills, looking for insects. Just out from shore, an osprey dove and rose again from the water's surface, clutching a wriggling trout. Tanner watched the bird of prey settle into its giant nest of sticks high in a dead lodgepole pine.

"Why can't things be like this all the time?" Tanner asked. "Where have we gone wrong?"

"I've got too many questions as it is," Jackson said, popping his gum. "I can't answer them either."

Tanner thought about Amy Ellerman and her offer to work with him. "Do you think she can help us?" he asked Jackson. "How do you feel about it?"

"Suit yourself," Jackson said. "I'll be sitting in my office for some time to come, filling out forms. If you want to see if she can be of help, by all means do it. Whatever it takes to get this figured out."

Tanner stared out over the lake. Jackson looked at his watch. "Sally should be here any time," he told Tanner.

"I know," Tanner said. "I just wanted to relax a minute."

"You don't want to see that mess very bad, do you?"

"Not very bad." He turned and took a deep breath. "But that's what I came for."

seven

At the Freeman Site park rangers had secured the area, but the news media were everywhere. In addition to state and local people, every major newspaper and television network was represented. Cameras rolled and reporters wrote furiously. The center of attention was Leland Beckle.

"I can't believe this," Jackson said as he parked. "Beckle's got no business talking to the media." He got out and slammed the door.

As Jackson and Tanner approached, the cameras and newspeople turned. Tanner waved them off.

The media knew John Tanner well, ever since the shoot-out with the poaching ring. They saw him as a real expert on the mountains, someone who didn't quit until he had found what he was looking for. They asked him if he was working the case and why.

Tanner continued to ignore them. Jackson held up his hand. "We can't tell you anything yet. Give us some time."

One of the reporters stepped in front of Jackson. "That's not what Leland Beckle said. He's told us a lot. What are you hiding?"

Jackson stopped and took a deep breath. Beckle was working his way through the crowd toward them. Jackson met Beckle and took him aside. A group of rangers converged and ushered the media back from the crime scene, warning them against pressing too hard.

While Jackson admonished Beckle about giving interviews, Tanner stared at the scene. Tarps and plastic lay everywhere, covering anything that might be evidence. It appeared as if a tornado had swept through, churning everything in its path into rubble.

Jim Clark stood to one side. The young ranger, of medium height and strongly built, was used to rugged hikes in the wilderness. But this was a different kind of test, and it had left him exhausted.

"I'm sorry you have to see this," he told Tanner, "but I have to confess, I'm glad you're here."

Others present at the scene were two park rangers who would also assist with the evidence gathering, the coroner from Cody, Wyoming, and Martin Linders, the Park's bear biologist.

Jackson and Beckle came over and everyone slipped under the yellow ribbon. Beckle crowded past everyone and walked onto the site, his hands on his hips.

"Let's not disturb the scene any more than we have to," Jackson called to him. "Come back over here with us. We'll wait for Sally."

Beckle reluctantly obeyed. Jackson wasn't anxious to have Beckle involved at all, but since it was Beckle's district, there was little he could do.

There were those who said Beckle's personality was a direct reflection of his looks. Ten years past, during fieldwork for his master's thesis, Beckle had been clawed along the right side of his face by a grizzly. His eyebrow hung at an odd angle over the eye socket, and he had lost the corner of his mouth. He was virtually unable to show expression on one half of his face.

With no private life, Leland Beckle concentrated on his professional career. There was no question about his knowledge or abilities: he had achieved his master's degree and enough years of experience in Canada to have published six papers. He knew bears and their behavior. It was his own behavior that was in question.

Beckle stood next to Tanner, glaring at him. He turned to Jackson. "You've made this complicated, bringing Tanner along."

"You know very well why he's here," Jackson said. "Why should it bother you?"

"Because he's bound to make things harder," Beckle replied. "He thinks that killer grizzly was a pet."

Tanner spoke evenly to Beckle. "It appears to me that you've never cared about the bears you've studied. That's too bad. You might have learned something."

"You'd better drop the sentiment," Beckle said. "This bear ripped a man to shreds last night. What if we run into another one like him? Maybe you don't belong here."

Martin Linders stepped forward. He looked like he wanted to say something to Beckle but only stared at him in anger.

"What's your problem, Linders?" Beckle asked.

"Mr. Tanner cares about animals," Linders said. "We all should. That's our job."

Linders walked off and stood a short distance away, staring out across the lake toward the distant peaks.

Those who knew Linders wondered what he would be like if he ever got really angry at someone. Linders was built more like a professional wrestler than a field biologist, yet he was known for his open mild manner. Since Beckle's arrival, however, Linders had become noticeably upset on several occasions.

Linders had become the park's bear biologist a year earlier, replacing an employee who had died in a skiing accident. He had spent his early professional years in Canada and Alaska and had just turned thirty. His records showed he had an undergraduate degree in biology from Wisconsin and was completing a master's degree in biochemistry from Montana State University.

Linders had been a welcome addition to the park staff. His experience in the lab, as well as fieldwork trapping and relocating both black and grizzly bears in Canada and Alaska, had made him a good selection for the position.

When not at his desk or in the field, Linders liked to work out. On occasion, he would go down to Bozeman and the weight room at Montana State University. It was rumored that he could bench-press more than most of the football players and could climb a rope from the gym floor to the ceiling in less than ten seconds.

Linders was a flashy dresser and, according to many of the rangers, could flirt with precision. Despite this, he was seldom seen in the company of a woman. He said that he had been married once but would never make that mistake again.

No one knew much more than that about him, for he spent most of his off time alone. Everyone who worked with him believed he preferred the company of animals to people.

The chief ranger had tried to nudge him into a more public life. There were many requests for someone to talk on grizzly issues, but Linders always begged off, preferring that someone else handle the speaking engagements.

Now Linders had turned and was staring hard at Beckle. "Maybe anyone who *doesn't* care about this bear *shouldn't* be here," he shouted over. "That's *my* feeling."

Beckle shouted back, "Tanner doesn't work here with us. He shouldn't be here."

Jackson spoke up. "Mr. Beckle, you know damn good and well that I requested Mr. Tanner's assistance, and that I went through proper channels. I don't want any more of this. Do you understand?"

Beckle looked around. There wasn't a face that showed support for him. He turned to Jackson.

"When Sally Hays arrives, you and the others go ahead and help her. I've got things to do." Without waiting for a response, he turned and shouldered his way back toward his vehicle.

The tension eased. Martin Linders rejoined the group. He spoke to Tanner directly.

"I don't like to see grizzlies die. I hope this is the last one."

"I do, too," Tanner said. "We don't have enough of them left to throw away like this."

A large gray Suburban with the Wyoming State decal on the door pulled into the campground. Sally Hays had arrived.

Martin Linders clapped Tanner on the shoulder. "Now we'll get to the bottom of this."

eight

SALLY HAYS was tall and trim, with an easy but determined manner. She knew what she had come for and wanted to collect it as quickly and efficiently as possible.

Though her step was as lively as ever, twenty-five years as a forensic biologist and pathologist had brought streaks of gray to once jet-black hair.

As deputy director and lab supervisor of the Wyoming State Crime Laboratory, Sally had solved or helped solve innumerable cases for the state of Wyoming, as well as many other states in the West and Midwest. Outside of the FBI lab in Washington, D.C., the lab in Cheyenne was as well respected as any in the country.

She got out of the Suburban and directed her assistant, a petite woman named Carol Williams, to help the rangers unload the bags and satchels. In her late twenties, Carol had worked with Sally for nearly five years. She was one of the best lab technicians in the region.

Sally surveyed the scene. Covered evidence was scattered over a large area. She shook her head. "Did a bomb go off here?"

"You would think so," Jackson said. "We've got a human and a grizzly fatality. There's a woman in Lake Hospital who was injured."

"I understand you believe there was human involvement with the grizzly, that it was painted, possibly by someone outside the Park Service."

"Yes, the grizzly was painted," Jackson said. "We can't understand why. I brought John Tanner in to help us. He's been studying the grizzly for a number of years."

Sally turned to Tanner. "I'm glad you're in on this, John. I'm sorry about your bear, but we'll get this figured out."

Tanner thanked her for her compassion. He had worked closely with Sally and the lab people on the poaching case. She had been able to verify that gunshot wounds to the elk had come from the rifles taken from the poachers at the shootout scene. She would certainly be able to get some answers to this.

"Do you know any more about the woman we found at Grizzly Lake?" Jackson asked her.

"I'm sorry, Nate, but nothing yet. I've sent photos of the reconstruction everywhere I can think, including Canada and Mexico. She's still in the cooler."

"I know you're doing your best," Jackson said. "That's all you can do."

Sally assembled everyone who would be gathering evidence and split them into teams of two. Martin Linders was paired with Jim Clark. Tanner and Jackson would work together, assisting Sally and Carol with the photography and the work on Barney and Allen Freeman.

When the tarps were removed from Barney and Allen Freeman's remains, Tanner left the scene and stood at the lakeshore, staring out over the water. Jackson soon followed.

"Are you all right?" Jackson asked.

"It just brings things back, that's all."

"Maybe I shouldn't have insisted you come," Jackson said. "I'm sorry."

"No, I'm glad you pushed me," Tanner said. "I have to get over it sometime."

"I appreciate it," Jackson said. "I hope you know that."

They walked back to where Sally was examining the paint marks on Barney. "Doesn't he look like an Indian painted him? I mean, I've heard of that sort of thing, for religious ceremonies." She looked up at Tanner. "You know more about that kind of thing than me."

"I don't think an Indian did it," Tanner said. "It follows Native American bear ceremonial designs, but the colors are wrong. At least, it seems to me. I never heard of yellow and black together. Usually red and black. I don't know for sure, though."

"Well, we can't say that the paint caused the bear to attack anyone," Sally said. "We'll just have to gather every bit of evidence we can and see what we can make of it."

Everyone began scouring the site. The teams worked slowly and methodically, tagging an assortment of bags and containers. At Sally's request, Tanner sketched the area, while she took pictures of everything from every angle and used large red markers, sequentially numbered, to show how the attack had unfolded.

When he had finished with the sketch, Tanner took hair samples from the lower limbs of the tree where Barney had struggled to reach Amy Ellerman. He climbed into the branches to collect skin and hair samples left by Amy.

Tanner peeled dried and bloody fragments of skin and hair from the bark, placing the pieces into a small plastic bag. As he worked, Julie's screams came back to him.

He looked down. Sally and Jackson were working near Barney. Clark was bent down near the ground, using a pair of tweezers. Martin Linders was staring up into the tree.

Tanner's vision began playing tricks on him. Linders became his dead wife, Julie, looking up at him pleadingly, as the grizzly dragged her away.

Tanner scrambled down, nearly falling. He hurried away from the site, his breath coming quickly.

Jackson hurried to him. "Can I help you, John?"

"No," Tanner said. "I just can't make it go away."

"You've got to let her go," Jackson advised. "That's what I learned. I couldn't hold on to my brother. He's gone. What did your counselor say?"

"The counselor told me a lot of things," Tanner said. "The department was good in allowing me to see him as long as I wanted. But it's not that easy to deal with."

"You've got to believe that she went when her time came," Jackson said. "You couldn't help that."

Tanner turned. "And what about our baby? What time did the baby get? Huh? What time did that little baby get? None!"

"I'm sorry, John. Maybe you ought to call it a day."

Sally Hays approached them. She held a latex paw imprint she had taken from her vehicle. "I'll understand if you don't want to continue, John," she said, "but I've discovered something important."

Tanner took a deep breath. "What have you got?"

Sally showed him the imprint. "Carol and I made this from a plaster cast of a track on the Grizzly Lake shoreline. Jim Clark sent the cast to us. I've just compared this imprint to one of Barney's paws. I believe they match."

Tanner remembered seeing the huge grizzly tracks at Grizzly Lake and thinking they were large enough to be Barney's. He didn't want to think his bear had killed two people, though.

Jackson studied the imprint. "Are you saying that Barney killed the woman we found in June?"

"I'm quite certain of it," Sally said. "Would you both follow me?"

Tanner and Jackson followed Sally to Barney's body, where she compared the latex imprint to one of Barney's paws. It seemed like a perfect match.

"We'll do plaster casts of the paws and teeth in the lab," Sally said. "Then I'll know for certain. But right now, I'd have to say yes, it looks like Barney killed the woman, too."

"Then that should end the maulings," Jackson said. "That should make things a lot easier for me."

"It won't make anything easier for you," Tanner said. "This is just the beginning."

"The paint won't make a difference if the maulings end," Jackson said.

"I'm not talking about the paint, necessarily," Tanner said. "Something else has to have happened to him. His behavior is what bothers me."

"C'mon, Tanner," Jackson said, "He might have broken a tooth. He might have a thorn in a paw. Who knows?"

Tanner glared. "Barney shouldn't have been way down here in the first place. That's the point!"

"Look, it's been a hard day," Sandy said. "I know how badly both of you want this to be over, but it's too early to be certain about anything yet."

Jackson rubbed his neck. "Hey, I'm sorry, John. Sally's right."

"Well, it's *not* over," Tanner said. "Take my word for it."

Barney was loaded onto a flatbed trailer in exactly the position he lay on the ground. Sally wanted no fluid transfers to hinder the necropsy results.

Allen Freeman's ripped and torn remains were transferred into the back of the Suburban in the same manner.

"His left hand is missing," Sally said. "Has anyone located it?"

No one had found the hand. Sally led the team around the perimeter of the scene, looking for the hand and sharing her conclusion that Barney had come along the lakeshore and had circled up through the trees before attacking Freeman from the front.

When she had finished, she and Carol began loading their things for the long drive back to Cheyenne.

"We'll have to determine whether Barney had infected teeth or old wounds," she said. "But at this time, I have to believe that the food lured the bear here and Allen Freeman was in the way. We'll know a lot more in the lab."

"What about the paint?" Martin Linders asked.

"We'll have to look into it," Sally replied.

Linders was looking at the scene. "Do you think this is the end of our nightmare?"

"I surely hope so," Sally replied. "I don't want to ever have to come up here again for something like this.

nine

DARKNESS HAD fallen. The moon, nearly full, was rising over the lake. The late-evening breeze was as soft as a fawn's breath. The water, smooth as cold glass, stretched toward towering peaks, rising jagged in the shadowed sky.

The media had left. Jackson was sitting in his Suburban, filling out forms. Tanner knew he would have a lot of forms to deal with himself. He hated the thought of it.

Tanner had not spent such a trying day since Julie's death. He stood on the lakeshore, gazing across the water, trying to forget the unsettled feeling.

Jackson closed the door to his vehicle and joined Tanner. "Nothing changes out here, does it?" he said. "To feel this peace, you'd never think last night had happened." He offered Tanner a piece of gum.

"Thanks, but you're going to need all of it." Tanner sat down on a log.

"I noticed you looking hard at Barney's remains, and the spot where he died," Jackson said, sitting down beside him. "What was that all about?"

"I know that something terrible happened to Barney,"

Tanner said. "The paint has something to do with it. I can't say what, though."

"Have you got enough to take to Grandfather?"

"I don't think so. There are different types of paint markings. They all mean different things. I don't know enough about it. I need to know more about what happened to Barney."

Tanner was fighting the urge to return to the site and spend time there. If Grandfather were here, he would go and sit for a long time in the darkness. He could learn things that way.

Grandfather had urged him to do the same thing. "You have a gift," he had told Tanner. "You should use it. The Creator doesn't give that kind of gift to just anyone."

The idea still frightened Tanner. He hadn't wanted the gift; he certainly hadn't asked for it. Why should he be obliged to use it?

"Are you thinking about going back over to the site?" Jackson asked.

Tanner shifted on the log. "Something tells me I should."

"Maybe this is all over," Jackson suggested. "Maybe you should just relax."

"You can think it's over, Nate, that's fine with me," Tanner said. "But I know better."

"Do you think Sally's wrong?" Jackson asked. "Are you saying Barney's not the bear that killed the woman?"

"No," Tanner said. "I'm saying that I need to know *why* Barney killed that woman. There has to be a reason."

Tanner turned his face into a slight wind that rose and cried in the trees, bringing a hint of moisture to the air.

Jackson was feeling the breeze also. "It seems just like last night out here, doesn't it?" he said.

Tanner was silent. He turned toward the site and stared into the darkness.

"I don't want to tell you what to do," Jackson said, "but maybe you should take a chance. Like you say, maybe you'll get something. It's something that's in you. You know, my mother—"

"I know," Tanner interrupted. "I've heard the story before. So why don't you try it with me?"

"Oh, no," Jackson said, "I don't have any gift like that. But I could stay, if you wanted. I could wait for you."

"No. I should be alone. No distractions. Tell the rangers on guard to go up to Lake Village and get some coffee. I'll tell them when I'm through."

"I mean it, John. I could stay, if you wanted."

Tanner smiled. "Nate, I know you. This kind of thing spooks you. You don't want to be here."

"Yeah, you know me," Jackson said. "I guess my older brothers scared me too much as a child down home. But you might need some help."

"No," Tanner said. "I'd rather be alone."

"You sure, now?"

"I'm sure, Nate. Go on. Get out of here."

Jackson sighed. "I'll take the rangers and go up to Lake Village. We'll wait. You radio me when you're through."

"Okay," Tanner said. "But it's going to be awhile."

"I've got nothing better to do," Jackson said. "Take your time."

When Jackson was gone, Tanner sat down with his back against a tree and looked out across the water. The breeze was stirring the surface and moonlight danced off the ripples. In the distance a loon called, a high, lonely scream. From somewhere another answered.

Tanner closed his eyes. He would sleep for a couple of hours, to settle himself into a quiet state of mind. When the time was right he would awaken, and he would enter the campground.

His mind would be open and he would feel what had happened the night before. He would know Allen Freeman's terror and, he hoped, he would learn what had happened to the grizzly he had studied and called a friend for so long.

* * *

The air was damp with a light mist. Tanner woke and rose. He entered the campground, and stood in the darkness, his body calm, his senses alert. He was open to what lay around him, feeling the heavy pressure of what had happened the previous night. Beyond the misty breeze that filled the trees, there were terrible screams just across from Tanner's conscious mind.

He started from the beginning, trying to imagine the party: the laughing and singing; happy people. He walked slowly, barefoot, feeling the ground that had witnessed horror.

There was an area where people had stood, flattened soil and plants against the bottoms of his feet. Potato chips, chunks of potato salad were mixed with pine needles and fragments of tree limbs accumulated over the years as mulch.

He felt something hard and small, sharp on one side, against the heel of his right foot. It wasn't a rock. He stooped and picked up a human tooth, and held it in his left hand.

The shattered picnic table lay just ahead. His feet touched splinters of wood. He closed his eyes. In his mind it was all a blur, just black whirring motions. The smell of death was as thick as rotten garbage.

The ground was soft and sticky in places. The blood hadn't fully dried; tiny bits of shredded flesh hadn't been found yet by nosy ravens. The wind seemed to cry here. The air seemed filled with sadness.

Barney had died nearby, beneath the tree that Amy Ellerman had climbed to save her life. Tanner stood on the spot and looked up into the tree, through the branches, into a sky filled with roiling clouds and fractured moonlight.

He sat down at the base of the tree, staring at nothing. He tried to imagine the bear rising, standing tall and terrible, ripping at Amy Ellerman's leg. Though he could feel the rage left behind, he couldn't envision the bear as Barney. But it had been Barney.

Tanner moved over to where Allen Freeman's remains

had been found. More sticky soil. More crying wind. He lay down on his back, his eyes closed, holding the tooth tightly.

The smell of blood and body fluids filled his head. As he lay, he knew the event was embedding itself along his spinal column, flowing into his brain, forming scenes that would come to him another time, when he least suspected it—likely in his sleep.

The wind cried over him and the whirring motions descended. His stomach knotted. He seemed to fall into a large, swirling hole.

Tanner rose, dizzy, almost nauseated. The darkness around him seemed thick with moving shadows. For a time after Julie had died, he would see her in his sleep. Sometimes he thought he had seen her when awake. He didn't want to see anyone here tonight. It would all come to him soon enough.

Tanner left the scene, returning to the lake. He stepped into the shallows, splashing his face with icy water. He heard something and turned, seeing an image in the shadows coming toward him.

"John? You all right?" Jackson stepped from the trees.

"I thought you were going to wait for my call."

"I got worried. You've been here a long time."

"No. I just got here."

"John, it's nearly three A.M."

Tanner was startled. He knew he had moved slowly and deliberately, to absorb the most that he could. And he had taken his time on the ground. But three hours?

"That's impossible," Tanner said.

"That's what I thought. So I came back. What's going on?"

Tanner came on shore and sat down on a log. His mind was swimming with blurred images and impressions.

"What's going on with you?" Jackson asked.

"This is like nothing I've ever felt before," Tanner replied. "It reaches me way down deep inside."

Jackson sat next to Tanner. "What do you mean?"

Tanner was leaning forward, as if he were trying to get rid of a headache. "It's beyond anything I've ever dealt with. I've done this before on mauling sites and murder scenes. But there's something here that I can't understand. Something real strange happened to Barney. He was a different bear than the one I knew. Very different."

"Is it time to talk to Grandfather yet?"

"No."

"When are you going to talk to him?" Jackson insisted.

"When I know what to ask," Tanner replied. "I'll have to wait for my dreams to come." Tanner winced as he spoke. He realized that what would come to him would be nightmares like he had never imagined.

"What do you think you'll see?" Jackson asked.

"I haven't any idea," Tanner replied. "But I feel like whatever comes will be straight from hell itself."

ten

HE SAT alone near the fire, knowing that John Tanner and Nate Jackson were probably at the mauling site, talking about what had happened. He couldn't afford to have them know his secrets.

Here, in his place, the forest was a haze of shadows and half-images, where the moon shone as thin beams of white through the dense canopy. Here the traffic on the park roads and the activity of the campgrounds could not be heard, only the eerie sounds of a world lost within itself, governed by the laws of prehistory.

Central Plateau was an isolated section of rock and dense timber, a lost world where the steam from thermal pools rose along primitive pathways never touched by man. Here the grizzly reigned supreme, lord of the forest.

Mary Mountain rose along the divide at the head of Hayden Valley, where the main trail crossed over to Nez Perce Creek. The trail was often closed due to bear activity, and few ever visited the area.

On the shore of Mary Lake stood the Mary Mountain cabin, deserted for some years. It was a suitable place for him, a man who had always wished to live as a primitive being. It was here that he played out secret rituals, chanting incantations that only he knew or understood, calling to the Great Bear spirit, so that one day soon he might assume the physical and spiritual likeness of the supreme ruler of the forest, the grizzly bear.

This had always been his desire. Then and only then could he absorb the spirit of his dead mother, a spirit that never left him alone.

His fantasies to become a grizzly had begun at the age of five, when he had first witnessed the bear's incredible power. His mother had taken him to a circus, where a grizzly had been chained to a tree.

"Isn't he warm and fuzzy looking?" his mother had said. "Just like your own teddy bear at home."

His mother had held him fast around the wrist, as she always did. Never by the hand. Always fast around the wrist. It had made him feel like the grizzly, with its front leg bound in iron.

The keeper had come to feed it, prodding it with a long pole to force it away. The grizzly had suddenly roared, lunging toward the keeper, hitting the end of the chain with the force of a train.

The chain had popped and the grizzly reached the keeper, hitting him so hard with a forepaw that his head had exploded. The bear had run through the grounds, destroying stands and concessions in its path.

He remembered clearly how his mother had loosened her grasp on his wrist and had run away, leaving him behind. It hadn't bothered him. He had felt like the grizzly: free! The shackle gone!

But his mother had soon realized her mistake and had found him. Once again the shackle had been placed on his wrist.

He had never known what happened to the grizzly. He liked to think it had gotten far away and was roaming free.

Now he had his own dreams of ruling unchallenged in a world far different from the one of his childhood, far away from the noisy, crowded streets with their dark alleys that held him fast and helpless. Far away from the iron fingers clamped on his wrist.

In those early years he could only imagine and dream about what he saw and felt. Each trip into the damp, dark basement with his mother, each atrocity against him multiplied in his mind a thousand times.

Often he would imagine his teddy bear, having turned huge and vengeful, tearing chunks of dripping flesh from those who had hurt him. He had come to see himself as that bear, reigning supreme over those who would harm him.

He had grown into puberty; the fantasies had grown with him. His obsession with bears had become constant. He had learned to kill as a grizzly might—stray cats and dogs had been his targets, sharpened garden tools were his claws.

By the time he was twenty, small pets no longer brought satisfaction. The taste for the kill had grown stronger within him, his fantasies wilder and darker. He knew that to avenge in the manner demanded by the Great Bear, his quarry would have to be bigger. His quarry would have to be human.

The Great Bear demanded it.

To avenge as the Great Bear, in a proper manner befitting its spirit, he had moved west, into the country where the bear lived in the flesh. There, he strove to learn the bear's biology, better able, then, to cross over into the grizzly's spirit realm.

He had also delved into Indian shamanism, learning what he could from books and documentaries, and then approaching Native American spiritualists; they had been kind, but had never shared with him.

Theirs was the world of the mind, a place where he wanted to be. But over time, he had come to believe that he didn't need them. He didn't need anyone. He had his own ways of contacting the spirit. His day would come, and he would be fulfilled.

Thus he had come to the mountains, ever closer to his mission. He had prescribed his own rituals, selected drugs and herbs himself. Little by little he had come where he now stood, ready to cross the last threshold and join with the spirit of the Great Bear.

When the right selections were made and the kills done in the right manner, he would satisfy the demands of the Great Bear spirit. Then and only then he could consume the spirit of his mother and rid himself of her forever.

Now, deep in the shadowed wilderness, he sat cross-legged near the fire, covered with the head and cape of a grizzly. His eyes had circles of yellow and black around them, and under the cape lines of yellow and black ran down his back.

Before him lay another grizzly's head, the eyes circled with black and yellow paint. With the night deep and dark all around, he made his offering. He asked that the spirit not be offended by the change in plans he must make. He needed additional time. He must be cautious. He didn't want John Tanner, with his Indian mind, learning their secrets.

Only the Great Bear could help him now. He chanted, leaning over the bear's head, and then placed a human arm between the teeth.

The arm had come from a young woman who had worked in a concession store in Canyon Village. He had watched her for some time, learning her habits, before approaching her. She had been delighted to hike into the backcountry with him.

When the right day had arrived, he had taken her into his realm and done what he had to, fulfilling himself for a time.

Now her remains lay beside him, such as they were.

No one knew about her. Not yet. They would, though, when the time was right.

Up to now, he had believed his association with the Great Bear spirit was blessed. He had chosen a massive

grizzly from which to learn. The bear had been wearing a
radio collar and had been easy to find.

He had trapped the bear in a large pit and had sedated
it several times, so that he might talk to it and feel its massive body. He had painted the grizzly in the manner demanded by the Great Bear spirit.

But his selection of victims must be precise. Each
woman must meet certain specifications: between five-four
and five-five in height, under 120 pounds, with dark blond
hair and blue eyes. Their hands must be small, their feet
almost dainty. They had to be in their early twenties.

There was also the requirement for the name. This was
imperative for success in his mission. Ellen had been the
first woman's name. Young and pretty; just right. Ellen
Lorraine Marks. She had fit all his needs, and she had met
the grizzly.

He had found Ellen during the first month, waiting tables at Old Faithful Inn. She had thought it interesting to
go into the backcountry, to see wondrous sites guided by
a man who seemed so polite and assuring.

He had left her along the shore of Grizzly Lake. To
date, she had not been identified.

Valerie had also fit. Valerie Jane Waters, the second one,
whose arm he was now offering to the grizzly's spirit. After the ritual, he would place her remains in a special place
within his secret realm. Then, when the moon was right,
he would leave the woman elsewhere, to be found by the
already troubled authorities.

Following this, a third and final woman must be found
to fulfill the requirements for his spiritual transfer. But before he could offer her, he must find another grizzly to re-
place the one who had deserted him.

Completion had been so close. How could he have
known Barney would escape? How could he have known
the big grizzly would be smart enough to dig its way out
of the pit? It had been plenty deep enough. But Barney
had wanted out so badly, even from the beginning.

The resultant death of Allen Freeman had made his mission complicated. Perhaps the spirit had demanded this offering as well. To question it served no purpose now; he must proceed with his plan in the manner that had been laid out.

Now he would have to dig the pit out again. He would have to find another grizzly as big and as knowledgeable as Barney, one he could also learn from. Barney had taught him many things that he would need during his transfer into the Great Bear spirit. He would need to know just a little more. He had been so close.

Then it would be time to bring the woman to complete his final ritual. He had already made the perfect choice: Amy Lee Ellerman.

But serious complications existed. Amy Ellerman had been injured by Barney, and she might not be able to hike into the backcountry for some time to come. It was distressing to think that she might not be available. She was the most perfect of all. Somehow, some way, he would have to bring her to his secret place.

Now a lot of attention was focused on the park. That would make his mission harder to complete. It would be a great challenge. Perhaps the Great Bear would see him in a better light and allow the transfer to come easily.

As he finished the ritual, he took the arm from between the teeth and placed it within Valerie Jane Waters's torso. She had been disemboweled by the grizzly, her legs and arms torn and tattered. Her head had been crushed in its mouth, and her face now bore no features whatsoever. She was beyond human recognition.

As with the first woman, he had never regarded her as anything more than an object he needed for his mission. Now she was not even that, only something he must dispose of in a manner fitting to the Great Bear.

He rose to begin dancing in a circle around the fire, stopping each time around to touch the dead woman's remains. He must conclude this part of his mission quickly, he realized, for dawn would be coming soon.

When the sun rose, he must be ready to assume his

daily position among the people with whom he worked. As always, they would not know who he really was or anything of his mission.

He needed to manage his time carefully now. The second woman would have to be left for the authorities to find. Meanwhile, he would need to clean out the pit and trap another grizzly.

Then he would bring Amy Ellerman to the pit, and she would be consumed, as the other two before her, by the Great Bear spirit. She would be the final step in his mission. She would help him enter a new world where he, and he only, would be king. After that, he would never have to hear his mother's voice again.

eleven

TANNER SLEPT fitfully. After four hours he awakened and sat up, disoriented, slow to realize he was in his cabin. There was sunlight at the window; it was eight o'clock. He finally realized he had been driven home by Nate Jackson. But he couldn't remember it very well.

Rather than rest, his sleep had been a battle within his unconscious mind, leaving him more exhausted than when he had gone to bed.

Tanner had decided to talk with Martin Linders before seeing Amy Ellerman again. Linders had gathered a lot of data on the travels of grizzlies through the remote areas. Tanner hoped to learn where Barney had come from before reaching the lake.

Tanner dressed quickly. He had no appetite. In Grandfather's Indian way, he had gone, in his sleep, to the place he was looking for, and had learned something about Barney. He couldn't remember being there, for the dream hadn't come to consciousness. But wherever he had gone, it had been abnormal and very frightening.

When Tanner was a boy, Grandfather had told him that

he would take an unusual path in life. Somehow Grandfather had been able to see Tanner's future. "You just know these things," he would tell Tanner. "Someday I believe you will know what I mean."

Tanner drove his state Jeep through Gardiner and into the park, trying to clear his head. He felt oppressed, as if something thick and sickening had worked its way into his soul.

At Mammoth Hot Springs, he parked in front of the visitors' center and crossed the short distance back to the administration building, one of the largest of the stone buildings built at the turn of the century. Three floors of office space held much of the park's administrative staff, plus personnel from other agencies.

Tanner entered the building, trying to bring his nerves back to some state of normalcy. After the previous night, he wondered if he shouldn't just try to forget his Indian ancestry.

But that was something he couldn't do. His past was a part of him, a part of his future, for whatever reason. It was rushing to greet him, he couldn't deny that. Somehow, as he grew older, his desire to learn about his forefathers was growing stronger.

Linders was located on the third floor, in the Backcountry Office. The space was shared by a number of people who worked the trails and remote campgrounds. Finding the woman's body, and now Allen Freeman's death, had interrupted a lot of studies, though, and everyone wanted the problem to end soon.

Linders had partitioned himself off from the others, secluding himself in one corner near a window. One partition was covered with a map denoting bear management areas and another showed the location of bear incidents throughout the park. Tanner noted that the Freeman Site had already been marked in large red letters.

Two walls and the second partition were covered with pictures of grizzlies and a number of Indian chiefs and warriors, including the Nez Percé leader Joseph, famous for leading his people through Yellowstone Park while evading U.S. Army troops in late summer of 1877.

"Brave man, he," Linders said.

"They were all brave," Tanner said. "A tragedy."

"Yeah, it's too bad all that had to happen," Linders said. He moved from his cubbyhole to a nearby table. "Care for a cup of coffee?"

Tanner politely declined. His stomach was churning.

Linders sorted through various papers scattered on a nearby desk. He pointed to the front page of the Bozeman *Chronicle*. Leland Beckle's picture was in the middle of the page.

"This guy's out of control," Linders said. "Who docs hc think he is, John Wayne?"

Tanner read the headline: PARK RANGER LEADS HUNT FOR CLUES IN ACTOR'S DEATH.

"I don't like a guy who tries to be a showboat," Linders went on. "I wouldn't ordinarily speak out against a fellow employee. But, you know what I mean? This guy's an ass."

"That's something you people in the Park Service will have to deal with."

"Yeah, I suppose so," Linders said. "But it's no secret he hates your guts."

"And I don't even know why," Tanner said.

Linders laughed. "Sure you do. He wants your stature. He wants the glory you got for catching those poachers two years ago. He wants that in the worst way. And he's going to have it, by God, one way or another."

"I'm not concerned with Beckle," Tanner said. "I'm trying to learn some things about Barney just before he died."

"What do you want to know?"

"Where he was before he came down to the lake. Hopefully *why* he came down to the lake."

Slurping coffee, Linders pointed to the map. "This is where I last saw Barney."

Tanner frowned. Linders was pointing to the base of

Observation Peak, near Grebe Lake. That also seemed way out of Barney's territory.

Tanner had never known Barney to leave upper Hayden Valley. But Linders's data showed that the huge grizzly had been roaming along the headwaters of Alum Creek, stretching over to Mary Lake and into Nez Perce Creek.

"Barney always seemed to like his home territory," Tanner commented. "I wonder why he would move?"

"I can't say," Linders replied, "but that's where I tracked him to. His collar was giving out strong signals. I've got a lot of data logged." Linders opened his desk and pulled out a folder.

"That's another thing that bothers me," Tanner said, reviewing the information. "Barney's collar was missing. It wasn't anywhere near the site. Whoever painted him must have taken it off. Maybe we can pick up the signals and find it. That would tell us where Barney was before coming down."

"Do you suppose we can figure this out?" Linders asked.

Tanner handed the folder back to Linders. "I hope so. It bothers me a lot. I can't help but think whoever did it might possibly want to do it again."

"Do you really think so?" Linders asked.

"I wouldn't be surprised," Tanner said. "Somebody had to have a reason to do that. A strange reason, I would say."

"There's been some strange things going on in the back-country for some time," Linders said, visibly upset. "Poachers. We can't get rid of them. We can't even keep up with the new ones coming in. Before long, they'll have wiped out the gene pool for the elk. Who knows what's next?"

"I don't believe a poacher had anything to do with this," Tanner said.

"That's exactly my point," Linders said. "It wasn't a poacher who painted Barney. Someone else did, for whatever reason. The paint and the poachers made Barney very,

very angry. He and the other grizzlies back there are fed up with everything."

"I don't follow," Tanner said.

"It seems clear to me," Linders said. "I think Barney just wanted to rid the world of one more crazy human. You can bet the rest of those people won't be back—those crazy city slickers who know nothing about the outdoors. He had to teach them all a lesson."

"Be serious."

"Listen, I am being serious. You know as well as I do that the human race is going to make this planet totally worthless in just a little while. It's almost too late now."

"I'm not talking about the whole planet," Tanner said. "I'm talking about this case. One thing at a time, please."

"And I'm trying to tell you that it all ties together," Linders said. He went to a file and pulled out another document. Tanner sat down with him. "Let me tell you a story. This happened three weeks ago. You listening?"

"I'm interested in *this* case, Martin."

"This is about a grizzly like Barney."

"I want to know about Barney," Tanner said. "Not a bear *like* him."

"Please, give me a chance," Linders insisted. "I'm answering your question. Don't you believe that?"

"Okay, I believe you," Tanner said. "What's the story?"

"It was close to midnight, a nice summer evening," Linders began. "I was headed home when a call came over the radio. Grizzly trouble at Lake Campground. When I got there another ranger was trying to keep this big, middle-aged woman from pounding him to death. She was holding a growling poodle in one hand, swinging at the ranger with the other, screaming that she was going to sue the park. A grizzly had wrecked her travel trailer.

"You see, what she'd done was lure this big grizzly into her camper with a dish of dog food. Then she'd sat at her little table, watching that bear eat the dog food right in front of her. When the bear was finished, he couldn't find a way out. So he slammed a paw against the side of her trailer and knocked all the rivets out of a seam, then just jumped out. She wanted to hold the park to blame."

"Are you saying that grizzly was Barney?"

"I can't say. I didn't see the bear. It left."

"Then what does the story have to do with Barney?"

"Don't you see? People are getting so stupid they don't know when their lives are in danger. Don't you think those bears hate everybody coming through the park? Sure they do! People gawking and staring and asking stupid questions. People throwing their shit everywhere. You know, people can't go anywhere without trashing the place. The animals hate that."

"Don't you think you're giving the bears human attributes?" Tanner asked. "Maybe you just want them to think the way you do."

"Well, they *do* think that way, John!" Linders's eyes were large. "You know that. You know they have a specialness about them. In your way of thinking, you should consider them very sacred."

Tanner wished everyone would quit referring to his Indian background. He was proud of this small fraction of his heritage, but he didn't want people to think he was different from them.

"Yes, animals are entitled to respect," Tanner said. "But I don't think they sit around and think up ways to get rid of people."

Linders picked up the piece of paper. "Who can say? Who really *knows* what's going on in their minds?" He got up and replaced it in the file. "You know, John, bears are so close to humans. You take their feet, you know, without the claws, just the pads. They look human, but backwards."

"That's true," Tanner said.

"And you've seen bears skinned and hanging up," Linders said. "Except for the shape of the skull, they could be human. They look *human,* John!"

Tanner got up. "I care about bears as much as you do,

Martin. You know that. That's why I'm continuing to pursue this. I don't want any more people *or* bears killed."

"Nobody does, John. All I can say is you've got to give the bears more credit for their thinking. You know how smart they are. They can stalk. They can reason. You know that. In many ways, they're far superior to us."

Tanner stared at the map. "You're sure you saw Barney up at Grebe Lake?"

"Anybody who's seen Barney would remember him," Linders said. "It wouldn't take a bear biologist for that."

"I don't question your word," Tanner said. "I just don't know why Barney would move, that's all."

"He had a mind of his own," Linders said. "That's obvious."

"Thanks for the help," Tanner said. He turned to leave.

"Jackson says you're going to Cheyenne for the necropsy," Linders said. "Is that true?"

"Yes, I intend to," Tanner said.

"What do you think you'll find?"

"I won't know until I see it."

"People say you were out at the site last night, having dreams."

"I was out there."

"Tell me what it's like, John."

Two summer employees walked in the door. They stared at Tanner and Linders.

Tanner said, "Thanks again for your help." That was all Linders was going to get.

"I'm glad you're working so hard on this, John," Linders said. "If there's anything to find, you'll find it."

twelve

TANNER DROVE back down toward Lake Village. The radio was alive with the news of Allen Freeman. His relatives had been notified, and now the whole nation was in shock. Hollywood had sustained a tragic loss.

Tanner turned the radio off and drove in silence. The world on all sides was mountains, vast and wooded, with peaks pushing into the sky. This land he knew so well now seemed foreign to him, and he couldn't understand why. What secret did the forest hold? A secret he could feel but not understand, too horrible to imagine.

The day was open and sunny. The park roads were lined with campers and trailers, sightseers and hikers shooting rolls of film of all the natural wonders. If the events of the weekend had frightened anyone away, it wasn't noticeable.

In fact, nothing about the park indicated that something terrible had happened. Bison and elk grazed peacefully along the rivers, Norris Geyser Basin was alive with activity, and the upper and lower falls of the Yellowstone River had as many watchers as usual. Even the scheduled trail rides and hikes were in progress.

As Tanner crossed Alum Creek he thought about Barney. On his right the land spread upward in steep mountains and ledges choked with lodgepole pine, breaking into meadows and valleys covered with grass and wildflowers. Few trails traversed the vastness, which rose steadily to Central Plateau.

As he passed the lower reaches of Hayden Valley, Tanner wondered again how a bear once so averse to humans would migrate from deep in the backcountry toward a noisy, developed area. It made no sense to him.

Tanner reached Lake Village and eased his way past campers and boat trailers to the front of Lake Hospital. Amy Ellerman was sitting outside on a bench.

"Beautiful day, isn't it?" Amy said. "Allen loved these kinds of days. He said he'd never seen skies so clean and pure."

"You sure you feel up to this?" Tanner asked her.

Amy stood up and leaned on her crutches. "I want to know why Allen died. Maybe then I can put it behind me."

Tanner helped her into his vehicle. At the site, Amy sat for a time, staring out the window. The lake was tranquil, and a flock of gulls were skimming the shoreline for food.

"This can't be where that terrible thing happened," she said. "It seems so peaceful. It just doesn't look the same."

"We don't have to do this," Tanner said. He wasn't certain what good it would do anyway, at this point. But he realized how much she wanted to help.

"I'll be fine," Amy said, blinking away tears. She took a deep breath. "I just want to see if I can remember the details."

"You were probably numb," Tanner suggested. "No doubt you acted on instinct."

"I acted according to how I've been trained," Amy said. "I guess that's instinct to me now. But it took me so long to shoot that bear." She pointed out the window. "I sat up there in that damn tree, too scared to move. If I'd only had a few guts, Allen might not be dead." Amy bowed her head into her hands.

Tanner put a hand on her shoulder. "Listen, Amy, it wasn't your fault. The truth is, Allen Freeman likely sustained mortal wounds within seconds. You couldn't have saved him no matter what you did."

"But I heard him screaming for help. It was terrible. I'll never forget it."

"People can scream when they're unconcious. He was probably doing that."

"You don't have to smooth things over for me. I've seen people die before." Amy told Tanner about her training in Idaho and the death of her fiancé. "Both men I cared about died horribly," she said. "That makes me feel awful. I just wish I could have stopped that grizzly."

"I'm asking you not to blame yourself," Tanner repeated. "If you'd stayed on the ground, that grizzly would certainly have killed you as well. You wanted to live. That's nothing to be ashamed of."

Tanner got out and helped Amy from the vehicle. Amy hobbled over to the exact spot where Allen Freeman's remains had been discovered.

"What happened to the body?" she asked. "Was it shipped to Ohio? That's where his parents live."

"Do you know his parents?"

"No. I just knew Allen for a couple of weeks. I wanted to know him a lot longer." She turned and made her way to the foot of the tree and looked into the branches. "I don't know how I made it up there. Pure adrenaline, I guess."

Tanner noted the hole where the patch of bark had been ripped free. "Do you remember which way Barney—I mean the grizzly—came from?"

Amy turned. "Barney?"

"I've been studying that bear since my graduate days in Fish and Wildlife Management. I'm on this case because I knew that bear. He wanted nothing to do with people. This shouldn't have happened."

"Do you think he shouldn't have been killed?"

"There was no choice. I'm just saying that something is wrong here. That grizzly normally stayed in the backcountry. In fact, he's never been observed within five miles of any road or campground. He wanted nothing to do with people."

"Oh? Not until the other night." Amy turned and pointed. "We were over there near a table. He came up behind us, woofing and growling. I thought he'd come for the food. I tried to warn them."

"Did everyone run immediately?"

"Not until the bear came into the camp. One of the cast had a terrier. It ran out from the trees and everyone laughed. No one took me seriously. She turned and glared at Tanner. "Why wasn't someone watching? Why wasn't the Park Service here?"

"I'm sorry you have to go through this," Tanner said. "I know it's very painful."

"How could you know?" Amy asked.

"I know."

"You're not going to just smooth things over so easily," Amy said. "You tell me you know. You tell me to relax. How can I relax? I saw someone I cared deeply for torn to pieces out here."

Amy turned away, tears streaming down her face. She made her way to the lakeshore, sobbing, demanding that Tanner get away from her. She wanted to be alone in her grief.

A Yellowstone Park Suburban came to a stop next to Tanner's Jeep. Leland Beckle got out. "I need to ask you some questions, Tanner," he yelled. "Where's the report on your pet bear? I need that on my desk right away."

Tanner left Amy as Beckle stomped over, continuing to yell. "I haven't heard from you, Tanner. You're supposed to be working with me on this case. I've been looking all over for you. I don't even know what you're up to." His distorted features were twisted in anger.

"You must have changed your mind since our meeting

at the lab," Tanner said. "I got the distinct impression that you weren't interested in working with me at all."

"I don't think you belong on this case," Beckle said, "but it looks like the higher-ups have made up their minds against me. Since I'm the main investigator on this thing, and this is my district, we're going to have to coordinate on everything. Do you understand?"

"Why don't we talk about this later?" Tanner suggested. "I can meet with you in your office first thing this afternoon."

Beckle looked over at Amy. She was turned the other way, peering out over the lake.

"Oh, I see," he said. "I know what you're up to."

Tanner stared at Beckle. "What are you saying?"

"What are you doing out here alone with her?"

"We were going over what happened," Tanner said. "That's part of the investigation."

"We all know what happened," Beckle said. "What can she tell us?"

"She wants to be of help. What's wrong with that?"

Beckle laughed. "She looks like she wants *you* to help *her*." He nudged Tanner with his elbow, commenting that women needed help, especially after a trying time in their lives. "They get over the sorrow quicker, eh, Tanner?"

"I don't understand your behavior," Tanner said. "I've got work to do here with Amy Ellerman, nothing more. She's waiting for me."

"Not so fast," Beckle said. "I don't want you doing anything or going anywhere without my knowing about it. Do you understand?"

"No one told me to report to you."

"I'm telling you, Tanner. I'm telling you now. I told you, this is *my* district. *I'm* in charge here."

"I'll need it in writing, from Jackson's desk."

Beckle's face flushed. "Who do you think you are? I'm in charge of this entire investigation."

"You bring me a letter from Nate Jackson. I'll need that from you."

Beckle gritted his teeth. "You might not be on this case much longer, Tanner. I can get things done. You should know that."

Tanner smiled. "This one goes past your daddy's influence, Beckle. There's a whole lot at stake here. Check it out, if you don't believe me. Push it and see where you get."

Beckle glared. "Okay, Tanner. You win for now. But this isn't over. If I can't get you off this case, I'll take care of things myself. You're in no-man's-land here, if you know what I mean."

"Just what do you mean, Beckle?"

"I'll spell it out, Tanner. You'd better be as good in the woods as they say you are. If you're not, you're liable to be bear bait lying out in the trees somewhere."

Beckle turned and stormed back to his vehicle. When he was gone, Tanner rejoined Amy.

"I'm sorry about the interruption. I'll take you back to the hospital."

"You and he must be old friends," Amy said. She turned from the lakeshore and started for the Jeep, with Tanner beside her. "I can't see how anyone will figure this out. You're already fighting among yourselves. Typical bureaucrats."

Tanner offered to help Amy in, but she refused. He got in on his side and started the engine.

"Maybe it was a bad idea to bring you out here," he said.

"No, I needed to see this place again," Amy said. "I just don't feel confidence in you people. I don't see how you're going to make things safe out here."

"We'll do our best," Tanner said, driving out of the campground. "I know this will probably cost you the rest of your field season. I'm sorry about that, too."

"No, it won't cost me anything," Amy said. "I intend to get back collecting plants by the end of the week."

"You won't be in any condition to use that leg by then."

"Oh, yes I will."

"How do you think you're going to get into the back-country?"

"Same way I always do, either on foot or horseback."

"The Park Service won't allow it, not until this grizzly problem is solved."

"I've read the paper, Mr. Tanner. And I've heard the talk in the hospital. Everyone thinks your Barney was the killer bear. Everyone thinks it's over."

"You can't believe everything you read."

Amy turned and glared. "The problem isn't mine, Mr. Tanner. The responsibility lies with you and the Park Service. I have a job to do, and so do you. I intend to get mine done on time."

"Time has nothing to do with it, Miss Ellerman. Two people have died in less than three months. This is a dangerous situation."

"I'll have ranger escorts with me, like I always do," Amy argued. "I have to work. The plants won't wait until your bear problem is solved."

Tanner drove into the hospital parking lot. Amy had the door latch open even before the vehicle stopped. "I heard you and that ranger back there talking about me. How you could get your way with me."

"What?" Tanner got out to help her.

"Just stay back, Mr. Tanner. I can help myself." She slammed the door.

"Listen, I said nothing like that."

"I don't know who said it, Mr. Tanner, but I heard laughing. I don't think it's funny."

Amy Ellerman left on her crutches. She looked back once, to glare, and entered the hospital just as Nate Jackson drove up. He appeared to be in a big hurry.

Jackson jumped from his vehicle. "John, we're going to Cheyenne. Right now."

"Isn't the necropsy Wednesday?"

"I just got a call from Sally Hays. She's pushed things up. It seems that an Indian policeman from the Shoshone reservation got a look at Barney. You know him. His name's Sam High Bear."

"I know him well," Tanner said. "I caught a prisoner of his who escaped and was hiding out with the poachers we caught. What's he doing in Cheyenne?"

"Something to do with the autopsy Sally was telling us she had to get out of the way. Anyway, Sam High Bear got a look at Barney and wants to talk to you personally."

"He's not just a policeman," Tanner said. "He's also a spiritual leader. He knows shamanic ways. He's likely found something that could help us."

Jackson took a deep breath. "It seems you were right. This isn't the end. It's just the beginning."

thirteen

Jim Clark's going-away party was well under way. Laughter and applause echoed from the old YCC and YACC cafeteria building, where a number of park personnel had gathered.

The talk, however, was not about Clark's new job at Yosemite but the absence of Nate Jackson, who had hurried to Cheyenne, Wyoming, with John Tanner.

Something major was taking place. Many were saying that the mauling death of Allen Freeman had been the result of something terrible that was happening in or around Yellowstone—something terrible that was happening to the grizzlies.

He had come down from his domain for a time, then had slipped out of the party. He now moved slowly through the first floor of the administration building, up the first flight of stairs. A light shone from an office on the second floor. He was careful in going past. Someone was moving around in there preparing to leave.

He waited inside an empty office as a young ranger

came out and hurried down the steps, his boots clumping as he left the building.

When it was safe, he eased out into the hall. Carefully, he climbed to the third floor and entered the Backcountry Office. He approached the small corner desk that had been set up for Amy Ellerman.

This was a special place, right here by her desk. She hadn't been here since Barney had hurt her, though, and her absence made him angry. It also made him nervous; he wanted her to come back to work as soon as possible. He needed her.

He stared at her desk, noting the stack of botany books, the coffee mug adorned with black-capped chickadees, the notepad with the little yellow flowers on the cover. He had seen these items before. He had touched them before.

He had also seen the picture of the man she had wanted to marry. He was no longer alive. It was right and fitting: he had left so that she could help him on his mission.

He touched Amy's chair, running his fingers along the smooth wood. He held his breath, released it, and stepped back from the chair, staring at it. The sensations were becoming stronger with each new trip to her desk.

The more he thought about it, the more Amy seemed like his mother. So very much. He could almost feel his own mother's essence in the wood.

He cracked a drawer and found an open box of cough drops. Some lay loose. He picked up two of them and stuck them in his shirt pocket.

In the same drawer he noticed a box of tissues. He pulled one free. It smelled of perfume. He held it to his nose, then placed it in his pocket with the cough drops.

He wanted to linger, to find a photograph of Amy. He had never been able to find one, preferably a small one that she wouldn't miss. He couldn't take anything large—she would certainly miss it and know that she hadn't misplaced it. She was careful about things.

The other two had been careful about things as well. They had been tidy in their dress and in the way they handled their jobs. He had watched them. They just hadn't been careful enough.

He couldn't stay now, for there were footsteps coming up the stairs.

He hurried from the office and out a back door from the hall onto the third floor porch. It was dusk. There were shadows. But he wouldn't know what to say if someone came out and saw him.

He felt relief. Whoever it was didn't stay long in the office. Footsteps out and down again. Everything clear.

He eased down the steps to the first floor, and out the back door. It was time to go to Lake Village. He had further plans for the evening.

During the drive he thought about Amy Ellerman and how he would get her up to his domain. It had taken some good planning with the other two. He had talked them both into a backcountry hike, the easy part. Having them meet him somewhere had been harder.

He had been careful not to let anyone see him with them, not at any time. He had picked times to talk to them when tourists were everywhere. None of them would make any connections. Besides, they had all likely left the park by now.

He had picked them up at designated areas, where he had agreed to meet them. Dressed in leathers, he had helped them onto the back of his dirt bike. Nothing fancy; nothing anyone would notice.

He had driven with them behind him, clutching tightly. It had been hard for them to ask questions with the wind in their faces.

Once up the trail, it had been easy to shoot them with a tranquilizer dart. They had looked at him so strangely. They had tried to run away, but the drug had quickly dropped them.

He knew that getting Amy Ellerman into the backcountry wouldn't be a problem; she went back there all the time—when she was healthy, that is.

He hoped her injured leg would recover very soon. He

didn't want to have to find a way to take her from the hospital.

It was late when he reached Lake Village. He sat for a time, near the helicopter pad, watching the hospital. He wanted to go in and look at her, but he didn't want anyone to see him there. Maybe later.

Tired, he lay back in his seat to rest for just a moment. His head nodded forward. A voice came into his mind: *Touch me. . . . I want you to touch me.*

"No, Mommy . . . no!" he choked.

He was in the basement of the old farmhouse, where they had lived when he was very young. He lay on his face, his small body naked, his ankles bound and his hands tied behind him.

His mouth was stuffed with a rag tied to a black handkerchief that was wound tightly around his head, the knot in the back like a hard rock at the base of his skull.

She began to roll him around on the muddy basement floor, the filthy dirt floor saturated with urine and excrement. He knew what was coming, in this fourth year of his life. It had been happening ever since he could remember.

During the fall of each year, when the moon rose full over a cold sky, her game would commence. At a specific time in the night, the light would shine through the basement window at just the proper angle. The filthy floor would become her place of ritual.

He had never been able to understand her chanting, her strange, wild voice, crying out to someone or something he could never see or hear. She would roll him, while wailing loudly. When she had finished her cries, she would take him to her.

He tightened in his sleep, the dream coming from deep within him. She was holding him up to the window, showing him to the moon, her filthy hands clutching him tightly.

In his sleep, he struggled to breath.

He could feel her shaking him, crying, "Come back! Come back!"

Again she rolled him in the filthy mud. She was lifting him to her. He could hear her voice again: *I want you to touch me. I want you to be my fuzzy-wuzzy teddy bear.*

He cried and wailed in his sleep, his hands gripping the steering wheel. If he didn't say yes, she would shove him back between her legs. He was nodding, agreeing to touch her.

She was untying him, forcing his hands between her thighs, crushing his small genitals with her free hand.

"Don't stop!" she was saying. "Don't stop!"

He jerked awake. His window was covered with steam. He was certain there was a face engraved on the glass, staring at him.

He yelled, bursting from the vehicle. "Mother! Go away!"

The night was calm, a slight breeze touching the pines. The moon was rising. He turned his back; he couldn't look at it.

He held his head with his hands, shuddering. A short distance away, a dog ran toward him, barking.

Carefully, he looked into the vehicle. The steam had left the window. It was clear. She had been there, though. His mother had been there. He was certain of it. But where had she gone?

Turning in circles, he looked to see if anyone had heard him. The dog was gone. All was quiet. He had been lucky.

He looked toward the hospital. He had come to catch a glimpse of Amy Ellerman.

But he couldn't. His mother was watching him. He knew she was. He could see her, there, just off to his right, standing next to a pine.

He turned away. Now she was to his left, standing in the grass near the helicopter pad. She was playing her tricks with him again. She was moving around, everywhere, trying to scare him.

He jumped back into his vehicle and raced from the parking lot, determined now more than ever to complete his mission. He must. He had no choice. He must enter the bear and partake of its power. He must consume his mother's spirit, or very soon she would consume him.

fourteen

THE WYOMING State Crime Laboratory sits near the center of Cheyenne, within the capitol zone. The sprawling brick structure, filled with forensics laboratory space, is a regional hub for crime work involving animals as well as humans.

There were more people present than had ever been involved in a bear necropsy before—in the entire history of the state or of Yellowstone Park. Despite the late hour, the work would be intense and thorough.

Sally Hays and her staff would coordinate the effort, with help from personnel from the Wyoming Veterinary Lab in Laramie, including Ben Ross, a toxicologist, and Don Wilson, a specialist in hair identification.

Tanner stood with Nate Jackson, staring at the huge bulk that had been Barney. He was seeing for the first time outside of the wilderness the big grizzly that he had studied for so long. Barney's remains made him feel strange, as if some ancient moral code had been horribly violated.

Barney lay on his side, in the exact position in which he had died, on a six-by-ten cut of three-quarter-inch plywood atop a large gurney. Next to the gurney was a table covered with knives and scalpels, all lined up neatly.

Everyone began to gather around the gurney. Sally Hays came in and approached Tanner.

"Mr. High Bear is out in the hall. He wants to talk to you there. He said he's seen enough of Barney."

Tanner excused himself. Sam High Bear was a short, well-built man in his early fifties, with warm but strong eyes and thick black hair. He was wearing his reservation police uniform, rotating his hat nervously with his fingers.

Tanner had never seen him so shaken. "Sam, I'm glad you stayed to talk to me," he said, shaking his hand. "I appreciate it."

"You've helped me before, and I wish to help you, if I can," High Bear said. "But I don't want to say much. You know that I'm a traditional Indian. It's not good to talk about these very bad things."

"You got a good look at Barney?"

"I saw enough."

"What can you tell me?"

High Bear squeezed his hat tightly. "I will tell you this. My grandfather was Ojibwa, and knew about these things. Barney was painted a certain way. They call this kind of man, who would do this, a bearwalk. He seeks to do evil things with the bear's power."

"Do you mean kill people?"

"Yes."

"How can you tell that?"

"I don't want to see the bear again," High Bear said. "I will not sleep as it is. But the paint markings show that somewhere in Yellowstone Park, a man wants to become a grizzly. The paint around the eyes shows that the bear will see something and bring it to him. The lines up from the mouth, around the head, and down the back mean that what the bear takes in through his mouth will be absorbed fully, made not to exist anymore. It's hard to put into words."

"Are you saying that the markings symbolize complete destruction of the victim who is eaten?" Tanner asked.

"Not destruction," High Bear corrected him. "Spirit cannot be destroyed. You know that. Of course he will destroy the body. But I would say that this man wants *control*. I would say he wants to become a grizzly and use the power to control someone's spirit. That's what I would say."

"Do you think he wanted to kill Allen Freeman?"

"That's impossible to know for sure," High Bear replied. "But whoever it is would have had to take the bear to the place where the actor was killed. I don't think so. I think the bear got away."

"Allen Freeman was just in the wrong place at the wrong time."

"That's likely."

"So the man who wants to kill someone is still out there?"

"It's very likely."

Tanner shuffled. "What sort of man do you think did this?"

"Very sick, very misdirected. The markings show me that he didn't learn the right way, that he doesn't know really what he's doing. He has read from books and maybe talked to a shaman, but mostly he has tried to learn by himself and is calling bad spirits."

"Now that Barney is dead, he has no grizzly to use anymore," Tanner said. "Maybe he can't continue."

High Bear shrugged. "I can't say about that. Maybe he will look for another bear. Someone who does this, someone who is a bearwalk, is very hard to stop. It's a terrible thing. That's all I can say."

"You've helped me a great deal," Tanner said. "I thank you. Can we get together and have something to eat when I'm through here?"

"I've got to get back to the reservation," High Bear said. "I've got my own problems. Good luck."

Tanner shook High Bear's hand and watched him leave,

his mind racing, his stomach churning. Sam High Bear wasn't someone who guessed at things.

All eyes were on Tanner as he entered the room.

"We're ready to start the necropsy," Sally said. "Did you want to say something first?"

"I don't know where to begin," Tanner replied. "I have a lot of respect for Sam High Bear. He's a top-notch lawman and not one to go off the deep end about anything. He just told me that he believes Barney was being used for ancient ritual purposes, by someone whose intent it is to kill someone else. I know we have no hard evidence, but I believe we've got a crazy person on the loose."

"What do you mean?" Ben Ross asked. "What kind of rituals?"

Tanner pointed to the markings on Barney. "Each circle and stripe has a specific meaning. Whoever did this intended to use ritual power in some fashion, likely to commit murder. Sam says that his grandfather told him about it. The Ojibwa people call this kind of evil shaman a bearwalk."

Tanner explained that ancient Plains and Mountain Indian ceremonies included homage to bears, particularly grizzlies. Often a warrior or a shaman's medicine helper would be a bear, and that person would have to undertake certain bear-centered religious ceremonies before going into battle or trying to heal someone.

"These people," Tanner continued, "are considered to be touched by sacred powers and are held in high honor. But in the case of a bearwalk, the power is used for evil intent."

"Are you saying that an Indian did this?" Jackson asked.

"No," Tanner replied. "But someone who wants to be *like* an Indian might have done it."

"That sounds illogical," Sally said. "How could the paint make a bear do anything?"

"Of course the *paint* can't make a bear do anything," Tanner said. "It's the *person* who did the painting. According to Sam, this person wanted to kill someone with Barney. In the person's mind, there was a reason for using a grizzly. Possibly that the grizzly is the most powerful animal on the continent and cannot be stopped.

"But Barney escaped from whoever painted him, then wandered down to Bridge Bay, where Allen Freeman happened to get in the way. Barney killed Freeman and mauled the woman."

"So what kind of person could have done this?" Jackson asked. He was staring at Tanner. "And how could he have done it without sedating Barney first?"

"That's right," Ben Ross said. "Barney would certainly have to be sedated first. How would he know about sedating bears if he hadn't worked with them before?"

"He, or they, could have watched someone working with bears," Tanner said. "They wouldn't necessarily have to be trained."

"But it's likely whoever did this *has* been trained," Jackson argued. "Otherwise, they wouldn't know how much chemical to use without killing Barney."

"You're probably right," Tanner said. "They would have to know how to handle a grizzly after it was sedated."

Sally commented, "This brings up the woman who was found. We're sure Barney killed her. So, does that mean Barney was painted then as well?"

"It sounds like we've got a lot of questions to answer," Jackson said. "I'm going out to call Milt Canby. We'll have to bring in the FBI."

"And what about the drugs used on Barney?" Sally continued. "It seems to me that Barney was one angry bear when he reached the campground."

Tanner was looking into Barney's mouth, noting bits of torn and bloody skin between the teeth, along with fragments of bone and hair. The bear had clamped down so hard he had pulverized parts of Allen Freeman's body.

"What kind of drug do you suppose he used?" Jackson asked.

Tanner looked at Jackson. Everyone in the room knew

what they were thinking. Though the drugs presently used to sedate bears and study them, or move them from one location to another, were proven quite safe and effective, some of the earlier drugs had caused controversy.

PCP, or a derivative, had been used for a time during the seventies and early eighties. Commonly referred to as angel dust, its use in bears soon became the center of a huge controversy.

There were those who believed that grizzlies would have flashbacks, much the same as humans, and become enraged. Others believed the bears didn't get strong enough doses, even if sedated frequently, to cause this condition.

Tanner had never made up his mind one way or another. He didn't care to sedate Barney, or any other bear, any more than absolutely necessary.

He knew that whoever had been holding Barney would have had to keep him sedated for long periods of time in order to paint him and carry on rituals. It took very little time to gather data on a bear in the field, but what Sam High Bear had described would take much longer.

Carol Williams, Sally's main lab assistant, rolled a cart into the room. The top of the cart was lined with a large quantity of vials and bottles of all sizes. Toxicology samples would be taken in great quantity.

"We can't look for everything over in our lab," Ben Ross said. "We'll need help from U.S. Fish and Wildlife."

Sally Hays shook her head. "This is the strangest case I've ever seen in my entire life."

They began the necropsy. Tanner stood beside Sally while she cut through the skin covering the skull, then sawed through to the brain, dictating to her tape recorder as she worked. The brain would be analyzed for many different kinds of drugs and poisons.

She then proceeded down the body. Having talked to Milt Canby, Jackson had returned to take special notes from the forms being filled out by the various lab personnel. Barney's stomach contents were of particular interest.

Besides plants and animal matter, the list included pebbles and rocks of various sizes, splinters of wood, and a number of pulverized bones.

"We'll analyze them," Sandy said. "I imagine most of them are human."

"It amazes me what those grizzlies can put in their stomachs," Jackson said. "You'd think they'd have terminal indigestion."

"You should've been here in the old days, when the dumps in the park were open," Ben Ross said. "You can't imagine the things those bears had in their guts—tin cans, bottles, razor blades. It's a wonder they weren't all killers, the inflamed mouths and bad teeth they had to endure."

When Barney's stomach was nearly empty, Sally reached in and pulled out a right hand. The wrist had been snapped free of the arm, leaving the connecting bones in mangled splinters. Only the thumb and first two fingers remained intact.

"This answers the question of Freeman's missing hand," Sally said.

The group continued work far beyond the scope of a normal necropsy. Tweezers and eyepieces were used for close observation. Material was extracted from between the paws, in the snout, between the teeth, in every small pocket of hair or skin from head to foot, everything from pine needles and minute soil particles to fragments of insects and plant pollen.

When they had finished, there wasn't a single square inch on the inside or outside of the grizzly that hadn't been checked and rechecked.

"We've taken more data on this bear than any ten we've ever looked at," Ben Ross said.

"Just so we don't have another bear come in," Jackson remarked. "It's bad enough that we're losing bears from poachers and angry ranchers. Now we've got someone who's going to make things extremely hard for us. This is going to create a whole new round of screaming against bears."

Ben Ross was nodding. "The press is already suggesting mad grizzlies in Yellowstone. We've got a real problem."

While the others had been discussing the problem, Sally had been conversing with an office assistant who had hurried into the room. The assistant left and Sally held up an envelope, making an announcement.

"The woman killed by Barney in June has just been positively identified."

Sally led the group into an adjoining room. A table stood along one wall, covered with head and facial reconstructions of unidentified accident and murder victims, complete with wigs and, in some cases, earrings. They looked a lot like mannequins' heads, except that the eyes were glass and the clay was colored more like real flesh, making the forms more lifelike.

Sally had cleaned each skull and had reshaped the heads and facial features to fit the bone lines. She had reconstructed most of them from crime-scene photos. In some cases, there had been little left to go on.

Tanner asked her how she got the muscle and skin tissue free from the skull so she could work with reconstruction. "Some labs use dermestid beetles," he told her. "They keep the head in a warm environment and the beetles eat everything down to the bone."

"Oh, no, I don't like that," Sally said. "I use a Crock-Pot. Dish soap and water does wonders. I turn it on high overnight, and the next morning, everything pulls free."

Sally lifted one of the heads. The reconstructed face was slim, with a small nose and mouth. A wig of shoulder-length blond hair had been fitted over the skin-tone clay. A set of glass eyes, deep blue in color, had been inserted into the sockets.

The head represented the victim they had found at Grizzly Lake in June.

"Ellen Lorraine Marks," Sally said. "Her picture just arrived. She left Boston two years ago for California. I guess it doesn't matter how she got to Yellowstone."

Tanner and Jackson viewed photos from the envelope.

The woman had been young, with shoulder-length blond hair and haunting blue eyes. The reconstruction was almost identical to the victim's real-life face.

"I've got to hand it to you, Sally," Jackson said. "You did an incredible job."

"I hope it's the last one I have to do from up there," Sally said. "But probably not."

Jackson looked up from the picture. "Oh, God. Don't say that!"

"I really hope I'm wrong," Sally said, "but this man surely wouldn't stop at one woman. I can't see how he would."

"Now you're talking about serial murder," Jackson said. "Do you suspect that?"

"All I know is that anyone who would even think of this is incredibly deranged," Sally replied. "Why would he stop with just one woman?"

"Because his bear is dead now," Jackson said.

Sally's eyebrows went up. "Don't you have any more grizzlies in the park?"

Tanner was thinking, his stomach churning again. Sally was echoing the thoughts of Sam High Bear. High Bear hadn't suggested serial murder, but he had been convinced the killer was still roaming the woods.

"Sally has a point," Tanner said. "I really believe Ellen Lorraine Marks was killed by Barney when he was a captive. You can't control what a grizzly does, or where it goes. He would have had to keep the woman captive and somehow turned Barney loose on her. I can't figure how he did that."

"We'll let the FBI help us with that," Jackson said. "We'd better get back. Canby is scheduling a conference tomorrow morning."

"I imagine the FBI will send some specialists in on this one," Sally commented. "I'll put a rush on the results from today's work. It looks as though you've got the worst problem in the history of Yellowstone National Park on your hands."

fifteen

HE LOWERED himself into the pit by means of a rope tied to a nearby pine. He had to clean out the pit, partially filled in now by Barney's digging. It was a nuisance, but it had to be done.

As he set to work, he wondered how he might have prevented the huge bear's escape. The pit could have been deeper, but that would have made getting in and out impractical. He needed to enter to talk to the grizzly, to perform the right ceremonies. The pit size couldn't be changed.

What other solution could have existed? It had been impossible to make the trip daily to check on him. There were places he had had to be to keep up his public image. And he couldn't have kept the grizzly sedated constantly; that would have killed him.

Nothing could have prevented what had happened. But it mustn't happen again. He had precious little time before he must offer Amy Ellerman to the Great Bear.

He groaned as he worked. Things had gotten complicated. He hoped to find another grizzly very soon. Yet he couldn't keep it in the pit so long that it, too, dug its way out. The timing must be perfect.

Perfect was the key word. He was being forced to finish what he had begun under some duress, for earlier in the day he had learned that the backcountry trails had been shut down—*all* the backcountry trails.

That meant there would be authorities roaming around. They would be looking for the reason their problem existed. He couldn't allow them to solve any mysteries. Not just yet. He would toy with them, give them something to chew on, so to speak, but he couldn't allow them to learn about his mission.

While the park personnel were busy planting stakes and tacking up posters everywhere, he would just go on with things. The chances were good he wouldn't be in this fix if it weren't for John Tanner. It was John Tanner's fault. Tanner's Indian mind had certainly been at work.

He knew without question what had alerted Tanner. Tanner had understood the meaning of the rings around Barney's eyes. He had known the significance of the stripes down the huge bear's back. It didn't matter. He would complete his plan anyway. Nothing else mattered.

Just after dark, before he had come to the pit, he had taken the remains of Valerie Jane Waters to a special place. He had left her, knowing that the Great Bear approved.

Now he could begin his quest for Amy Ellerman.

He wiped his brow and looked into the sky. Clouds were building, and there was a lot yet to dig out. He had to hurry and get things ready for her.

Though he might be able to take Amy from the hospital grounds, it would be very risky. Now, with the alert out, it would be very difficult to make things work smoothly.

He dug furiously now, promising himself that he would work with the efficiency he had developed over time. He would use the techniques that had brought him success with the first two women.

He had used the tranquilizer gun often on bears. And on women.

His experience with women had been in another place, where he had grown up, the place he had left to come west and begin his mission.

The experiments on those women had been successful. No one had ever known. No one had ever found the bodies. He knew just the dosage to use on a woman his mother's size, for he had experimented on his mother many times.

As she had tied him as a child, he had tied her. He had kept her in the basement at the old house in the country, testing his theories over time, until he knew just how much it took to sedate a woman of her stature.

Even when he reached adulthood she had called him Fuzzy Bear. She had wanted to do things to him, and have him touch her. In turn she would touch him, but it didn't bring the pain it had in childhood.

It was a game he had come to enjoy, even crave.

He had agreed to allow her to cover him with the mud from the basement, and he would test his drugs on her. He learned how much of the drugs to use and how long they would last. Different chemical mixtures gave different results.

"Fuzzy Bear, you can stick me with your needles if you want. Just be careful. You want me here to touch you, don't you? Yes, and I want you to touch me. . . . Yes, touch me there. . . . Don't stop until I tell you."

He had never worried about killing her during his experiments. He knew chemistry. He wouldn't make that mistake.

It seemed like she saw it as a game, allowing him to do his testing on her, feeling herself falling into a soft darkness while he touched her, then leaving the basement and returning to a normal life.

There had never been a concern about anyone ever knowing. All her life she had seemed like more than one person—many different people—who could be anyone she wanted whenever she wanted.

Then one day something had gone wrong. They had both been covered with mud, touching, he letting her fall back slowly to the basement floor, as she always did.

But she hadn't awakened. He had shaken her for hours, but she still hadn't awakened. When she had begun to turn cold and hard, he knew she would never awaken.

The problem was, she hadn't died.

He had known immediately that in order to consume her spirit, she should have died in the jaws of the Great Bear spirit. As it was now, her lifeless eyes wouldn't stay closed. He saw her continuously, staring at him in his sleep.

Even after he had buried her beneath the filth of the basement, even after months and months had gone by, she would stare at him in the night. She would find him, wherever he was, and grin at him, asking him to touch her.

He had even returned to the old house on a cold fall evening and had gone into the basement with a shovel. He had dug her remains from beneath the filth and had poured oil and kerosene over them, after first severing her head with a hunting knife.

After positioning the head with the sunken eyes toward the window, he had waited for the right moment, when the moon had risen full, its light shining into the basement. Then he had touched a match to the body. It had exploded in flames, filling the basement with smoke.

Late the next day, after burying the charred remains, he knew he hadn't killed her spirit. It was still with him.

He had taken the head and had placed it in a bearskin bag, painted the bag with black and yellow lines, and tied the bag tightly with rawhide. He would open it when the time was right.

He had realized that his mother might forever remain alive, stalking him. It was not just the darkness that brought her; often, in the daylight, he would see her looking at him from out of the faces of women who resembled her—blond, blue-eyed women of medium build.

She was inside them. He knew it.

The only animal who could stop her was the mighty grizzly, the most powerful animal alive. After seeing a picture of a bear-eaten woman in a tabloid, he had decided that he must learn how to make the kill. He knew of the bear's power, for he would never forget the day at the circus. Now he must learn the secrets of the grizzly's powerful teeth and claws.

Since coming west, he had spent a lot of time in the forest, watching the bears, learning their ways. He had enjoyed seeing them make their kills, slapping a huge paw against the head of a moose or an elk, debraining the animal with one powerful swipe.

They did it so easily. It was so much like the bear trainer who had died at the circus.

Barney, the big grizzly he had trapped, had been so willing to help him. He had sedated Barney and had talked to him often, had touched his enormous claws, felt his giant teeth.

Barney had been wonderful. Everything had gone as planned. He had almost finished his mission. So why had the big bear wanted to leave?

It didn't matter. He would find another grizzly, a grizzly more willing to help him. Then he would bring Amy Ellerman into the forest.

He climbed from the pit, dreaming. Overhead, the sky was dark and filled with rumbling. The final moments of his plan became vivid in his mind.

He would join with the Great Bear, right before Amy Ellerman's eyes. With the grizzly's power, he would tear his mother's image from within her very being. Then it would be time to open the bag that contained his mother's head. He had embalmed the head according to an ancient formula. He had done quite well for his first time.

The head, now buried safely in the forest, would be painted, the brains within it consumed. This would come immediately after consuming the grizzly's brain. Then the union of all spirits would be complete. The power would belong to him.

His plan would be completed, the last and most important elements satisfied. Yes, it would all be final and he would be rid of his mother's staring eyes. Forever.

sixteen

THE HOSPITAL lay still and quiet under a roiling sky. Thunder rumbled overhead and streaks of light pierced the darkness.

Amy Ellerman tossed and turned in her bed. Despite the heavy sedation, her sleep was fitful. The dream that came to her was in full color.

The grizzly stood over her, its jaws wide, its mouth drooling. It roared, making her ears ring. She couldn't move. She waited for the bear to come down on her, ending her life.

Instead the grizzly shook itself ferociously, sending showers of debris from its fur. Dirt and forest mulch covered her from head to foot.

Again she tried to move but couldn't. She opened her mouth to scream and choked on clumps of plants that exploded from the grizzly. Pieces of leaves and stems stuck to her lips and tongue, embedded by little spines, like bee stings, that shot pain through her mouth.

Amy tried to move her hands. Her body was locked, as if some invisible force had tied her down. The plants continued to fill her mouth, smothering her, and she reconciled herself to death.

Suddenly she was standing in front of herself, looking into her own face, as if she were the grizzly closing in for the kill. She could see herself trembling, waiting for the fatal moment.

Then she peered into her own mouth and saw flowers—small flowers with pinkish white petals and deeply divided leaves. Geraniums.

Amy sat up, gasping for breath. All around her was silence, while outside a storm's thunder boomed. Her eyes wide, she turned on a light and jumped from her bed.

Pain in her leg caused her to collapse. She rose to her knees and pulled her crutches over to her. *The closet!* rang through her mind. *I've got to get to the closet!*

She eased her cotton shirt from its hanger. Trembling, she ran her hands over the material. Her fingers clasped a fragment of plant stem and she held it up in front of her.

"Oh, my God!" she yelled aloud.

The stem had to have come from the grizzly's coat. Though her mind had been clouded the night of Allen Freeman's death, and even during the following couple of days, she now realized that the plant fragment might be from the species of geranium she had been looking for.

On her hands and knees, Amy probed the closet floor with her fingers. Finding another small segment of stem, her heart leaped. More stem fragments followed and half of a leaf. Then, to her complete amazement, she discovered a nearly complete if wilted flower.

"Yes! Oh, yes!"

A nurse appeared at the door. "Miss Ellerman, what's wrong?"

"Nothing. I'm just fine," Amy said.

"We heard you yelling."

Amy held the plants gingerly, hopping to the bed on one leg.

"Where are my things? I need something that was in my jeans pocket."

The nurse pointed to the bedstand. "Look in the top drawer."

Amy rummaged while the nurse watched speculatively. She found a small eyeglass and began to examine the plant fragments.

She spoke to herself aloud: "The calyx is bristle-tipped. Okay, good. Yes, densely glandular along the flower stalk. Very good!" She turned to the nurse. "*Geranium bicknellii.* It is! I'll just bet it is!"

"Ger—what?" the nurse asked. "Miss Ellerman, are you all right?"

"Couldn't be better," Amy answered. "I believe this is *Geranium bicknellii.*"

The nurse frowned.

"I believe this is the geranium I've been looking for to complete my plant study," Amy said. "I'll have to try and find a complete specimen, though. I want to be certain these aren't fragments of *Geranium carolinianum* or *Geranium dissectum.* It *has* to be *bicknellii.*"

The nurse said, "Miss Ellerman, you should go back to bed now."

"I'm fine," Amy said. "Just fine."

"Yes, but please go back to bed."

Amy complied. The nurse made certain she was comfortable. "If there's anything we can do for you, just push your night button."

"Thank you," Amy said. She threw off the covers. "There is one thing. Could you help me to a phone? I need to put a call in for John Tanner."

"Miss Ellerman," the nurse said. "It's very late."

Amy was already to her crutches. "I know. I just want to leave him a message. I'm certain he'll want to know just as soon as possible."

Amy started down the hall toward the office. The nurse started after her. She asked, "What could be that important this time of night?"

Amy turned. "Geraniums. Those geraniums I was looking at. Nothing could be more important right now."

seventeen

THE ADMINISTRATION building in Mammoth Hot Springs was alive with activity. The superintendent's conference room was the site of a formal meeting. Maps had been brought in for easy reference.

Tanner walked in, looking at the photos of past park superintendents that lined the walls near the ceiling on two sides of the room. The men in the pictures seemed more stern today than usual.

Tanner realized that a lot lay on his shoulders. He was putting his professional reputation on the line in believing that a murder, or a series of murders, had been committed in the park, based solely on a friend's words about bearwalks.

As a rule, Native American mythology would not be the basis for a criminal investigation. Yet Tanner knew that the law enforcement community respected him to the extent that they wanted to hear him out.

Somehow the press had learned of the meeting. They were sending messengers back and forth from Mammoth

Hotel, wondering when a news conference was going to be called.

So far they hadn't discovered his suspicions; the headlines had all focused on a rogue grizzly, finally killed. If they ever learned the reality of the situation, it would be world news.

Park Superintendent Bill Canby and the chief ranger took their seats together. Leland Beckle and Martin Linders sat across from Tanner and Jackson, who sat on either side of Bill Young, an FBI agent stationed in Bozeman, Montana.

In his midforties, Young was good-sized and in good shape. During his earlier service in the Midwest, he had been involved with a number of open-country murders, some of them serial.

This case, however, already had him shaking his head.

He was reviewing photos of Ellen Lorraine Marks. Closeups of the victim revealed that head and facial wounds had obliterated most of the hair and flesh. Her torso was devoid of internal organs, and her arms and legs were stripped of nearly all the muscle tissue.

"It looks to me like the bear ate her completely," Young said. "You've got a bear with a large appetite."

"Yes, but there's a problem here," Tanner said. "It has to do with bear behavior."

Tanner explained that a normal grizzly mauling death includes partial or total consumption by the bear, especially when the victim has been killed in the backcountry and hasn't been discovered, which was obvious from the photos.

"It's what's *not* in the photos that bothers me," Tanner added. "A grizzly will often bury part or all of its victim, so that it can come back later and feed again. Look closely at Ms. Marks's remains. Do you see any evidence of her having been buried?"

"She looks pretty clean from that standpoint," Young agreed. "So how does that lead you to believe some deranged killer was involved?"

"I know we haven't got a lot to go on yet," Tanner said, "but I know Barney was being used by someone, or more than one, for ritualistic purposes. This killer, or killers, was using the grizzly to claim victims. A friend of mine who's seen this kind of thing before told me he believes the object is to gain spiritual control over the victims."

Martin Linders studied Young. "What do you make of that? A man feeding a woman to a grizzly?"

Young seemed stunned. "I've never heard of it. Ever. I'm not saying it hasn't happened somewhere before, but not in my experience."

"This happened in my district," Leland Beckle said. He leaned forward in his chair, frowning at Young. "We're counting on you to figure this thing out. We've got to get things back to normal around here."

Milt Canby had been listening intently. He said to Beckle, "Let Mr. Young have a chance to analyze things. He'll do his job, if we let him."

"Another thing," Young said, "I can't say a lot about this kind of thing, anyway. If, indeed, there is some guy doing this, then I'll have to call on somebody who can get into his head. I'm not a behavioral specialist."

"When will you know how to proceed?" Beckle pressed.

"Depending on what I discover in the field, I may ask for someone to come out from Quantico," Young replied. "I'll need some evidence to support Mr. Tanner's theory."

"Where do you want to start your investigation?" Jackson asked.

"I want to see the site at Grizzly Lake where you found this victim," he said. "I'll also want to talk with anyone who knew her." He turned to Tanner. "And I'd like to speak with your Indian friend."

"I'll arrange for interviews," Jackson said.

Beckle suddenly announced that he had to get back into the field. "Let me know when you're coming into my district. I want to be along." He left, with everyone staring after him.

"He doesn't seem to fit in here," Young commented.

"You've got that right," Jackson said. "His daddy's a U.S. senator. He works where and when he wants."

"Interesting," Young said. "He doesn't feel comfortable in crowds, does he?"

"He dislikes me being in on this," Tanner said. "I haven't figured out why yet, but he can't stand it."

"Have you forgotten what I told you?" Martin Linders said. "He wants the headlines. You usually get the headlines. He's been working to see that he gets them, not you."

"Maybe so," Tanner said. He reached into his pocket. "I got a message from Amy Ellerman, the woman who was injured by Barney the other night. I talked with her this morning and she believes Barney definitely came to the party site from, or passed through, an area where a fire burned two years ago. If we can find the area, it might help the case."

"How would she know that?" Young asked.

Tanner explained about the geranium that grew on fresh burn areas and that Amy was collecting them for her Ph.D. in botany. "She found pieces of the geraniums on her clothes. She fell from a tree onto the bear and they stuck to her."

"So the grizzly had to have come through a burn area before it got to the campground?" Young asked.

"No doubt about it," Tanner said. "The geraniums were flowering. That's significant, as the geraniums are biennial, which means they only live for two years. And only in the second year do they flower."

Young rubbed his chin. "So that's why the fire area has to be two years old. I get it."

Tanner nodded. "Exactly. And that narrows the area down considerably."

Young was impressed. "It sounds like Miss Ellerman has an eye for details."

"She trained for police work," Jackson explained. "She pulled out when her fiancé was killed."

Young turned to Tanner. "Do you think we can find where this grizzly came from?"

"I think we have an excellent chance," Tanner said. "If we do, it could give us a lot of answers."

Jackson got up and pointed to a map. "The only burn area from two years ago near the lake is at the head of Alum Creek, on Central Plateau." His finger ran straight across to the Freeman Site. "Barney could easily have come from there to where he killed Freeman."

"When can we go in?" Young asked.

"How about now?" Tanner said.

Young stood up. "We'll have to ride in. Let me change clothes. I'll be in front of the building in ten minutes."

Jackson got on the phone to arrange for horses, and Tanner studied the map with Linders.

"I don't think I can go in with you," Linders said. "I've got a lot of calls to answer and a lot of troubleshooting to do. It seems like everyone has seen a grizzly in their camper lately."

"I can imagine," Tanner said. "We'll keep you informed of what we find."

Jackson got off the phone. Tanner followed him out the door and retrieved a set of latex paw prints he had brought from the crime lab in Wyoming. They had been taken from Barney. He would use them to check against the tracks he hoped to find in the backcountry.

Young reappeared, carrying notepads and a camera, dressed for the backcountry. Together, they got into Nate Jackson's Suburban and started down, beginning their trip to Central Plateau.

eighteen

J IM C LARK entered the administration building at Mammoth and hurried up the steps to the Backcountry Office. Martin Linders had radioed him in the field, asking him to come in as soon as possible.

Clark had less than a week left before his transfer became effective, but he would stay on in Yellowstone as long as they needed him. Yosemite Park had already sent three rangers over to help. Other national parks would be sending personnel before long.

In the Backcountry Office, Clark found two of the Yosemite rangers standing with Linders, staring at a map.

Both rangers were in their midthirties. The taller of the two, Mark Robbins, had worked in Yellowstone for three years before leaving. The other, a blond man of medium height named Dale Berry, had been in the south all his career and had just arrived at Yosemite. He had never expected to start his first week this way.

"I would go with you," Linders was telling them, "but I've got to get over to Tower Falls and check out a reported grizzly sighting."

"A grizzly at Tower Falls?" Robbins asked.

"There are a hundred reports a day now," Linders said. "They come from everywhere. I can't take any of them lightly."

Linders was edgy and anxious to leave. Clark noted that his features were drawn and his uniform rumpled and stained, as if he had slept in it since the night of Allen Freeman's death.

It was no indictment of Linders; everyone was worn to the breaking point. Linders had to be under the most pressure.

Linders pointed at the map. "Jim, I was just telling these guys that you've got to get to Obsidian Cliff. There are some hikers wandering around down there. We can't have that."

Linders' finger traced along the hiking trail that ran from a picnic area at the base of Obsidian Cliff, past the east front of Roaring Mountain, and out at Norris.

The trail did not go into the backcountry. Possibly the hikers saw no danger in a brief outing. They hadn't considered that death can happen anywhere, and very quickly.

"There's a woman and two men," Linders continued. "They're *crazy* to be out there!"

"Maybe they just arrived in the park," Berry suggested. "Maybe they didn't know about everything that's happened."

"Bullshit!" Linders said. "They had to know. The signs are posted everywhere. Everyone knows!" He jabbed his finger into the map.

"How'd you find out about them?" Clark asked.

Linders took a deep breath. "Leland Beckle just radioed it in, so they're likely still back there. You know that area, and I wanted to ask if you'd take these guys with you. You've got to hurry."

"Why didn't Beckle chase them out himself?" Clark asked.

"I don't know," Linders said. "You know Beckle; he

probably thought he had more important things to do. He wouldn't tell me." He picked up a clipboard and his hat.

"Do you want us to chase them out of the park?" Clark asked.

Linders was at the door. "Just tell them to stay out of the backcountry. Make it clear to them that their lives are in danger. Tell them they'll be eaten, even if they stand around on the road."

Clark frowned while the other two rangers laughed.

"I don't care what you tell them," Linders said. "Just scare the shit out of them. If they're not smart enough to listen, draw them a picture."

Linders was out the door. Clark followed with the other two rangers. Linders got in his Suburban. Clark watched, thinking that Linders would soon be yelling at tourists, calling them names. Linders hated tourists; he shouldn't be dealing with them.

Clark drove his Park Service pickup, leading the two rangers in their sedan toward Obsidian Cliff. The radio was alive with dispatches. The park was filled with tension and fear. Even with help from other national parks in the region, there still weren't enough personnel to cover everything.

Clark pulled in at the picnic area below Obsidian Cliff. Robbins and Berry stopped next to him. The only vehicle in the deserted campground, a small red sedan with Michigan plates, sat empty near one of the picnic tables. Clark led the other two rangers onto the trail.

The view spanned the park's north-central region, rocky slopes dense with lodgepole pine. The fires of '88 had hit some areas hard and left others untouched. Scattered locations had suffered only light burns, where the fires had rushed through quickly, doing little or no damage to most of the cover.

"Keep your eyes open," Clark told the two rangers. "They may or may not be on the trail."

They skirted a slope lined with blackened pines and came into a meadow where the soils were deep. Scarlet Indian paintbrush covered the ground under the dead trees, mixed with the showy yellow flowers of arnica and the brilliant pink of fireweed. Dense patches of bluebells and lupine also caught the eye, and a covey of blue grouse rose from between two fallen logs.

After twenty minutes of hiking, just before Lake of the Woods, Clark spotted a young woman sitting along the trail. She was slumped over, with her head in her hands. A small knot formed in Clark's stomach.

Clark and the other two approached her. She was red-haired, dressed in a blue T-shirt and black hiking shorts. Her hair and back were covered with pieces of grass, as if she had been lying down.

"Ma'am, is there a problem here?" Clark asked.

The woman looked up. Her face was ashen. "What?" she asked blankly.

"Aren't you feeling well?" Clark asked. "Did something happen here?"

The woman pointed up the trail. "She's . . . dead. . . . It's terrible."

"What happened?" Clark asked.

The woman was shaking her head. "There's not much . . . of her left."

Clark pulled his radio from his belt and called the dispatcher. While he talked, the woman began to rock back and forth, babbling incoherently. She lay down in the grass, her hands over her eyes.

Robbins and Berry tried to comfort her. She sat up again and began sobbing.

Clark knelt down beside her. "Help is on the way." He squeezed her hand. "Can you tell me, is there anyone else out here with you?"

The woman stared at him blankly.

"Was there anyone else hiking with you?"

"Gary said he would," she replied weakly. "He . . . he got the week off. . . . She's dead . . . eaten."

Robbins asked Clark, "Aren't there supposed to be two men with her?"

"That's what Linders thought," Clark replied, standing up. "You two stay here with her. I'm going along the trail and see what I can find."

"Won't you need someone with you?" Berry asked.

"If Beckle was right, there should be two men out here somewhere," Clark said. "One or both of them might show up. I'll call if I need help."

Clark started along the trail. A minute later, Lake of the Woods came into view, a small body of water surrounded by grass and sedges. Two grebes rose from the water and winged their way into the blue sky overhead.

When he was nearly at the lake, Clark found a man lying on his back beside the trail. The knot in Clark's stomach grew larger.

Clark approached him slowly. The man's eyes were open, staring into the sky, and he appeared to be singing to himself.

"Sir, can you hear me?" Clark asked.

The hiker was in his midtwenties, well built, with long, dark hair. His shirt and hiking shorts were covered with dirt and mud. He appeared to have urinated on himself.

"Sir?" Clark repeated. "Sir, can you understand me?"

The hiker sat up. "Her face . . . it's gone. She's in pieces. Who is she?"

"Where did you see the body?" Clark asked.

The hiker lay back down and began humming.

Clark called Robbins and Berry on his radio. They reported back that paramedics had arrived.

"I'm going to try and bring this man down there," Clark said. "I'll be in touch."

Clark helped the hiker to his feet and struggled to get him to walk. The man was afraid to move, fearing a bear was nearby and would come out of the brush after him.

"Did you *see* a bear?" Clark asked.

"It could still be here," the hiker said. "It ate her."

The hiker began to whine loudly. He started to run. Clark tackled him and held him down until he quit struggling.

"Just relax," Clark said. "Nothing's going to hurt you."

Clark sat him up and was talking to him when three paramedics hurried up to them.

One of the paramedics was a woman named Jackie, whom Clark had seen before at Lake Hospital. Gray-haired and usually smiling, she had worked for the hospital since it had opened. She was strongly built and confident in her abilities.

"Let me give him something to calm him down," she said. "He's by far the worst of the three."

The man began to struggle again. Clark and the other two paramedics held him while Jackie administered a drug. The hiker slowly relaxed and began sobbing.

"You found the other man?" Clark asked Jackie.

"We found him wandering on the highway," she replied. "They're all in deep shock. They must have seen something pretty horrible."

The knot in Clark's stomach grew tighter. "Can you take care of him? I'm afraid I'm going to have to locate a body."

"What do you think happened here?" one of the other paramedics asked. "Another grizzly attack?"

"These two both talked about a dead woman," Clark said. "They both suggested she had been eaten. I don't know what else to think."

"This has got to be the craziest summer on record," Jackie said. "Do you want one of us to go with you?"

"You've got your hands full as it is," Clark said.

"There's a lot more help on the way," Jackie said. "I'll come with you."

The other two paramedics agreed. Clark and Jackie started along the trail. As they reached the shoreline, both gagged from the smell of decaying flesh.

Clark and Jackie covered their noses with handkerchiefs. "Are you ready for this?" Clark asked her.

"There's no choice," she said, tears starting from her eyes.

Rising slightly above the water, partially hidden in tall

grass, lay human remains covered with flies. The body lay on its back, its head twisted at an awkward angle. Its face and most of the hair were gone, with little but skull and bone remaining.

The left arm lay beside the body cavity. Everything inside the torso was gone, from the pelvic region to the throat, including the breasts, and the muscle tissue on both legs had been shredded into fragments.

"Is it a woman?" Clark asked.

"I think . . . so," Jackie said. "But there's no breasts . . . to be sure."

Jackie turned away, sobbing and gagging at the same time. Clark took a few steps away from the body. The knot in his stomach seemed to consume his entire being, throbbing, working its way up his esophagus.

He stumbled sideways and bent over. The knot exploded from his mouth and he sank to his knees, thinking of humming a tune.

nineteen

TANNER RODE in the lead, with Jackson and Young following. They were deep in Hayden Valley, nearing Central Plateau.

Tanner stopped his horse to dismount and check grizzly tracks he had found in the trail. As he had done all day, he took the latex paw imprints to verify that the tracks had been left by Barney.

They had started their ride at the Freeman Site, backtrailing signs left by Barney coming down from the high country. Tanner had lost the trail many times, but he now followed deep tracks left under a heavy tree canopy, where the rains had done little damage to the imprints.

The country was covered with lodgepole pine, interspersed with open hillsides and meadows. Here and there isolated stands of whitebark pine formed colonies in rocky areas. It was a prime food for grizzlies, and the area showed a lot of bear use.

The meadow flowers were profuse. Earlier in the summer, clusters of arrow-leaf balsamroot had covered the slopes with masses of bright yellow. These plants had by now dried out, giving way to the sky-blue colors of lupine and bluebell, mixed with the red of sticky geranium and Indian paintbrush. Many varieties of tiny white perennials filled in under the taller flowers and grasses, forming a carpet of intense color.

The day would have been pleasant and the scenery enjoyable had it not been for the reason they had come and the stress and hard work associated with it. Four hours of riding had taken them in a lot of circles and zigzags. The grizzly's tracks had been easy to follow under the tree canopy, but Tanner had been forced to dismount often in the open.

In some locations, thunderstorms had washed imprints from around rock-covered hillsides, leaving Tanner to guess where Barney might have gone. Though the going had been slow, Tanner had been lucky in relocating the grizzly's trail.

The pattern made by the tracks was unusual and had led them into steep country, where the bear had fallen down hillsides and gone off in many different directions, often in circles, as if confused about where he was going.

There were many places where Barney had lain down for significant periods of time, and had thrown up stomach contents, indicating to Tanner that the bear had been suffering internal problems.

Tanner also noted that Barney had passed up entire meadows filled with roots and rodents. A hungry grizzly should have dug the area like a rototilled garden.

Instead, the trail was littered with small pines that had been flattened and trees that had lost huge strips of bark. Tanner realized that Barney had been wandering about, enraged and disoriented, for at least two days before he had reached the campground.

Tanner had hiked or ridden through this country many times, trailing the big grizzly, listening for frequencies put out by the radio collar Barney had worn since becoming a yearling.

The area also reminded him of a spot outside the park,

high in a private pasture, where he and his wife, Julie, had been hiking two years before. They had carried garden tools and plastic sacks, intent on digging wildflower bulbs for transplanting in a rock garden.

Tanner had suggested putting off the hike for one day so that he could finish some paperwork. She had talked him into going, as she wanted to collect the bulbs before the leaves were totally dry. Once the leaves had dried up, they would have been almost impossible to locate.

They had never made it to the wildflower patch.

After the funeral, Tanner had sold their home. He hadn't wanted to continually see the garden Julie had planned and dreamed over.

Later, he wished he had kept the property. He wanted to collect the bulbs and finish the work in her garden, to build a form of memorial to her. Now it was too late. He couldn't make it up to her, no matter how hard he tried.

They neared Central Plateau, reaching higher ridges that rose above Hayden Valley. To the east and south, a wide expanse of forest sloped down into Yellowstone Lake, immense and glassy blue in the afternoon sun.

They passed through Highland Hot Springs, where steam rose from pools bubbling with sulfurous water and mudpots that popped, thick and brown. The ground was covered with layers of salt and lichen, white combined with blues and greens, yellow, orange, and red.

Past the geyser basin, across a small ridge, they looked into Alum Creek, where they sat their horses and studied the area.

The Alum Creek fire had burned a wide swath. The trees were no longer dense and green but charred and lifeless. The understory, however, was thick with grass and flowers.

Tall stalks of fireweed were everywhere, their brilliant pink-red blossoms flaring in the afternoon sun. Chipmunks ran through the cover, stopping to chew on aster and arnica leaves and to search out pine nuts that had burst from heated cones.

Just below the trail a small herd of deer stood staring, their mouths filled with browse.

"That's a nice buck," Young said, pointing to one of the deer. "He doesn't care that this area burned."

"The forest gets old in places and ends up as firewood," Jackson said. "A certain type of habitat dies out and gives life to another type. It's been going on since time began."

Tanner checked his map. "I didn't know the fire came this far east. The map doesn't show that."

"Leland Beckle mapped it," Jackson said. "He must have guessed. I doubt if he ever got out of his office to look."

"Does it make that much difference?" Young asked.

"Probably not as far as this case goes," Jackson said. "We need to keep accurate records, though, for our own internal use."

"Let's worry about that later," Young said. "I want to know why it's so hard to find where that grizzly came from. We've been riding a long time."

"I thought it was important to track Barney all the way," Tanner said. "There's too much country up here to be guessing."

"How much farther do we have to go?" Young asked.

Tanner pointed to grizzly tracks along the trail. "Barney came through here, just as Amy Ellerman predicted. We should be finding what we're looking for soon."

"Are you sure that finding this place will help solve the case?" Young asked.

"What about the evidence at the scene?" Jackson asked. "We're bound to find something we can use."

"I hope you're right," Young said.

Tanner dismounted and led his horse, checking Barney's tracks closely. They were difficult to follow here, as the grass was thick, hiding them effectively.

Jackson called attention to a place where the vegetation had been disturbed. Tanner and Jackson looked closely at it and agreed that Barney had been digging in the soil and rolling in it.

"What was he doing there?" Young asked.

"It's common behavior for bears and other carnivores," Tanner explained. "They often role in the dirt or in something rotten to hide their odor. That makes it easier to sneak up on prey."

Tanner studied the area, noticing a number of small plants in bloom: small geraniums. *Geranium bicknellii.* Amy Ellerman would go wild with glee when she heard of this site.

Tanner had just climbed on his horse when an urgent call came over his radio. The dispatcher relayed that Jim Clark had found a woman's body near Obsidian Cliff. The area had been sealed off and was now under heavy guard.

"We need to get back down there," Young said. "This will have to wait until later."

"You two go on back," Tanner said. "I'll see if I can find where these tracks lead."

"Are you sure that's a good idea?" Young asked.

"I go on wilderness patrol alone all the time," Tanner said. "We need this evidence just as badly as the rest of it."

"John, I wish you'd wait on this," Jackson said. "No one should go out alone, not under the circumstances."

"I'm worried that we may not get back to this area again for a while," Tanner said. "I need to know what Barney went through up here."

"I worry about what you could go through up here," Jackson said. "If your hunch is right, you could be in grave danger tackling this alone."

"I won't take any chances," Tanner promised. "Once I find what I'm looking for, I'll radio out. I won't stay; I'll just come on down then."

"I'll radio in for backup," Jackson said. "I wish you'd come back with Bill and me partway, at least until the backup arrives. Then you can all come up here together."

"It'll be dark by then," Tanner said. "Send someone in here to catch up with me. But I've got to keep going."

"I hope you don't mind my saying so, John, but you're

acting a little reckless," Young commented. "We don't want to see anyone get hurt."

"I've got nothing to lose," Tanner said. "I'm not married. This is a job for single guys."

Jackson frowned deeply. Tanner's vision of life was gloomier than he had thought. He shouldn't have asked Tanner to come in on the case.

"I know this area as well as anyone," Tanner continued. "I should take the risks."

"I won't tell you not to do this," Jackson said. "I promised you I'd give you free rein. I just don't want to be responsible for something I could have prevented, that's all."

"None of us could have prevented what's happened," Tanner said. "I just want to protect people—*and* bears—from someone who's obviously crazy beyond any definition of the word. I think my finding what's up here will help do that."

"I'll give you my opinion, for what it's worth," Young said. "We don't know anything about this killer yet. We don't know his habits; we don't know his fears. It's entirely possible that you could be getting yourself into something far worse than a standoff with a grizzly."

"Nothing's worse than that," Tanner said. "And now that I've seen what this maniac can do to a woman or a bear, I hope I do meet him. I'd like to share with him my idea of hell."

twenty

TANNER CHECKED his sidearm and eased his horse down the hill toward Alum Creek. The tracks were deep and easy to read. Barney had come from somewhere on the other side of the burn.

The sun was dropping in the west, hanging over the tops of the trees like a pale, round melon.

Just like the day his wife had died.

He turned away from it, dread filling him. Soon the light would start to fail rapidly, leaving the forest filled with shadows.

Tanner wished it were earlier in the day, but he had no choice. He reached the edge of the burn. Alum Creek lay just below. Beyond, the burn ended and the trees were again filled with green boughs.

He sat his horse, listening. The birds had quit singing. In the shadows along the trail, a squirrel chattered.

Something else lay ahead in the timber. He could feel it. In the open burn area, all had seemed normal. Suddenly things had changed.

Tanner eased his horse forward. The air was still. All was quiet. Too quiet.

As he rode, Tanner thought back on the night he had spent at the Freeman Site. He hadn't slept well since. The nightmares rumbling in his head seemed nearly ready to surface. They would be coming out very soon.

It was all too quiet, the way the forest becomes when a grizzly is watching prey from the trees. The quiet before the storm.

But Tanner didn't think it was a bear. He was certain someone was watching him. It didn't feel like a bear.

At the creek, Tanner dismounted. The horse drank deeply. The air remained still. Quiet. Things had been quiet far too long. It bothered him more and more.

Overhead, a raven flew lazily into the west, cawing its deep, throaty call. Seeing something on the ground, it turned in flight, made a circle in the air, and continued on.

Tanner stood and listened. His horse snorted and reached for grass along the bank. Tanner thought about tying the horse and moving a way distant, just to feel the area.

A slight sound in the forest made him turn. He certainly wasn't alone.

It wouldn't be good to leave the horse, Tanner decided. He was too tired to know for sure what was watching them. He couldn't take any chances.

It could be a grizzly that was watching them, wondering if he was game, knowing for certain that the horse was. He had to stay with the horse.

After remounting, Tanner crossed the creek. Barney's tracks had come nearly straight downhill from a heavily wooded terrace of land just off the creek bottom. He knew he had to be nearing the Mary Lake cabin.

The air remained still and quiet. The shadows thickened, filling with steam from the small thermal pools that dotted the ground. Bubbling water broke the silence. Tanner relaxed a little.

Tanner urged the horse up the hill. Once on the terrace,

he stopped the horse to peer through the steam. A large pit lay just ahead of him, like a huge mouth gaping in the shadows.

The pit was easily ten feet square and nearly as deep. A rope attached to a nearby tree hung down over the edge. Barney's tracks showed clearly in the soft earth around the opening. There were also boot prints everywhere.

Tanner examined a mound of fresh earth that lay just outside the pit, separate from the weathered mound obviously left from the original excavation. Someone had been digging here very recently.

Tanner concluded that the huge bear had undercut one side of the pit, causing the rim to collapse. After more digging and tearing of soil down into the bottom, Barney had managed to climb out.

Whoever had trapped Barney had then come back to clean out the pit. That meant he intended to trap another bear.

Tanner peered over the edge and into the bottom, squinting, wondering at what he was seeing. In one corner there appeared to be a pile of garbage, possibly rags of some kind. He couldn't tell for certain in the shadows.

As he leaned over for a closer look, a rank, permeating smell invaded his entire being. It made him want to turn and leave.

Tanner grabbed the rope and eased himself down the loose soil, certain now of what he would find. The rags he had mistaken for garbage were fragments of bloody clothing.

Scattered through the clothing were pieces of bone and a finger. A few feet away lay remnants of a small necklace, next to a decaying hand. The fingers lay open, attached to the hand bones only by filaments of shredded tendon.

Tanner scrambled out of the pit, visions of his dead wife filling his head. He turned and stared down into the shadows, knowing that Barney had killed someone in the pit, a woman, killed her in the same manner as he had killed Allen Freeman.

Without question, the human killer had to be someone who knew the park backcountry, who could have trapped Barney without being mauled himself. He had to have known how to lure Barney into the pit. It had to be someone who knew bears very well.

Tanner called in on his radio, but the reception was broken and weak. He was too far back in the timber.

After moving around, trying several more times to call in, he became aware that his horse was watching something in the trees.

Tanner was certain he saw movement. He pulled his pistol but, after thinking, decided not to pursue anything. He would not look again in the pit or investigate the nearby cabin. Instead, he mounted quickly and started back toward an open area where he could radio in effectively.

Back down the slope, nearly to the bottom, he suddenly felt very strange. Eyes were boring into his back.

Too late he turned the horse. Something struck him in the middle of his back, just under his shoulder blade, something sharp, like the sting of a large bee.

Tanner reached back, struggling to grab the needle, frantic to pull it free. It hung from his skin, the plastic drug canister bouncing against his back as the horse snorted and turned.

Finally, Tanner pulled it out. He held it firmly, kicking the horse into a dead run. He heard someone grunt behind him, followed by the soft whoosh of an arrow before it clipped through the branches of a tree just over his head.

Tanner rode low over the horse, still gripping the little canister. He broke the needle off at the base with his thumb and stuffed the canister into his pocket. He was getting dizzy.

He held on in desperation, the horse jumping the creek, weaving its way through the timber and across the burn site.

On the other side of the burn, Tanner pulled the horse to

a stop and looked back. His eyesight was hazy, his thinking muddled. Colors exploded in his head.

He pulled his radio and told the dispatcher his location. He could hear her asking for clarification. He tried to talk but found himself laughing. He slid from the horse.

The horse skittered sideways and trotted away. Tanner came to his knees but could not control his muscles. He was certain someone was walking toward him, then began to run toward him. He fell flat on his face.

Unmistakably, someone was rolling him over. He couldn't see clearly and couldn't speak in any rational sequence of words. He didn't know what they were doing. It made him angry. He felt the urge to lash out.

There were more of them now, whoever they were. There was a noise in the sky above him. Enraged, he vowed to himself that they would not take him. He would fight to the death.

twenty-one

HE SAT just under the crest of a tree-covered knoll, watching them through binoculars. The foliage was dense and the lighting was poor, making for difficult observation, but he couldn't risk getting closer.

Three rangers had arrived by helicopter. They had to have been sent by Nate Jackson and the FBI man. Lucky for Tanner they had arrived.

He had nearly gotten John Tanner where he wanted him. There had been no choice other than to try and stop him in any way possible. Tanner had been far too curious, far too eager in his own mission to discover what had happened to Barney.

Tanner was good in the mountains, however. He had been very observant and had known someone was watching him. This had saved his life.

He wished now that he had shot Tanner initially with his compound bow instead of trying to sedate him and take him into the pit. He had wanted to hit Tanner in a large muscle, in the buttocks or upper thigh, but the needle had struck far too high. There hadn't been enough of the drug entering Tanner's system to knock him out.

He would have liked that—to have dragged Tanner to the pit and kept him until he had captured another grizzly. He would have fed Tanner to the grizzly, helping his mission a great deal.

He would have to try for Tanner again later, because Tanner would never give up. Especially now.

He watched the rangers struggling with Tanner to get him to calm down. He watched through his binoculars, a smile on his face, as Tanner lifted a huge rock and hurled it at the rangers, scattering them like a flock of frightened chickens. The strength that drug could muster!

Tanner was chasing one of them now, screaming oaths. Another one tried to subdue him from the back. Tanner tossed him aside like a sack of groceries. Finally, with three of them on him, Tanner ran wild and slammed into a tree, knocking himself unconscious.

He smiled and lowered his binoculars. The show was over—for now.

He wondered how the show had gone down below, the one on the shore of Lake of the Woods. He wondered how everyone had reacted to finding the remains of Valerie Jane Waters. He smiled.

One thought troubled him, though. He had dumped the body carefully, but he had had to do it quickly. He hoped he hadn't made any mistakes.

He started back toward the pit. Tanner was being loaded into the helicopter. There was nothing more to see, and more important things to be done.

He had a lot of work to do now, compliments of John Tanner. He would fill in the old pit and find a suitable location for a new one on the other side of the burn site. It had to be close to where Amy Ellerman would come, but he couldn't have the authorities snooping where his mission was taking place.

The helicopter lifted off and turned in to the darkening

sky. *Good-bye, John Tanner. Take your time recovering.*
When you do come back, you know I'll be waiting.

Dealing with the old pit would occupy a good deal of
time. They would have to dig it all out and analyze everything. They would look like a bunch of archaeologists—
digging and sifting, digging and sifting. It would slow
down the investigation.

By the time they had finished, he would be one with the
Great Bear Spirit.

He stayed in the shadows as he moved back toward the
cabin. He needed to enter the cabin before he left. It was
part of the preparation. It was a special part of his mission.

Thermal pools gurgled and bubbled along the trail, the
steam rising through the dense forest. He felt elated, so
close was he to achieving his goals.

He stepped into the cabin and fitted himself with the
grizzly head and cape. It was once again time to see the
things he had collected for viewing. It was time once again
to remember what had happened before, to see those
events that had contributed to his mission.

It was dark in the cabin, as it must always be when he
viewed these things. Only a certain lantern, which had
been blessed by the spirit, could be lit. It was very old—
from the last century—and it was smeared with blood.

He had covered the lantern with his own blood, mixed
with that of his victims and Barney. It was fitting that everything should join together in the proper way.

When he trapped the second bear, he would add its
blood to the lantern.

Tied to the lantern's base were crow feathers and human
hair from his victims. Everything fit together just right.

After chanting to the Great Bear Spirit, he ambled, like
a grizzly on its hind legs, across the floor. He would make
the circle around the interior walls, viewing his collection
of items in the special order.

Near the east wall he raised the lantern. Newspaper clippings had been taped in neat rows, the stories arranged in
sequence. His eyes followed front-page headlines from the

Billings Gazette. BEAR ATTACK IN YELLOWSTONE CLAIMS HOL-LYWOOD SUPERSTAR! stood out in bold, black type.

Other, major papers from around the country were taped in a group that covered this wall from top to bottom. In the initial story about Allen Freeman, there were references to Amy Ellerman. He had underlined the *A* in Amy each time it appeared in the story.

There were separate stories about Amy and her attempt to save Freeman. There were pictures of Amy, too. He had touched them up with paint, making her look like an Indian headed for a raid.

Another headline in another paper read: YELLOWSTONE BEAR VICTIM IDENTIFIED. The *E* in Ellen Lorraine Marks was underlined heavily throughout that story. He looked forward to underlining the *V* in Valerie Jane Waters very soon. He knew the authorities would discover who she was quite quickly.

When he had offered Amy Ellerman to the bear, he would place the story of her death in the space he had left, just to the right of Valerie's story. All three would be in a perfect line.

He traced his finger around the border of the papers. He had drawn grizzly tracks in his own blood.

He moved on, chanting. What lay ahead was even more pleasing to him.

The wall opposite the door was covered with pictures of death. He held up the lantern and stared at them, moaning softly to himself. They reminded him of events past, events that fueled his fantasies, fantasies that grew darker and required more and more attention.

A few of the pictures were from the distant past, of bodies he had long since forgotten. The pictures served only in comparison to the recent events of his mission. They all stimulated him, however, and he took great pleasure in knowing he had come so far along.

He had developed the latest photos very recently; a number of them were eight-by-tens. They showed Barney, in the pit, tearing at the first woman, Ellen Lorraine Marks.

They were in sequence. In the beginning, the grizzly was coming out of sedation, clawing its way toward the trapped woman. Then the initial contact—the woman raising her arms to ward off the horrible blows. The woman fainting. Then Barney doing his work, his terribly satisfying work.

He nodded to himself, smiling, once again viewing the various stages of her death. He was learning from the grizzly. Soon he would be able to do it himself.

He also had video recordings of the work, for he had set up two cameras. There was no way to watch them here, because there was no electricity. He sometimes viewed them in his apartment, but only when everyone else in the complex was out, or late enough at night when everyone was sound asleep.

Those times were very rare. He couldn't take any chances. Viewing the films sometimes set him to chanting and growling.

The photos did for him what he needed. His moaning grew louder, and he moved his hands all over himself. He went to the sequence showing the second woman, Valerie Jane Waters. Very satisfying.

He moved to other photos, one showing him under the grizzly cape, holding Valerie's remains. He had set the timer on the camera and had given himself ample time to position himself. The shutter had clicked, perfectly, while he had been chewing at the base of her throat.

Another photo showed him with a mouthful of flesh. Still another found him mounting the woman's remains. *He was coming closer and closer to the completion of his mission.*

The photos weren't his only trophies. There were other items: earrings, necklaces, shoes. He looked now at credit cards that bore his tooth marks and a backpack that he had marked with his own special symbol—the Indian symbol for a grizzly's foot.

He had discovered it while researching ancient petroglyphs. He had added his own style: the claws were pointing down, not up.

He continued around the room, viewing everything with great satisfaction. He removed the head and cape, smiling. The time was coming fast when he would see all these things from the mind of the Great Bear. It would be soon, and it thrilled him to think of it.

Outside the cabin, darkness had fallen completely. He made his way to his trail bike, hidden well in the trees and brush. He would return soon.

The final day was drawing nearer. Ever nearer.

twenty-two

TANNER OPENED his eyes and focused on Amy Ellerman at his bedside. She was dressed in hiking shorts and cotton top but still had a hospital band around her wrist.

"I heard you moaning," she said. "You've finally come to."

Tanner tried to sit up but found he was restrained by straps that held his chest to the bed.

"What's going on here?"

"You had a pretty tough time of it," Amy replied. "You were like some kind of monster. They had to calm you down. It sounds to me like you were drugged."

Tanner looked around him, unbelieving. "What?"

"You can't remember?"

Tanner lay his head back. "I don't feel all that well."

"If you could see yourself in the mirror, you'd understand why," Amy said. "You looked like you met a bear yourself. Your head is bandaged. I guess you have a pretty severe concussion."

Tanner's head throbbed. Pieces of what had taken place

came to him, in fragments. He could see the burn area, as if he were there again.

Then he saw Jackson and Young. He remembered them riding with him, looking at the country. He remembered looking at bear tracks. He couldn't piece together why they had been riding. It was confusing.

"They won't even tell me how this happened," Amy continued. "I can't get anyone to talk about it."

Tanner groaned.

"They were thinking of flying you out to Cody. Somebody suggested Billings. You weren't doing well. They still might, I understand, depending on your improvement."

"How long have I been here?"

"Nearly two days."

"What's happened since I got in here?" Tanner asked. He suddenly remembered the radioed message. "Didn't they find another dead woman somewhere?"

"At Lake of the Woods," Amy said. "There's not much out about her. I guess they know who she is, though, and they're notifying relatives."

Tanner remembered a little more. He remembered being alone, knowing he had discovered something major. He remembered thinking that he should have gone back with Jackson and Young.

"I'm lucky to have gotten out," Tanner said. "I'm not clear on everything yet, but I remember feeling like I was prey."

"Did you go up to the Alum Creek burn area?" Amy asked.

"I think it was Alum Creek," Tanner said. He groaned again. "Have you ever lost your memory?"

"One time, as a child, I fell off a horse and banged my head pretty hard. When I came to, I didn't know anything. Took me about an hour before I started to clear up. I was lucky; it could have been days before I remembered anything. Maybe weeks. Maybe never."

"Thanks," Tanner said. "You give me hope."

"Well, nobody *has* to say anything, really," Amy said. "If I want to believe the papers, you were attacked by that serial killer."

"What are you talking about?" Tanner asked. Serial killer. The words triggered memories.

Tanner began to see the pit, the bloody clothes, the remains of a woman's hand. He remembered trying to radio out, getting on the horse and starting back, the sharp sting of the tranquilizer dart in his back. He began to breathe rapidly.

"Are you all right?" Amy asked. "I'd better call a nurse."

"No, no, I don't want any of them in here for a little while," Tanner said. "I just want some time to gather myself, that's all."

"Do you want me to leave?" Amy asked.

"No. I'd prefer it if you wouldn't. That's up to you."

"I'd like to stay," Amy said. "I need to know about this from someone other than the press."

Amy handed Tanner a New York paper. Huge headlines read SERIAL KILLER STALKS YELLOWSTONE PARK: VICTIMS EATEN BY GRIZZLIES UNDER SPELL OF PSYCHOTIC MURDERER.

"I thought they were all crazy," Amy said. "Then they bring you in here." She handed him a more recent paper.

Tanner gasped. Two photos, one a front facial of him in his uniform and the other showing paramedics lifting him from an ambulance, covered a third of the front page. The headlines read: JOHN TANNER NEARLY FALLS VICTIM TO YELLOWSTONE SLAYER: TANNER DISCOVERED FIGHTING FOR HIS LIFE.

" 'Yellowstone Slayer'?" Tanner said.

Amy laughed. "You know the press. Got to have a catchy name. I don't know how much of it is real. It would be nice to know what's really going on. I've got work to do up there."

Tanner tried to sit up. "Could you have someone come and take me out of this harness?"

Amy reached for the side of his bed. "Just ring your buzzer."

Tanner tried to laugh. "Yeah, that would work."

A nurse looked in the door. Her eyes widened and she did an about-face. After a minute, she had returned with a doctor.

"I need out of this," Tanner said. "You can't believe how claustrophobic I am."

The doctor moved to Tanner's bedside. He looked into his eyes with a small light. "You've improved dramatically. Good."

"Doc," Tanner said, "about the restraints."

The doctor leaned over the bed again. "You promise not to tear the place apart?"

"Sure. I'll do anything to keep from being tied down."

Tanner stretched his arms. The doctor asked him questions about his head, writing on a chart as he spoke. Amy watched with interest.

The doctor laid the chart down and peered under Tanner's head bandage. "I see the stitches are still in. You tore the first set out, you know."

"You're joking."

"It wasn't funny. You were in a very bad way, but you didn't want anyone to come near you."

"I apologize for behaving that way," Tanner said. "I don't remember it. Not yet, anyway, but I'm sure I will soon enough. When can I get out of here?"

"I'd like to keep you one more day for observation," the doctor replied. "If you have no problems, I can't see why you can't go then."

"Another whole day?"

"I'd keep you longer," the doctor said, "but we need the room."

The doctor hung the chart on the wall outside the door. The nurse followed him down the hall. Amy walked back over to the bed.

"I'm out of here tomorrow morning. Not a moment too soon, either. I've got a lot of catching up to do." She reached into her pocket and produced a small plastic bag containing bits of geranium. "Listen, I have to thank you. I'm glad you brought these back from the crime lab. They're the same species as I found on my clothes. Can you tell me exactly where I can locate them?"

"You can't go anywhere up there," Tanner said. "I didn't have such a grand time, you know."

"I can understand your irritation with me," Amy said. "I know that the last time we talked, I wasn't very polite. I apologize."

"That's fine. Just don't get any ideas about going into the backcountry." He was seeing the remains of the woman in the Cheyenne crime lab. He was seeing his wife's remains. He didn't want to see this woman lying on an autopsy table.

"I shouldn't have jumped to conclusions about you," Amy went on. "I've discovered for myself that Leland Beckle, the ranger who was with you, is pretty rude."

"He is rude," Tanner said. "Did you talk to him?"

"He came in here to see me," she replied. "He told me he could take me into the backcountry and help me gather my data."

"Really," Tanner said. "What did you tell him?"

"I don't like him. I need that information desperately, but I don't want to be around him—certainly not alone."

"He's not good company under any conditions," Tanner said. "If I were you, I would just tell him to forget any favors."

"Maybe you can help me, then."

"I don't have any authority here," Tanner said. "Besides, you should know better than to even think of going into the backcountry now. Do you want to end up like those other women?"

"It wouldn't take long. Just a day."

"That's too long. Especially under the present circumstances. Can't I make you realize what could happen?"

Amy read the tortured look on Tanner's face. "I appreciate your concern. And I also learned something else that

I need to apologize for. You *do* know what it's like to lose someone to a bear mauling who was very close."

"You heard about my wife?"

"I must confess, I did some snooping. People around here admire you. When the radio call came in that you were injured, some of the staff here thought it might have been a bear. Everyone was really worried. That's how I learned about your wife. I'm sorry."

"That's in the past," Tanner said. "I'm trying to move on."

"I know what it's like," Amy said. "I know what it's like double."

Tanner looked into her face. "Listen, you did all you could to save Allen Freeman. You realize that, I hope."

"I know," Amy said. Her voice remained steady. "I've done a lot of thinking. I thought I wanted to marry him. I'm not certain now that I would have, after seeing how he behaved at the party. Still, it's hard to see someone die like that."

"You couldn't have stopped it, any more than if a plane had crashed into your house."

"Yes, but don't you wonder how you might have changed things, how you could have done something different, so it wouldn't have happened?"

Tanner took a deep breath. "Yeah, I know."

Amy looked at him. "It's been two years for you, and you still can't deal with it, can you?"

"I'm doing the best I can."

"But it hangs on, doesn't it? No matter how hard you try, it sticks with you, like some kind of old cement that keeps turning up in the lawn."

Tanner stared out the window.

"And I'll bet this case isn't helping things, is it? I can't imagine having to view pictures of those poor women. Seeing them in person would absolutely be too much. How can you do it?"

"I have to," Tanner said. "There's a killer who needs to

be stopped. I know the country Barney came from very well. That's where the killer is."

"And that's where the geraniums came from. Right? Alum Creek."

"You can't go up there," Tanner said.

"I only have a limited amount of time to collect specimens," Amy said. "They'll be drying out very soon."

"Come back next year. Finish it then."

"I can't, John. Don't you see, they'll be gone by then. They're *biennials*! They're in their second year right now! There isn't another chance."

Tanner thought about it. He knew how important the study was to her, and this one species of geranium was the most important part. But the danger was too great. Amy's life far outweighed anything else.

"John, you've got to help me with this," Amy pleaded. "You understand my situation. You're a scientist."

"I also believe your life would be in grave danger," Tanner said. "I mean, look at me. Isn't that proof enough?"

"You were alone," Amy pointed out.

"Numbers don't mean a thing here," Tanner said. "I was foolish to stay up there alone, but this guy might do anything, at any time."

"I'll bet he doesn't stay in that area," Amy suggested, searching for anything to get her way. "Doesn't that sound logical? He knows you, or someone else, will be right back up there. You'll be trying to gather evidence. He'll move. I know he will."

Tanner thought a moment. "You have a point there. But it doesn't matter where he goes. You won't be able to go into the backcountry until he's caught. That's something you're going to have to understand."

"I've got to collect this data, John, one way or another. Can't Nate Jackson spare a few rangers for just one day?"

"You would need three or four men with you up there," Tanner said. "And at that, there would be lives in jeopardy."

"I suppose you're right," Amy said. "I don't want to endanger anyone's life." She looked out the window, staring through the trees at the lake. "But I don't want to lose everything now. I can't start over again."

"Try and hold on for a little longer," Tanner said. "We'll catch this guy soon. With the FBI in on it, we'll have a lot of resources to draw from. Besides, your leg could use some more rest, I'll bet."

"My leg can rest after I finish my study, I'll have all the time in the world then."

"I won't be in here much longer," Tanner promised. "We'll have a lot to go on when all the evidence is in. I'll keep in touch with you. As soon as it's safe, I'll take you up there myself and help you."

Amy stood at the door. "I'm leaving the hospital first thing in the morning. If you're up, I'll stop in. If not, I'll wait to hear from you. And please, John, make that very soon."

twenty-three

His MISSION was back on track. John Tanner was in the hospital, his head bandaged tightly. Even when he got out, he wouldn't be going into the backcountry for some time to come.

Two days had passed, allowing him to dig a new pit and to locate a male grizzly nearly as large as Barney. This bear had no collar and had not been studied, or likely even touched by human hands.

Perfect! A pure bear to finish the mission. No better luck could have befallen him.

The forest was filling with shadows. Through binoculars, he now watched the grizzly as it moved along a ridge, the late-evening sun highlighting the blond in its thick fur.

He lowered the binoculars. The bear was coming.

"Your name will be Medicine Heart," he said. "Your strength will soon be my own."

Time was precious now. The final day would soon be here. Things had to be perfect.

He checked the top of the pit thoroughly. It was well camouflaged with pine boughs, evenly spread so no holes were visible. The grizzly could have no reason to hesitate in stepping out after the meal prepared for it.

He hurried to a large pine nearby, where a plastic bag hung suspended at the end of a rope, some twelve feet in the air. The bag contained a dead fawn he had shot four days earlier with his bow.

He climbed partway up the tree and untied the rope. The bag thumped to the ground. He carried the bag and the rope to the edge of the pit, visualizing the grizzly coming up the trail toward him. *Soon! Very soon! I will rule the forest very, very soon.*

He opened the bag. The stinking gases didn't bother him. The fawn slid easily from the bag, filling the air with the odor of putrid flesh.

He poked at the dead fawn; its stomach was swollen and flyblown. *You've ripened just right. We'll have my grizzly brother here before long.*

He tied the rope to the fawn's hind legs, slung the loose end over a tree limb that hung over the pit, and adjusted the height to suit him. Satisfied, he stood back and viewed the dangling fawn, then climbed a tree twenty feet away to watch.

The grizzly appeared, ambling along the trail, its nose in the air. He grinned broadly as the bear approached the pit, sniffing and woofing. The grizzly rose on its hind legs and reached for the fawn, stepping out onto the limbs.

"Gotcha!" he yelled, watching the grizzly fall through the branches, landing with a thump in the bottom of the pit.

The grizzly roared, turning circles in the shadows of the pit, looking for a way out.

He climbed down from the tree and approached the pit. The grizzly was shredding the fallen branches into kindling.

He looked down over the edge. "Medicine Heart! You've come to me. The time is nearing."

The grizzly glared up at him, froth drooling from its mouth.

"Oh, my brother, my brother. You've come to help me."

The grizzly stood up and roared at him. He smiled with satisfaction. "Are you ready to meet Miss Ellerman? I have been preparing for both of us. We'll meet her together. Yes. Oh, yes, we'll eat her, you and I." He began chanting, *"Hiie-ya-ho-ya. Mmmnn-ho-ya-ho."*

Still chanting, he rose and took a tranquilizer gun from a nearby clump of brush. He pulled it from its scabbard. It was painted with yellow and black stripes. He had already filled a dart with the drugs he had selected.

He returned to the pit and leaned over the edge. Chanting over the tranquilizer dart, he inserted it into the chamber. The grizzly rose to meet him, swinging furiously at him. He marveled at the bear's incredible power, praying to his spirit.

"Medicine Heart, brother in death, give me your strength. Give me your power. Give me your heart."

He sent a dart into the grizzly's shoulder and waited. Within thirty seconds the huge bear had slumped down and over onto its side.

But the grizzly wasn't completely out. He had seen to that, calculating the dosage to keep the bear slightly mobile. The bear's eyes were open and its huge paws twitched.

Wearing his head and cape, he began to dance around the outside of the pit, chanting. When he was finished, he picked up a bag containing a brush and a can each of black and yellow paint.

The shadows were getting longer, the light in the pit dimmer. He threw another, heavier, rope over the branch that had held the fawn, letting the end settle against the ground near the grizzly's head. He made certain the rope was secure, and lowered himself into the pit.

The grizzly tried to rise but could only move its front paws and head slightly. Thin drool ran from its lips.

He tossed the shattered branches aside and knelt down beside the bear's massive head. He leaned over. "I greet you, Medicine Heart," he said, kissing the grizzly's face.

"You are the sweetness of death, my brother. You are the one who will give me your power. Soon. Soon."

The grizzly lay watching, helpless, as he ran his hands through its thick coat and over its body, feeling the heavy muscles, touching the long claws and running his fingers along the thick, exposed fangs.

He placed his hand on the bear's forehead. "I feel myself, as I will soon be," he said, his eyes closed. *"Hiie-ya-ho-ya. Mmmnn-ho-ya-ho."*

The grizzly opened its mouth slowly, wanting with all its being to clamp its jaws over the man's arm. But his muscles would not obey.

Chanting, he prepared his paints, dropping pinches of powder from a small bag into both colors, mixing it in thoroughly. Carefully, he painted black and yellow circles around the grizzly's eyes, then moved to the mouth and brought lines back under the throat, circling up along the jawbone, behind the ear, to the back of the head.

From the base of the skull, he drew black and yellow lines down the grizzly's back, working slowly, carefully.

When he had finished the painting, he kneeled before the grizzly and began a new chant. *"Ho-ah-umm. Mmmnn-ho-ah-umm."* He moved his arms about, laying his hands upon the grizzly's head. *"Ho-ah-umm. Mmmnn-ho-ah-umm."*

As he chanted, the grizzly began to get its mobility back.

He stopped as the grizzly suddenly lurched up on his front legs, his head hanging, froth drooling from his mouth. He tried to raise his back legs but couldn't.

"Medicine Heart, my Medicine Heart. You are a strong one, aren't you? You are the right one." He pointed to the rising moon. "Yes, you are the one."

A rumble began in the grizzly's throat.

"I will leave you now, for you do not yet understand. In time, you will."

His paints in the bag, jammed under his arm, he grabbed the rope and began his ascent out of the pit.

Breathing a throaty snarl, the grizzly turned sideways, swiping awkwardly at him. A single claw barely nicked the calf of his left leg. The sting was sharp.

Startled, he nearly lost his grip on the rope but caught himself. His mother's face flashed before his eyes. *Where do you think you're going, my little Fuzzy Wuzzy?*

"I wasn't going anywhere, Mother. I wasn't. I promise."

He held fast to the rope, frozen, waiting for his mother's face to reappear. Just below, the grizzly roared, frightening him into motion. He climbed to safety, while the grizzly fell forward trying to rise.

Out of the pit, he got down on his hands and knees. He crawled to the edge. The grizzly's face was half in darkness.

In his mind, his mother appeared again, her face distorted in rage. *Try to run from me, will you?*

"No, Mother. I promise." He held his teddy bear against him, shielding himself from her. "No, Mother. Don't. . . . *Please!*"

She pulled his bear from him and began ripping the arms from the body, twisting the head violently. *Never tell your bear to hurt me! Never do that!*

He was crying, his hands covering his face. "Don't kill my bear! Please, Mommy, don't kill my bear! *Please!*"

She was ripping, tearing the head free, ripping, pulling the stuffing from his little teddy, her eyes ablaze. She tossed the pieces aside and reached for him, dragging him to her by his ankle. She placed her fingernails against the calf of his bare leg.

Want to know how a real bear scratches? Want to know, do you?

She raked her nails down his leg, biting deep, leaving furrows of blood and torn skin.

"Stop, Mother! Please stop!"

In the pit, the grizzly was to all fours, then rising up on his hind legs, mouth drooling froth, eyes glaring intense rage.

He stared into the pit. The grizzly roared.

He stopped his crying. His eyes widened. He smiled.

"You're alive! She didn't kill you after all!"

The grizzly leaned forward, trying to reach him with a paw. He reached down until his fingers were inches from the huge claws.

"Brother Medicine Heart! You will help me get her. She cannot stop you. She cannot stop me!"

The bear roared again, straining, huge paws reaching up.

Lifting his face to the sky, he began to chant. As darkness fell completely and the moon rose, he began to dance, mimicking the grizzly in the pit. He circled the pit, going to all fours, shaking his head in rage, coming up, swiping the air with his paws, going to all fours. . . .

He told the grizzly to sleep well and started toward the cabin. Once again he would view the pictures and see the trophies he had gathered. He was getting ready for Amy Ellerman. Soon she would be coming up. She would meet the Great Bear, and he would be free from his mother. Forever.

twenty-four

FROM HIS hospital bed, Tanner stared out his window into the twilight. He heard a knock at his door.

Jackson stuck his head in. "I hate to say I told you so," he said, chomping gum. He and Bill Young entered. Both looked worn and irritable. "Your doctor says you're coming around. How are you doing?"

Tanner's bandage had been removed, but he had yet to get into a shower. "It's a bad hair day."

"Looks better than when you came in," Young told him. "It could have been a no head day."

"You were right," Tanner said. "I would rather have run into a mad grizzly. They don't shoot you in the back with tranquilizer darts."

Young held up a piece of paper. "We've got some results on what you were shot with. Phencyclidine, for starters."

"You were 'dusted,' as they say," Jackson added. "I'll bet you've been seeing some pretty bright stars."

"It was phencyclidine, not a derivative," Young went on. "There was also ketamine, and some mescaline."

"Mescaline?" Tanner said.

"Yes," Young said. "That comes from the peyote cactus, doesn't it?"

"Yes," Tanner said.

"This guy is taking Indian spiritualism to the hilt," Jackson commented. "It's the weirdest thing I've ever heard of. And John, my friend, you were nearly one of his victims. How do you feel about that?"

Tanner didn't answer.

Jackson chewed his gum hard. "According to Jim Clark, you were a raging madman, trying to kill everyone. Three of them couldn't hold you. Fine way to be, Tanner. Why didn't you radio in when you discovered the pit, like you said you would?"

"I tried," Tanner said. "I was back too far. I couldn't keep a steady signal."

"Then why didn't you just come out?"

"That's what I was doing," Tanner said. "I *was* leaving. I saw what was in the pit and I couldn't handle it. I would have *flown* out of there if I could have."

Young took out a notebook. "About this pit you found, can you be specific?"

"A big hole in the ground, not far from Mary Lake cabin," Tanner said. "He kept Barney in there, until Barney dug his way out. There's a lot of evidence up there—bones, clothes, a lot of stuff."

Young was writing. Jackson chomped hard on his gum. "How long after we left you did you find the pit?"

"Less than an hour," Tanner said. "It wasn't much past the burn site."

"Did you see the killer at all?"

"Never. Not once. I knew he was there, though. I could feel him in the trees." He saw Jackson and Young frowning at him. "I should say I knew something or someone was there. He stayed well hidden. If I had known it was the killer, I would have turned right around."

"Sure you would have," Jackson said.

"We can't have any more fatalities, human or bear," Tanner said.

Young popped the notebook against the palm of his hand. "Human includes you, John. You endangered yourself. If I didn't know better, I'd think you don't care a lot about living."

Tanner stared at him.

"I asked Nate about that when we left you," Young said. "We radioed in for backup, then I learned about your wife. I'm sorry. Still, you can't endanger yourself like you did."

Tanner took a deep breath and folded his arms across his chest.

"John, there are a lot of people who care about you," Jackson said. "You can't do us any good on this case if you're dead. Most of all, you can't do yourself any good. Think about it."

"I had to know what happened to Barney," Tanner said. "Now I know, and I know all of it's going to happen again if that killer isn't stopped. Now. When are we going back up?"

" 'We'?" Jackson said. " 'We' doesn't include you, I'm afraid."

Tanner didn't argue. He turned and looked out the window, waiting for Jackson to say that he was taking him off the case.

"You could stand a few more days of rest," Jackson continued. "We'll see where things are then."

"The doctor says I can go in the morning."

"Make sure you're healing up," Young said.

"Things are under control, John," Jackson added. "Don't take it all on yourself."

"There's a team going up to look at the pit in another day or two," Young said. "They're working at Lake of the Woods now. We had some trouble the first night the body was found, and we've been slowed up."

"Two grizzlies wanted to come in and feed on the remains," Jackson explained. "They had to move the body out before they wanted to. There's a chance we lost some evidence, but it was either that or kill the bears."

"I think it's important to get right back up on Alum

Creek," Tanner said. "What if he kills again before someone gets up to the pit?"

"We flew over it this morning," Jackson said. "It's been filled in. He didn't waste any time. We'll have to dig it anyway, but right now we're thinking he'll dig a new pit somewhere else."

"He's going to stay on Central Plateau," Tanner said. "He can't readily move anywhere else."

"What about the east backcountry, behind the lake?" Jackson asked. "And what about the Thorofare area? Those areas don't get much travel, either."

"There are a lot of places he could move to," Tanner admitted. "Where will we start?"

"I've contacted the behavioral science people," Young said. "They'll make a profile from the MOs. We should know a lot more then. Right now, we know he's very organized. But we don't know specifics yet, so we can't waste our time speculating. We have to watch the campgrounds and the concessions, to be sure no one else gets picked up."

"I feel helpless here," Tanner said.

"No use getting excited," Jackson said, turning for the door. "We'll be back to see you before long."

After Jackson and Young left, Tanner sat up, looking out the window, watching them as they talked on the lawn in front. Beyond was the lake, broad and blue in the afternoon sun.

A nurse brought Tanner his dinner. He picked at it, then set it aside. He rose and dressed himself. His head had stopped throbbing, but a dull ache persisted. No painkillers for him. He hated drugs.

The hall was filled with rushing people. A nurse stopped and asked Tanner why he was up.

"Where's everyone going?" Tanner asked her.

"Please, get back to bed," the nurse insisted. Her face was distorted with anger and exhaustion.

Tanner allowed her to usher him back into his room.

She waited, making certain that he undressed and got back into his white gown.

Tanner pulled back the covers. "What's the emergency?"

"A call came in from Old Faithful," the nurse replied, "and another from Grant Village. Heart attack victims. There have been five since the serial killer thing hit the news."

Tanner slipped into bed.

"Everything has gone crazy," the nurse continued, throwing up her arms. "Everyone is seeing him. The killer is in every campground, every night. Everyone is seeing a grizzly coming at them."

"Maybe they shouldn't be here," Tanner suggested.

"Oh, but that wouldn't do," the nurse said. "I'm not sure this whole thing hasn't attracted *more* tourists than usual."

"I believe you're right," Tanner said. "There's no way they could stop them from coming, though, even if the Park Service wanted to. There's too much at stake to close the park down completely."

"Right. It wouldn't be a good profit-and-loss statement," the nurse said. "There's too much invested up here to stop the flow."

"Even without the present danger, this is wild country," Tanner pointed out. "People should realize that and behave accordingly."

"That will never happen," the nurse said. "Are you going to stay put now?"

"Do I have a choice?" Tanner asked.

"No. I'm tired and it's late. I'm supposed to keep you down. Will you please do me a favor and cooperate? . . . Please?"

"I'll stay put," Tanner promised.

"You're an angel," she said, turning out the light.

Tanner took a deep breath and lay back. His head ached, though not enough to keep him in a hospital.

But he'd promised. Just one more night. He could handle it. Maybe.

twenty-five

THE NURSE was gone, the echo of her heavy footsteps long past. Nothing stirred inside. Outside, a slight breeze rustled the treetops.

Tanner lay staring into the black ceiling, envisioning stars. He wasn't outside, but he would bring the night sky inside with his mind.

Tanner closed his eyes. The darkness began to swirl. Colors spewed from everywhere, mixing into a distorted panorama of the wilderness.

The sky was a lumpy gray, the clouds drifting in thick layers. The trees appeared fuzzy, as if the bark were brown cotton, the needles green felt. The earth undulated in waves, like a tempest-tossed sea, the trees rising and falling, the rocky ridges breaking apart and reforming like jigsaw puzzles.

From a hole in the picture came a grizzly, its features badly distorted. Its body changed from large and hairy to slim and white, back and forth.

The head never changed—until it reached the front of the picture.

The grizzly stopped. Its broad face came toward Tanner, the teeth exposed as the mouth came open in a roar. When the grizzly's mouth closed again it was staring straight at him.

But the eyes were not those of a bear. They were human.

Tanner arched in his sleep. The human eyes laughed at him. Narrowed and cruel, the eyes defied him.

Tanner remembered what Grandfather had once told him about dreaming: "Once you know that you are in a dream, you can interact with others in the dream. All that can be hurt in a dream is your mind. If you do not let your mind become hurt, then you can control the dream."

The huge head drew nearer. Tanner turned a palm upward and saw the letter *D* imprinted there. A dream; he was in a dream. Certainly. But it didn't feel like a dream. It felt real.

Tanner looked at his palm again. The letter *D* stood out, large and red.

After calming himself, Tanner reached for the grizzly's face, to touch it and ask what it represented. The human eyes seemed surprised. The head receded.

Tanner walked toward it. The grizzly turned and began to run into the rolling forest. Tanner called out to it, but the bear never stopped running.

This would not be the end of the dream, Tanner said to himself. He would trail the bear.

Below him were tracks, like petroglyphs on the forest floor. The tracks were red, and they led backward.

Confused, Tanner turned in the dream and looked behind him. There were no tracks. The grizzly had entered the rolling forest, leaving red, backward tracks.

Tanner started into the forest. The tracks were hard to see, hiding themselves within the moving ground. Tanner persisted, keeping his arms out to control his balance. He followed the tracks into the wilderness, catching occasional glimpses of the grizzly looking back at him through angry human eyes.

The forest began to change, to become darker. Tanner stopped himself, arms still out for balance. The tracks had taken him to a huge hole. It yawned like a giant, toothless mouth, waiting for him to step in, waiting to swallow him.

Tanner looked into the pit, seeing the human eyes staring up at him. The grizzly opened its mouth, roaring. He felt himself sliding forward toward the pit. A huge paw came out of it, reaching for his leg.

Tanner jerked awake. The hospital darkness was dead still. His gown and the bed were drenched.

Trembling, he climbed out of bed. He walked to the doorway and looked up and down the hall. It was empty. Then someone came around the corner.

Lights near the desk revealed an older man shuffling toward him. The man reached Tanner and stopped. Tanner looked into his face. His hair was disheveled, his eyes wide.

"He's dead," the man said. "The bear killed him, right there on the road. I saw it myself."

"Who?" Tanner asked. "Who was killed?"

The old man turned and started to walk past. He stumbled, and Tanner caught him.

A nurse arrived. Another nurse paged a doctor.

"What's going on?" Tanner asked. He checked the palm of his hand. There was nothing on it. He wasn't dreaming.

"There was a man killed by a grizzly tonight," the nurse said. "He was dressed like a ranger. People are saying the dead man was the serial murderer."

Tanner walked back into his room and dressed. A nurse met him at the hospital door.

"What are you doing?"

"It's time for me to go," Tanner said.

"But the doctor hasn't checked you out yet."

"I'm fine," Tanner said. "I promise, I'm just fine."

twenty-six

TANNER DROVE into Mammoth and entered the administration building through a heavily guarded front door.

He had radioed for Jackson on the way back from the hospital and had learned that the FBI and park personnel were meeting in the superintendent's conference room at 2 A.M.

Present were Jackson and Young, along with Leland Beckle and Martin Linders. Jackson had seated Linders on one side of the table and Beckle on the other, at opposite ends, so they would not be facing one another.

Beckle had not been seen much since Jackson had reprimanded him for speaking to the press without authorization. He had insisted on sitting in here, though, as he had boasted that he would be the one to catch the killer. Not the FBI. Not anyone else. It would be him.

Linders had told Beckle just prior to the meeting that popping off to the media had caused everyone a great deal of trouble. Beckle was still seething at the remark but would not physically challenge Linders.

Now Linders sat relaxed, while Beckle twisted his fingers into knots.

Young walked over to the coffeepot. Jackson stuffed gum into his mouth and pulled a chair out next to him for Tanner.

"Does the doctor know you're here?"

"I'm officially discharged," Tanner replied. "I just have to go back and sign the papers."

"That's good, because the doctor called here. He wants me to send you back."

"He told me he needed the room," Tanner said. "Besides, I was supposed to be dismissed this morning anyway."

"I suppose you figured anytime after midnight was morning," Jackson said.

"Yeah, close enough," Tanner said.

Tanner noticed Beckle glaring at him. Martin Linders was smiling. Jackson said, "It's good to have you back on the case, John. No one could ever accuse you of overstaying your hospital break."

"Breaks like that I can do without," Tanner said.

Young sat down and gulped coffee. "Let's call this meeting to order. We've got a lot to go over."

"A nurse at the hospital said the news was out that the killer was mauled to death by a grizzly tonight," Tanner said. "Has this thing finally come to an end?"

"Not hardly," Young said. "He was a copycat, posing as a ranger. He was trying to rope a bear near Norris. This just makes things worse."

"I've had it up to here with the insanity," Linders said. "I say we feed them all to the bears."

"Not a time for joking," Young said.

"No joke," Linders said. "Definitely no joke."

Beckle, who had been quietly rubbing his hands together, stared hard at Linders. "We need a professional approach. That's impossible for you, isn't it?"

Linders smiled crookedly. "Iron your shirt, Beckle, or at least change it once in a while."

"That will do," Jackson said. "We have serious matters at hand. Anyone who doesn't tend to them will have to leave this meeting. I hope I'm understood."

Linders and Beckle continued to stare at one another. After a moment, Tanner asked, "How did the copycat get a park ranger uniform?"

"He broke into a ranger's apartment," Young said. "He must have been planning it for a while."

Tanner shook his head. "Meanwhile, there's nothing new on the real killer."

"We're getting closer to figuring him out," Young said. "One of our behavioral specialists flew in from Quantico this morning. His name is Ron Grossman. He's one of the best."

"I thought he was coming to this meeting," Linders said.

"He's been studying MOs from both dump sites all day," Young said. "He should show up anytime now."

"You said you learned some more about the second victim," Jackson said. "Let's have it, so I can fill out another mountain of paper."

Young studied his notes. "We think we have an ID: Valerie Jane Waters, a summer employee from Nebraska. Her car was towed from Canyon Village in late June. She'd had a nosebleed, and the tissue blotches match her blood type. We got hair and dried skin from the car. We're having the lab check DNA against that of the victim."

"So both women came from the park?" Tanner asked.

Young pulled some photos from his pocket and handed them to Tanner. "They both worked for park vendors. Both tended counters all day. It would have been easy for the killer to scope them out, make sure they were what he wanted, without anyone paying the slightest bit of attention."

"He had to have gained their confidence as well," Jackson added. "We're sure he wears a uniform. Smooth boy."

"He has to work in the park, then," Tanner said.

Young nodded. "No doubt about it. He knows the system here. He's real efficient."

"Too bad the copycat wasn't the real thing," Linders said. "Then I could go back to my regular job."

"That would be too easy," Young said. "This guy is real clever."

Tanner studied the pictures. "Why didn't anyone report the first woman missing?" he asked, staring at Ellen Lorraine Marks.

"It was her first year here," Young answered. "She didn't have a car. You know that turnover's pretty high. It's not uncommon for these kids to just take off with someone and not show up for work the next day."

Tanner continued to stare at the pictures. Young and pretty, filled with vitality. He turned to Jackson.

"Amy Ellerman looks like these women. She's a few years older; but the looks are almost the same."

"Right down to the long hair," Jackson said.

Tanner fingered the photos nervously. "She wants to go back to Alum Creek and collect geraniums."

"She told me," Jackson said. "I can't help her until this thing is over. There's no way."

"She checked out of the hospital yesterday morning," Tanner said. "Where is she now?"

"Pacing her apartment," Jackson said. "She'll have to pace awhile longer. We're going to be watching her closely."

"There are a lot of other women who look like Amy Ellerman," Linders pointed out. "Why would he pick her over the others?"

"That's a question for the behavioral specialist," Young said. His eyes went to the door. "I think he's here now."

twenty-seven

THE DOOR opened. Ron Grossman was tall and thin, with graying temples. He walked with a loose but confident gait. His eyes were quick and filled with concern.

Young introduced him. Grossman set a briefcase on the table and sat down opposite Tanner. He took a deep breath. "Sorry I'm late."

"You're on," Young said.

Grossman opened the briefcase. He pulled out two files and laid them down. His eyes went up to Tanner and back to the files. "Mr. Tanner, I understand you have some notions about this case, as it pertains to bears and Native American mysticism?"

"I believe this killer is delving into shamanism," Tanner said. "I was advised by a friend that he wants to have the power of a bear."

"I tried to talk to your friend," Grossman said. "He said I wouldn't understand. He told me you would know how to explain it."

"I don't know anything specific," Tanner said. "The paint marks on the grizzly have symbolic meaning. It has to do with acquiring bear medicine. It's a spiritual thing. I was hoping you could figure out why he wants to be a grizzly."

Grossman laced his fingers together on the files and leaned forward. "Let me say that I don't put a lot of credence in that sort of thing, Mr. Tanner, but this is a case that I cannot comprehend. I've talked to a lot of people in my kind of work about it. They've seen everything, and I mean everything. Yet this is beyond anyone's wildest concepts. I'm going to need all your help."

Leland Beckle spoke up. "You'd better open your mind about this spiritualism, Mr. Grossman. It's the real thing."

"Do you have any ideas you'd like to share?" Grossman asked.

"I've studied Indians and their ways," Beckle said. "I know a lot about them. Probably more than Mr. Tanner, even though he has Indian blood in him."

Jackson spoke up. "What's your point, Beckle?"

"I'm saying that I want to be the main investigator here. I know more about it than anyone else. It's *my* district and I want to be in charge!"

"We'll all try and work together," Grossman said. "That's what's needed here. Okay?"

The room was silent, except for the humming of fluorescent lights. Everyone stared at Beckle, who was glaring back and forth from Grossman to Tanner.

"Is there anything else?" Grossman asked.

Beckle stood up. "I'm going back into the field. Nobody here knows anything!"

Beckle stormed out. Grossman turned to Jackson. "I'll need all the information on him I can get."

"Do you think he has anything to do with this?" Jackson asked. "His office is covered with pictures of bears and Indians."

"A lot of people around here have pictures of bears and Indians," Grossman said. "But we'll be watching him."

Grossman opened a file and began handing around photos. Tanner couldn't look at them for very long.

"I'm going to share what I presently know," Grossman said. "As you can see, both women were young, blonde, and blue-eyed. You saw the resemblance. Not twins, but close. This killer is searching out women who look like someone he knows, or used to know. He's probably after an authority figure from his past. Likely his mother.

"Now, as far as the work on the MO, the bodies have been compared in great detail. There are some notable comparisons.

"Both were sexually assaulted, both before and after death. Remnants of ritual markings were found on both women, including paint of the same colors and type found on the grizzly." Here he looked at Tanner.

"They also found human tooth marks on both women," Grossman went on. "It appears that the killer has been feeding off his victims, like a grizzly would."

"Eating them?" Tanner said.

"Parts of them. Around the throat, the abdomen. Places a grizzly would feed from. Am I correct? A bear will go for the soft parts first?"

"That's correct," Tanner said.

"How can a guy do that and function in regular society?" Jackson asked.

"He has no problems functioning," Grossman said. "His worlds are divided, like night and day."

Everyone was staring. Jackson drank coffee and added more gum to his mouth.

Grossman opened another file. "Here's the profile. It's as complete as I can make it, for now."

Everyone leaned forward slightly.

"The killer is a white male between the ages of thirty-five and forty-five years, likely the first-born son in a family where discipline was inconsistent. The father was likely away for extended periods of time, and he was left with his mother, who abused him in who knows how many ways.

"Despite this, he has a strong personality but is something of a loner. He is sexually competent but likely not married. He would be living with his mother, if she were alive. His problem is, he believes she is chasing him in spirit form. He has an urge to rid himself of her by killing women who look like her. Somehow he can't run far enough away."

"Do you think he's from within the park?" Tanner asked. "Or could he have come from somewhere else and is living in the backcountry?"

"That's hard to know for certain," Grossman replied, "but I believe he works within the Yellowstone Park system. He certainly possesses above-average intelligence, is articulate, and has to be strong and physically fit to do what he's doing. If he isn't a ranger, which I believe he is, he would need to have access to uniforms and equipment consistant with his crimes."

"Why is he using grizzlies?" Jackson asked. "Why not just kill with a gun or a knife?"

"What he's doing with the grizzlies is displaying his urge for control over everything around him," Grossman explained. "I don't know what Native Americans believe, but this guy wants to think he can incorporate the grizzly's power into himself, and then take his mother on and get rid of her."

"That's not what Native American spiritualism is all about," Tanner said. "Not even close."

"Well, then, he's twisting what he's read and heard to suit himself," Grossman explained. "It's likely he's watching the grizzly eat the victims, believing that the bear is consuming the woman's spirit. He follows after the bear, feeding in the same manner, learning from it.

"He will have a set number of victims, and he will watch the bear eat all of them. After the final victim, he will likely kill the bear and eat parts of it. He believes that by doing so, he has assimilated all the spirits the bear has within it. With this power he can then get rid of his mother's spirit, and end the haunting."

"I don't understand the thinking," Jackson said. "How does he believe he can get rid of his mother's spirit?"

"This is all laid out neatly in his mind," Grossman said. "He's likely hidden part of his mother somewhere—her heart, or head, maybe. After he's killed the right number of women and eaten from them as the grizzly hås, he will want to extricate the spirit of his mother from the trophy, and subsume her into his new being—that of a grizzly bear. Then he will have devoured her and gotten rid of her. He will have the power of a grizzly and his world will be complete."

"Someone like that should surely stand out," Tanner said.

"Not really," Grossman said. "To see this man in everyday life, you would never believe any of this. He interacts with everyone well, with the exception of a few quirks that anyone might have."

Jackson got up for more coffee. "We've got a lot of rangers here, especially during the summer season. How could we single out the one you've just profiled?"

"You can't," Grossman said. "We've got to make sure we know everyone working here, their backgrounds, everything."

"I have people on that now," Young said. "We'll sort through them and narrow the field down considerably in a couple of days."

"Of all the rangers," Jackson said, chewing hard, "there can't be more than a half dozen that fit the profile."

"Once they're tagged," Young said, "we'll have someone watching them twenty-four hours a day."

"Give all the watchers binoculars," Grossman suggested. "Maybe someone will get lucky and get a glimpse into a residence. We've solved some tough cases that way before."

"We can't go in," Jackson said. "What do you mean?"

"If we can find the guy's residence, it will be filled with a lot of strange items," Grossman said. "He will have collected newspaper clippings and a lot of trophies—items he's taken from the victims: earrings, necklaces, shoes, sometimes even body parts."

"What's that all about?" Jackson asked.

"You all need to know that this guy lives in a fantasy world," Grossman explained. "He wants to relive the events over and over, filling himself up with the feeling of the crime. He loves to see pictures and feel personal items taken from each kill. This spurs him to the next victim. It's a continual process."

"When do you think he'll strike again?" Tanner asked.

Grossman referred to a calendar on the wall. "The first two victims died on or near a full moon. Likely on. We've got less than a week to find him."

"He'll be very hard to catch in that short time," Linders said.

"He believes he will never be caught," Grossman said. "In his mind, he's unstoppable. Everyone and everything is beneath him. He'll make a mistake, maybe just a very small one, and that will be all we'll need."

Grossman stuffed the files into his briefcase and closed it. Everyone was watching him closely. He singled Tanner out.

"What are you looking at, Mr. Tanner?"

"I think you'd better open your briefcase again and take some notes," Tanner said. "I know where you're apt to find your trophies."

"You do?" Grossman said.

"I think we'd better head up to the Mary Lake patrol cabin. I bet we'll find a lot of strange things up there."

twenty-eight

YOUNG LOOKED down from the helicopter. "There's an awful lot of country up here. I can see how someone could do this without detection, but I'll never understand why someone *would* do it."

Grossman adjusted his sunglasses and looked out across the dawn skyline. "Because this is a crazy world we live in, Bill. There's nothing sacred anymore."

Tanner and Jackson sat across from them, holding tight while the helicopter landed. The pit was a hundred yards distant, through the trees. There was already a forensics team approaching the Alum Creek burn site from the ground.

"Pretty good timing," Young said. He looked at his watch. "Even with the early start, we'll be pressing to finish this before nightfall."

Young and Grossman got out, ducking their heads under the rotors. As he left the helicopter, Tanner felt an urgency. Though he knew he didn't have to scan the trees this time, he had the urge to look behind him, to watch for the barrel of a tranquilizer gun.

"You've got that look in your eyes," Jackson said. "I saw it when we left you up here by yourself the other day."

"I guess I should relax," Tanner said. "But I can't until this is over."

"If right about this," Jackson said, "we could be very close to it. Grossman says the killer needs his fantasies. He needs the trophies."

Tanner realized that the type of mind at work up here had little to do with humanity. All that had been lost. Grossman had explained how the killer's childhood had likely robbed him of life, or of any semblance of inner normality.

But that hadn't stopped him from imitating normality outwardly, and imitating it very well.

As they walked toward the pit, Tanner wondered who among the park rangers could do this. According to Grossman, there was no sure way to tell. You couldn't figure it out from someone getting angry, or by how many *Playboys* they had under their mattress.

The part that bothered Tanner the most was the fact that the killer might not have been detected. If it hadn't been for Barney killing Allen Freeman, no one would have had any idea.

At the pit, the forensics team organized for the dig. They had a lot of equipment designed to give field readings, and a lot of sifters for screening the smallest particles.

While they worked, Tanner led a team headed by Young and Grossman to the Mary Lake patrol cabin, a half mile through the shadows of an awakening wilderness.

Tanner studied the area near the cabin through binoculars. Though still on edge, he felt better today. There were birds, lots of them, flitting about the branches. Squirrels busied themselves on the ground, something they would never do with danger about.

"It looks clear to me," Tanner said. "Let's go in."

Along the way, Grossman asked about the thermal

pools, bubbling noisily, sending steam into the early-morning sky. He had never been to Yellowstone, where in places the earth has remained in the ancient geologic past.

"I've heard that Old Faithful erupts about every seventy-five minutes or so," Grossman said. "That's amazing. How do all these pots and basins work?"

Jackson explained that the molten rock beneath the surface heats water that has seeped underground, sometimes to a depth of two miles or more. The water cannot boil, due to the extreme pressure of the underground network, and rises back up.

As Jackson talked, Grossman stopped to study one of the pools, where crystal-blue water was spitting and boiling, its edges colored red and yellow and black.

"A lot of chemicals come up with the water," Jackson said. "You can smell the sulfur."

Grossman looked from the pool up to the cabin. "I'm afraid what we're going to find up there won't be nearly so pretty."

With guns drawn, the team circled the cabin. After approaching cautiously, Young called inside several times. When there was no answer, he kicked the door in.

Grossman and Jackson followed, their guns drawn. Tanner stood back and entered when they came to the door.

"I guess you knew," Grossman told Tanner. "Everything's here."

Tanner walked inside. It was dark and smelled of blood and rotting human remains. Young began looking for another body. He found fingers and pieces of flesh tacked to the walls.

"I've seen this kind of thing before," Grossman said. "But this is as bad as it gets."

Young lifted his radio and called for half the forensics team. They would take a lot of pictures and salvage a lot of evidence without really disturbing anything. The killer would be coming back; there was no doubt about that.

While they waited for forensics, Grossman began going over the walls with a flashlight, picking out details. Tanner stood with Jackson, listening to his remarks, viewing the inside of a very deranged mind.

When he saw the bloody markings around the newspaper clippings, his dream came back to him. He saw the backward tracks leading to the gaping hole in the ground. He saw the grizzly with the human eyes staring up at him, its mouth open, one paw reaching up for him.

"I need some air," he told Jackson.

"Wait," Jackson said. "Look at what Grossman found."

"This is interesting," Grossman was saying, referring to the newspaper clippings. "You see where he's underlined the first initial of each victim's first name? That's got to mean something."

Grossman took a pad from his pocket and wrote down the *E* in Ellen Lorraine Marks and the *V* in Valerie Jane Waters. Tanner's mind was spinning.

"Yes, he's got to be after Amy Ellerman next," Grossman said. "Look here. He's underlined the *A* in her name several times."

"I'm going out for a minute," Tanner said. "I've got to."

Outside, Tanner breathed deeply. The tracks were all over his mind, marking the inside of his psyche. He couldn't get rid of them.

The forensics team arrived. Young and Grossman gave them instructions. Jackson walked over to Tanner.

"Eva," Jackson said. "Grossman thinks the mother's name was Eva. E-V-A is everywhere in there."

"Is that how he escapes his mother? He feeds her to a grizzly?"

"That's what Grossman says. You've got to admit, he really knows his stuff."

"So Amy Ellerman is the last link in his sick chain?" Tanner asked.

"It looks that way," Jackson said. "Maybe we should have her get out of here altogether, at least until this is over."

"That would be a good idea."

"And you, too, John. Why don't you take awhile to relax? Let these guys finish this. You've done way more than your share."

Tanner rubbed his hands through his hair. "Maybe I should. I'm not a hundred percent yet."

"John, if you were to ask me, you aren't much over sixty percent. I know you."

"That low?"

"Listen," Jackson said, "you went through a lot. Take it easy for a while. No one will blame you."

The forensic team began a systematic but careful gleaning of evidence from the cabin and its surroundings. Lots to get, yet nothing obvious could be taken, for nothing tied anyone directly to the murders.

Grossman came out of the cabin. Tanner noted it was the first time he had seen the man smile. Not much, but enough to detect.

"Mr. Tanner, I guess we've got you to thank. If you hadn't put yourself at such risk, we wouldn't know about this place."

"I just hope it will bring an end to this," Tanner said.

"We all do," Grossman said. "Now that we've found this place, we should know who he is in a day or two."

Young came out and pointed through the trees to the helicopter. "Let's fly back and see what's waiting for us down below. We'll let forensics handle things up here for the time being, and leave someone on guard. I'd like to come back up later."

Tanner walked with them toward the helicopter. Young and Grossman were relaxed, confident that the cabin was the major breakthrough they had needed.

As they boarded the helicopter, Tanner took a last look around. He hadn't been able to relax, or even to settle down. The tracks were all over his thoughts. They flashed before his eyes. They were leading him somewhere, he knew, somewhere very dark.

twenty-nine

TANNER KNOCKED on Amy Ellerman's apartment door. She answered, her face expectant.

"I'm sorry," Tanner said. "I didn't come to tell you everything was over. Just about, though. We hope."

"Just about doesn't help me. It's just about fall up there. Those plants will be gone."

She let him in. He told her about the cabin and the forensics team that expected to find all they needed to pinpoint and arrest the killer.

Amy was only partially listening. She was standing by a table against one wall. There she had a microscope and an array of plant material she had been studying.

Tanner walked over. Amy was staring at a small plastic bag labeled GERANIUM BICKNELLII. She rubbed a tear from her cheek and went to the window.

"I seem to get just so far, and then something happens," she said. "I'm really sick of it."

Tanner sat down on the couch. "It's pretty hard to know what to do. They might know who he is today, or it might take a week. But there's one thing we are certain of: he's after you."

"Bad joke, John."

"I wouldn't joke about a thing like that."

"So, what do you mean?"

"I mean this guy wants you."

"What are you talking about?"

"An FBI profiler on the case says the murderer is trying to kill his mother," Tanner explained. "He likely did kill her, but he thinks she's still alive in some way. The profiler says he needs to kill women that look like his mother."

"A lot of women have long blond hair, John. Why would he single me out?"

"Well, let me tell you a story."

When Tanner had finished with the information about the killer spelling Eva with his victims, Amy laughed nervously. "That's so sick. You couldn't have made that up."

"I didn't make it up. You should have seen the inside of that cabin."

"I saw a few things like that while in the academy. A lot of it was on film."

"You can't smell it on film," Tanner said. "You couldn't breathe inside that cabin."

"I guess I'd just as well pack up, then. There's no use hanging around here any longer." Amy was looking out the window. Parked across the street was a car in which sat two men in suits. "If I stay here, I'm going to have agents looking out for me all the time. I don't want that."

"That's a necessity, no matter where you go, until this thing is over. Unless . . ."

Amy turned from the window.

"Unless you agree to let me take you to dinner. In that case, I'd be the agent watching out for you."

"Oh, really," Amy said. "And how do you intend to look out for me?"

"By taking you for a swim at Chico Hot Springs, and

then maybe around the area, seeing some sites, getting your mind off all this."

"That's the best offer I've had in a while," Amy said. "You won't succeed in getting my mind off this, but you may be able to distract me momentarily."

Chico Hot Springs resort nestles up against the Absaroka Wilderness, halfway between Yellowstone Park and Livingston, Montana. The main hotel was built at the turn of the century and is considered to have some of the finest cuisine in the region.

Tanner had made reservations. The midsummer crowd was noisy: a lawn wedding had just finished and the reception was spilling into the lobby.

"Allen wanted to take me here," Amy said as they waited for their meal. "He just never got around to it."

"You should have told me," Tanner said. "Maybe this wasn't a good place to come."

"Oh, no, this is perfect," Amy said. "I guess I cared about Allen. Actually, though, I really didn't know him all that well. I thought I wanted to spend my life with him, but maybe later I would have thought of it as a mistake. Do you know what I mean?"

Tanner leaned back while the waiter set their plates down. "Yes, I know what you mean. Don't they call that the rebound?"

"I don't think I was on the rebound. Maybe I was. It's been a couple of years since Jim was killed. Could I still be on the rebound?"

"You're asking me?"

"Yes," Amy said. "You look to me like a rebound expert."

"I played only a little basketball," Tanner said. "My sports were football and wrestling. You don't want any rebounds in either one of those."

"Rebounds are only good in trampoline and platform diving," Amy said. "I'm not good at either."

"We'll stick to nonrebound sports then," Tanner said. "Deal?"

"Deal," Amy said. "The fish is good."

"Flown in fresh every day," Tanner said. "Do you like Mexican?"

"Very much."

"I've got a friend over in a little town on the other side of the mountains," Tanner said. "He and his wife do a great job. Would you like to try it?"

"They must have some good Mexican restaurants closer than that."

"I need to get away from here as badly as you," Tanner said. "I could end up with more damage to my head if I don't let someone else take care of it."

"Are you saying that you can't let it go, yet you have to for health reasons?"

"Exactly. I still have a buzz in my ears, but I'd turn around and go back up there in a heartbeat if I thought I could find that guy. I can't do that. There are plenty of top-grade lawmen here now. They'll catch him."

They finished their meal in silence. A short way from the dining room, just out from the main building, was the saloon, where a band played rousing country tunes. At the back of the saloon was a large swimming pool and a smaller soaking area where warm mineral waters flowed.

"That looks inviting," Amy said. "But I'm not sure I want to fight the crowd."

"I've got a mineral pool up behind my cabin," Tanner said. "That would be a bit more relaxing."

Amy smiled. "You've got a mineral pool?"

"Yeah. It's no resort, but it's warm and cozy."

"Warm and cozy sounds good to me. I haven't been warm and cozy for a long time."

thirty

THE NIGHT was open and cool. Stars filled the mountain sky around a nearly full moon.

As they pulled up to Tanner's cabin, Amy looked around with interest. "Nice hideaway you've got here."

"It works for me," Tanner said. Inside, he took some iced tea from the refrigerator. "Do you like wild mint tea?"

"Very much," Amy said.

"I mixed it with rosehips."

"It sounds delicious," Amy said. "A tall glass, if you please."

Amy was interested to know that Tanner grew and collected his own herbs. A kitchen shelf was lined with containers with homemade labels: western yarrow, field mint, watercress, various sages, all were there ready to mix with regular teas. There were a number of containers filled with powdered roots, including alumroot, purple coneflower, and biscuit root.

"How did you learn about all these?" she asked. "I didn't know you could use all these for medicine."

"My great-grandfather told me about most of them," Tanner replied. "I've also collected a few volumes on medicinal plants. I've made it a hobby."

"Very interesting," Amy said. "Maybe you could have gone up and collected my geraniums for me."

"I can do some sampling techniques," Tanner said, "but I leave the heavy stuff to the botanists and range scientists."

Amy sipped her wild-mint tea and looked out the picture window toward peaks bathed in moonlight. "It's very peaceful up here, I must say."

Tanner took her to the back, through sliding glass doors onto a cedar deck. At the edge of the deck, he had installed a large hot tub made of natural stone. Warm water ran into one side through a filtering system, and out the bottom through another system.

Steam rose from the clear blue water into the night sky. He punched a switch and the water became activated, churning bubbles to the surface.

"It's connected to an underground thermal aquifer that rises just over there." Tanner pointed to where a column of hot water rose to the surface and formed a small stream. The air was filled with steam and the smell of mineral salts.

"Why did you go to all this trouble?" Amy asked. "Why don't you just soak in the natural spring?"

"I prefer to have the water on a thermostat," Tanner replied. "That way there are no surprises."

"Surprises?"

"Yeah, surprises. I once saw a guy get into a thermal pool up above Gardiner. It was warm when he got in. Then something happened and he was instantly boiled to almost nothing. I never get into a thermal pool, no matter how harmless it might look."

Amy leaned down and swirled her fingers in the churning water. "This feels great. I'll be perfectly safe in here?"

Tanner smiled. "Perfectly safe. But I can't say the same

for your swimming suit. The natural salts in the water can ruin the color."

"Oh, c'mon."

"Take your chances, if you'd like."

Amy laughed. "You never wear one in here?"

"Why should I?"

"That's true. Why should you?"

"There are towels in the bathroom," Tanner said. "See you in the tub."

Tanner undressed in his room and covered himself with a towel. Outside, he moved to the tub and dropped the towel, sliding down into the warm water. He watched Amy come through the sliding glass doors, a towel wrapped around her.

She stopped at the edge of the tub. "Turn around, please," she said.

"I'll cover my eyes."

"No, you'll peek. Turn around."

Tanner made an about-face, his eyes still covered, his elbows on the edge of the tub. If he had bothered to take his hands away from his face, he might have seen in the trees, just fifteen yards away, a pine bough that shook slightly.

Got to be careful, very careful. Can't afford any mistakes. He worries about bumping another bough. It is awkward trying to move carefully through the thick cover with his compound bow and arrow. Slung over his back is a tranquilizer gun, a dart in the chamber, ready to fire.

"You can turn around now," Amy said. She was in the water, her smiling face just above the bubbles.

Tanner slid down next to her. "These are the best accommodations in the valley."

"I won't argue that," Amy said. "This is *so-o-o-o* relaxing."

"I thought it might take your mind off other problems."

"Actually, it has," Amy said. "I've been thinking about it. I can't go on fighting what's happened. If I'm supposed to get back up there and collect my data, I will. If I'm not—well, there's nothing I can do."

It's time now, John Tanner, time for you to go. While she speaks, he moves in a circle through the shadows, around the perimeter of the deck, fixing an arrow to his bow. The deck railing could be a problem, but not if Tanner rises far enough up.

"I want my Ph.D. in botany in the worst way," Amy continued, "but I don't have any control over this. I'll just have to do the best I can."

"I'm glad to hear that you're not torturing yourself any longer," Tanner said. "I'm sure you'll get back up there soon. With what we've found already, they'll catch him before long."

"It sounds like you've reconciled to the fact that you can't do anymore, either."

"I hit my head awfully hard," Tanner said. "Harder than I wanted to admit at first. There's no use tempting permanent injury. It's time I backed away."

He is in position, waiting. He is ready to aim the bow. *Rise up a little, John Tanner. I need a better shot. Don't just lie there in the water, Tanner. Rise up for me!*

"This water is really warm," Amy said. "I guess I'm not used to it."

"Are you starting to get lightheaded?" Tanner asked.

"Maybe just a little."

"You can't stay in the heat for too long. You should stand up."

She smiled. "Help me up, then, would you?"

Tanner placed his hands on her hips, easing her up. Her breasts rose above the waterline. Tanner pressed himself into her as she put her arms around his neck.

Oh, Amy! What are you doing with him? You had better stop. Do you hear me, Amy? You had better stop!

Tanner kissed Amy long and hard. He turned himself partway around, leaning an elbow against the side of the tub. His lips went to her neck and down to her breasts. Amy's head went back, her lips parting in a soft moan.

Move away from her, John Tanner. She's been bad, but I'll deal with her later. You've got to move to your right just a little. I don't want the arrow going through you and into her. I can't take that chance. Move just a little, please. Hurry, please.

Tanner left Amy and swam to his towel. He reached into it. Amy saw what he held in his hand.

"You've got one that glows in the dark? Do you do this all the time?"

"No, Amy," Tanner said. "I got some today. I guess the drugstores cater to teenagers these days." He stood up in the water and began walking back to her.

He raises the bow. *Thank you, John Tanner. Hold still, please. Don't walk so fast. Stop. That's it.*

Amy stepped beside Tanner, offering to help with the condom. Tanner swung himself around so that his back was against the side of the tub. Amy straddled him, reaching her hand down into the water, guiding him into her.

He lowers the bow and clenches his fists. *You're making it hard for me, John Tanner. Look what Amy is doing! She will have to pay for this!*

Amy whispered in Tanner's ear. "John, you feel wonderful. But I'm a little uncomfortable."

"Let's move inside," Tanner suggested.

Amy left the tub first, with Tanner behind.

Very good, John Tanner. He raises his bow, beginning the draw. *Stay at that angle, please.*

Amy stepped in front of Tanner to get her towel. She moved ahead of him again. Just in front of the sliding glass doors, Tanner pulled her around and kissed her. She ran her hands up and down his back, and along his buttocks, wrapping a leg around him.

He lowers his bow. Can't take a chance. Can't hurt Amy Ellerman. She wouldn't be perfect for the offering. *You've betrayed me, Amy. I can't let that go. I'm going to have to take you from the house now. That will make things much more difficult, but I'm going to have to do it.*

Tanner closed the sliding doors. Inside, he pulled the

covers back on the bed. Amy climbed onto him, wrapping herself tightly against him in the darkness.

He stands on the deck, trying to decide how he will open the doors and take position. He has never seen the inside of Tanner's cabin. It will be a challenge to get in without being detected and kill John Tanner without a scuffle. There may need to be a scuffle. Whatever it will take to appease the Great Bear Spirit.

Inside, Amy and Tanner rolled on the bed, the sounds of their lovemaking carrying throughout the cabin. They did not hear the subtle squeak of the door sliding open and the slight thunk of the bow against the door frame.

The beeper on Tanner's nightstand went off. Tanner stopped. "I've got to radio in," he said. "There's no phone up here."

Tanner sat on the edge of the bed and took his radio from the nightstand. He called in and waited for a response.

The radio crackled, the voice on the other end using coded verbiage. Tanner stood up. "Repeat, please. It's a copy, but please repeat."

More crackling. Tanner turned to Amy, raising a thumb. "It sounds like they know who it is."

Tanner told the dispatcher that he would wait for Nate Jackson at his cabin.

He is nearly to the bedroom door, his bow ready. A few more steps and he will have a clear shot at John Tanner, standing beside his bed, but he stops himself. He has heard the transmission and knows what it means.

He stands for a moment, thinking. Everything has changed. The radio transmission has ruined his plans, all his plans. He cannot take Amy Ellerman now.

He turns for the door. Tanner will be turning the light on momentarily. He must leave. It will be best to get Amy Ellerman later. He will have to find a way.

He slides through the door and into the darkness.

Tanner found his towel and turned a lamp on. Amy sat up, her face beaming with open curiosity.

"They found some evidence that suggests who the killer is," Tanner said. "They've called a meeting right away."

"Who is the killer?" Amy asked.

"They didn't transmit that. I'll find out very soon."

Tanner's beeper went off again. He turned his radio on, speaking his call letters.

The voice from the Mammoth dispatch center came over the radio, telling Tanner that the meeting had been moved to 10 A.M. A few key personnel couldn't make it until then.

Tanner turned off the radio. "I didn't feel like talking to Jackson and Young tonight, anyway."

"That would have been inconvenient," Amy agreed. "Now, where were we?"

thirty-one

TANNER DROVE under the big stone arch at Gardiner, his mind troubled. He hadn't slept well. His dreams had been invaded once again by bear tracks—blood red and backward.

"I can't understand it," Tanner was saying to Amy. "I hear that the killer's been discovered, and I feel worse than I did before."

"Are you trying to say you don't think they found the killer, then?" Amy asked.

"I can't say that," Tanner replied. "It sounds like they have some pretty convincing evidence. That's what the meeting is for, to discuss it. Some of them want to make an arrest. Others aren't so sure."

"Can't they question him?" Amy asked.

Tanner stopped in front of Amy's apartment. "I think that's what the meeting's about. Pack some things. I'll be back right after the meeting. Then we'll go over Beartooth Pass. My great-grandfather lives in that country. I haven't seen him for a while. You'll like him."

"Does he have a hot tub?"

Tanner smiled. "It's a good thing he doesn't. He'd want to join us."

Tanner drove from the apartment to the administration building. The area was filled with cars. Though the media usually remained near the Mammoth Hot Springs Hotel, today they were all over.

Tanner shouldered his way through the press, into the front door, past throngs of security people, to the superintendent's conference room, where a number of law enforcement personnel and high-ranking officials had gathered, including a large man in a dark gray suit.

Mark Weston was a special assistant U.S. attorney from Bozeman, Montana. He had been called in to make the decision about arresting Leland Beckle.

Nate Jackson was seated next to Bill Young. Both were listening to Ron Grossman describing what kind of information he had, and how he would present it. Grossman seemed nervous and unsure of himself, something Tanner hadn't expected.

"I thought you'd want in on this, John," Jackson said. "I think we have our man. We're deciding if we have enough evidence to arrest Leland Beckle."

"So it all points to Beckle," Tanner said.

"A cleaning woman found a plastic bag under Beckle's desk," Jackson said. "It contained two fingers and Valerie Waters's picture. In addition, the investigation team found a ballpoint pen at Lake of the Woods, where Valerie Waters's body was found. The pen was personally inscribed to Beckle from his father. There was blood on the pen that matched the victim's."

"Where's Beckle now?" Tanner asked.

"Nobody can locate him anywhere," Jackson replied. "We have Jim Clark and two other rangers patrolling the cabin areas, but he hasn't showed."

"What about the cabin?" Tanner asked. "Didn't they find anything up there?"

"Nothing that really nails him."

Bill Young leaned over the table. "We're going to take

him in anyway. Any reasonable man would conclude, from
what we've found, that Leland Beckle is our murderer."

Ron Grossman was sitting quietly, poring over his notes.
He felt Tanner's eyes on him and looked up. "Do you
want to know my opinion?"

"If you'd like to give it," Tanner said. "You're studying
pretty hard."

"I've been going over Beckle's record, everything I can
find. He's got the potential to be a killer, I'll say that, but
I'm not sure in this case."

"But there's no doubt," Young argued. "We've found
enough already to convince anyone."

"It would appear that way," Grossman said. "I'll agree
that his background, to some degree, would indicate the
possibility of criminal behavior development. His parents
were divorced when he was ten, and he didn't see his father that often for four or five years. He was an only child
who took care of his mother—became the 'man of the
house' and took on a lot of responsibility.

"But he doesn't really fit the profile. I mean, I think
he's certainly capable of murder, but I believe it would be
spontaneous, not planned out. He wouldn't be that organized."

Tanner had to agree. Beckle was never that orderly. His
office and his appearance proved that. But there were a lot
of things about him that would make a person believe he
could kill.

Leland Beckle was a man liked by no one. Beckle's ir-
reverence toward women was something he had never hidden. He was Lake District Ranger, and always in the
backcountry, certainly giving him the opportunity to commit the crimes.

And there was no question that he knew bears; he had
worked with them many times. But one of them had hurt
him. Tanner wondered if maybe he had wanted to get back
at all the bears—and all the women.

"There are some other factors that make me wonder,"
Grossman continued. "There are no records of family

mental problems. His father is a powerful senator. His mother was one of the leading philanthropists in the West."

"Did you say *was*?" Tanner asked.

"She died four years ago," Grossman said. "The coroner listed the cause of death as a stroke. There was no autopsy. The body was buried on the family farm."

"Leland Beckle was the one who found her," Bill Young said. "Who's to say he didn't kill her and cover it up?"

"We would have to exhume her to find out," Grossman said. "From everything we've been able to learn, though, she had a lot of friends. Everyone who knew her says she was a charming woman."

"People lead double lives," Young argued. "You know that. You're the behavior expert, for Christ's sake."

"I'm just saying what I've learned," Grossman said. "Don't take it personally."

"And her name?" Tanner asked.

"This is the confusing part," Grossman replied. "Her name was listed as Martha Rae Miller Beckle on the death certificate. But Martha Rae was the name given to her on adoption by her foster family when she was five. It's known among her friends that her name was changed. We can't find anything to prove that, though."

"No birth certificate?" Young asked.

"None that we can find. She was born in the country. We just can't come up with one."

"What name did Beckle call her?" Tanner asked.

"There's no way to know. He doesn't even list her on his employment documents."

"So maybe he knew her by her real name," Young suggested. "Maybe they had some kind of 'thing' going."

"With Beckle, I would say that's a possibility," Grossman agreed. "But there's no way to prove it."

Mark Weston, the assistant U.S. Attorney, called for everyone's attention. He began speaking about the case and the importance of everyone's cooperation in keeping the contents of the meeting private. "What we decide will be public knowledge soon enough," he said. "We don't want Mr. Beckle taking off for Canada."

Bill Young was called on to give a summary of the investigation. He stepped to the front and used a map as he spoke, noting the location of the pit they had found and dug, and the Mary Mountain patrol cabin. He also mentioned that the killer had likely dug a new pit somewhere and that efforts were being made to locate it.

Tanner paid only partial attention; he was fighting off strange visions flooding his head.

Grossman was called to the front. He laid his notes on a podium and faced the gathering.

"I'm not sure what to say, only that I don't think we ought to say conclusively that Mr. Beckle is our man. We should watch him closely but not arrest him."

Grossman defended his position by again describing the kind of man they were looking for, addressing Beckle's similarities to the profile and what he believed to be Beckle's differences.

"Mr. Beckle's work record shows him to be quite unscheduled in his use of time," Grossman went on. "It doesn't seem to me that he could coordinate the effort it's taken to commit these crimes and go undetected."

"Maybe that's the side he wants to present to everyone," a ranger said. "Maybe he's not organized on one level and very organized on another."

"Anything's possible," Grossman said. "We can't pigeonhole guys like this. I'm just stating the reasons why I don't think we should conclude that Mr. Beckle is necessarily our man. He fits the profile in many ways; but in other, substantial, characteristics he doesn't fit."

Grossman began taking questions. He was patient, explaining in detail the mind of a serial killer to those who wanted to know, to those who thought they knew, and to those who couldn't bear the idea of someone like that working beside them on a daily basis.

Tanner looked around the room; every face was intent

and serious. Martin Linders, seated in a chair by one wall, was rubbing his chin, watching Grossman.

With Tanner on leave, Linders had been given the task, with Jackson and Young, of handling the press conferences. Tanner didn't envy him that position. The press could be very pushy.

Linders had always been shy when it came to public speaking. In fact, he had not appeared on camera. In the paper, though, Linders had been quoted as saying that there would have to be strict attention paid to detail if the killer were to be found. He had said he believed the one they were looking for had a decided advantage: there was a lot of backcountry in the park and little time to search it before the next full moon.

It had been Linders who had suggested that an investigation team return to Lake of the Woods and look for more evidence relating to the death of Valerie Jane Waters. Within an hour, the team had discovered Leland Beckle's pen. Linders was as eager as anyone to get this over with.

Tanner turned back to the front. Grossman was saying that he would continue to study Leland Beckle's background. When he sat down a series of debates ensued. At last Weston announced that there was not enough evidence to issue a warrant for Leland Beckle's arrest.

Jackson and Young stood up and joined the officials at the front. There was a lot of work to do. Grossman stayed at the table, studying his notes, running his hands through his hair.

"Maybe some rest would do you good," Tanner suggested.

Grossman looked up. "There's no time for that. I've got to keep on this until it's finished, if it ever is. We haven't much time until the next full moon. We need to find whoever's doing this before then. It could very well be Leland Beckle. Maybe he's more organized than I think he is."

"He certainly enjoys media coverage," Tanner said. "Isn't that one of their traits?"

"They like to follow the coverage, that's true,"

Grossman said. "And, yes, they often are there and help create the stories. But they never feel vulnerable. I think Mr. Beckle feels vulnerable."

"All I know is that he dislikes me a lot," Tanner said. "He resents my acquaintance with Amy Ellerman."

"I understand that Miss Ellerman had dinner with you," Grossman said. "She's being protected at all times?"

"She will continue to be with me until this is finished," Tanner said.

"I see." Grossman sorted through his notes. "We've been trying to collect the names of all blond women who work in or near the park. So far we've found nearly fifty, ten whose first names begin with *A*. It's impossible."

"He wants Amy," Tanner said.

"I'm afraid he won't be that selective this late in the month," Grossman argued. "He may feel he's lost his chance at Miss Ellerman and may want just anyone who's blond and whose name is right. He needs to escape real bad. He wants to go someplace and never come back. I hope he hasn't gotten somebody else by now."

Tanner thought about it. Grossman was right; there was no guarantee that the killer would insist on Amy. And if he had someone else, he would likely have her at the new pit site; he would certainly have prepared himself by capturing another grizzly.

"How many men are staking out the Mary Mountain patrol cabin?" Tanner asked.

"I understand that Jim Clark led a team in there last night," Grossman replied.

"It's good that someone is watching the area," Tanner said. "Jim's as good as the park can do for that. Our only real chance is to find the new pit where the killer is operating."

Grossman stood up and stuffed his notes in his briefcase. "That's the only way. I don't have a good feeling about it."

Grossman walked toward the front, to converse with

Jackson and Young and Weston. As Tanner left the room, Martin Linders stepped in beside him.

"Do you think Beckle's the killer?" he asked.

"It looks that way," Tanner said. "But I really don't know, not after hearing what Grossman had to say."

"I think we'd better cover our bases," Linders said. "You and I should go into the backcountry and find that new pit."

"Where do we start?" Tanner asked. "You, more than anybody, know how many square miles we'd have to cover. It's impossible."

"Not impossible," Linders said. "A person can get just about anything done once they put their mind to it." He turned toward the door that led into the corridor that reached his office. He stopped at the doorway and looked back at Tanner. "When you're ready, we'll go back onto Central Plateau. I'll bet we could find that new pit together. What do you say?"

"I'll be back in a couple of days," Tanner said. "We'll talk about it then."

Tanner left the building and walked to his Jeep, his mind on the backcountry. A search to find the second pit could take weeks. Linders seemed to think the impossible could happen, just because he wanted it to. There wasn't time. They would have to find the killer within three days or another young woman would surely die.

thirty-two

THE AFTERNOON was open and warm, the sky a deep blue in all directions. Tanner wound through traffic past Silver Gate and Cooke City, both crowded with campers and motor homes.

The Beartooth Highway stretched through tall pines and rolling meadows, along an alpine wilderness dotted with marshes and lakes. Blue gentians covered the hills and bottoms, mixed with the tender blossoms of marsh marigold.

Rocky peaks rose in all directions, as if the earth were but a sea of endless mountains.

"This feels like the top of the world," Amy said.

"The early Indians believed it was," Tanner said. "Some of them still do."

Tanner drove the highway patiently. Traffic was bumper to bumper in places. Campers and motor homes were strung in long, looping lines where the switchback highway rose to the top of Beartooth Pass.

Amy rolled down her window and let the breeze flow through her hair. She looked far out, to the north and east, across a panorama of rolling plains, where the Yellowstone River carved its way through sandstone rock toward its juncture with the Missouri.

From the pass, the highway dropped like a fallen rope, descending from eleven thousand feet downward to a little valley and into Red Lodge, Montana.

"This looks as if it should be a small town in the Alps," Amy commented.

"They've done a lot to make this town look that way," Tanner said. "Every summer they have the Festival of Nations, a week of food and culture from all the European countries."

After browsing a few shops, Tanner took a secondary highway that wound along the foothills, past remnants of old coal mines—sagging, weather-beaten buildings built against the hills—and along an abandoned railroad where early immigrants worked their lives away.

As they entered the tiny town of Bearcreek, Amy commented, "This is like a ghost town. I see only a few occupied houses. The rest are empty."

"There was a mine disaster here in nineteen forty-three," Tanner explained. "Seventy men died in an underground explosion. The town never recovered."

"There seems to be a pattern around here," Amy observed. "Every once in a while something terrible happens, something that stays in the history of the area forever."

"I just hope finding Beckle has put an end to it," Tanner said. "We don't need any more history like that."

Down from Bearcreek, they entered a little farming town called Belfry, filled with small, old houses, where husky German women worked in large vegetable gardens.

A short distance down the road, they came into Bridger. The streets were lined with people browsing craft booths.

"This town is named for a famous mountain man," Tanner said. "Maybe the most famous of them all. They have a celebration here every summer."

"Jim Bridger? I read about him," Amy said. "He always

brought presents to the Indians, so that he could open up friendly trade relations."

"That's true," Tanner said. "Were you thinking of getting a gift for Grandfather?"

Amy pointed. "Stop at that greenhouse up the road. I'll bet he likes strawberries."

Amy left the greenhouse with a four-pack of strawberry plants. They were flowering, and runners trailed out from under the leaves.

"He'll be impressed," Tanner said. "He'll want to keep you."

They turned off onto a gravel road that led toward the isolated and flat-topped Pryor Range. As they neared the mountains, Tanner was silent, his mind on his dreams and the image of red tracks that still lingered.

Past the Sage Creek Campground, they turned off on a narrow, winding dirt road. It led to a large draw with a small, spring-fed stream. Halfway up the draw, on a terrace covered with pine and juniper, stood a lone tepee and a small, dome-shaped lodge.

The sides of the tepee were painted with images, among them the sun, the moon, an eagle, a crow, a magpie, a buffalo, and a large bear.

"He lives out here all alone?" Amy asked.

"I have some relatives among the Crow people," Tanner said. "The women make his tepee from buffalo skins. He stays warm in winter and cool in summer. He's comfortable."

"What's the small round lodge?" Amy asked.

"It's a sweat lodge, mainly for ceremonial use. To Indian people, it's the same as a church—a place to pray and talk to the Creator."

Tanner took a twist of tobacco from a bag under his seat. He and Amy got out, holding their presents. There was no sign of anyone around.

"He may be up praying," Tanner said.

Amy pointed to a nearby hill. "Is that him?"

An old man dressed in deerskins and heavy elkskin

moccasins waved a cane overhead in greeting and made his way down a worn path.

"A-ho! It is my wayward great-grandson," he said to Tanner in Crow.

Tanner tried to remember the language. He held out the tobacco, doing his best to answer in Crow. "Grandfather, it's good to see you. It's a good day. I've brought you something."

The old man took the tobacco. "That's good, but you should work on your speech." Then he spoke in Cheyenne. "Did you bring me any pie?"

"I've forgotten how to speak Cheyenne," Tanner said in Crow.

"That will not do," the old man said in sign language. "You must keep in contact with your roots."

Tanner spoke in English. "This is my friend, Amy Ellerman."

Amy handed him the strawberry plants. "I'm glad to meet you. May I call you Grandfather?"

The old man's eyes twinkled. He spoke to Amy in English. "Yes, Grandfather would be good. Are you going to make me into a gardener?"

Amy blushed. "I'll plant them for you by your spring. They will do well on their own."

"Thank you." He nodded at Tanner. "How did you get mixed up with him?"

Amy laughed. "Bad luck, I guess."

"Terrible luck," the old man said. "Come inside and we'll have something to eat."

The tepee floor was covered with hides. The edges were folded up and a cooling breeze blew in. The walls held a variety of items, including various medicine bundles, a bow and arrows, and a shield with a bear on the front.

"Are you comfortable up here?" Amy asked.

"Very," the old man said. "I don't want for anything. This is the best way to live, out in the open, with the wind singing at your door."

"Then you've lived this way all your life?"

"Yes. I am Crow, Shoshone, Cheyenne, and Scots-Irish," he said. "That's why I have a bad temper."

"Not as bad as his," Amy said, pointing at Tanner.

"That's true. He should come up and see me more often. I would make a likable person of him. It would be hard, but I'm a persistent man. Can you make fry bread?"

Amy looked at Tanner. "Flour and water, some powdered milk, and salt," he said. He told her the proportions, and pointed to a large bag. "He keeps everything in there."

Grandfather filled a pipe with a mixture of tobacco and native herbs. He lit it and offered it to the earth and sky, and the four directions. He smoked and handed the pipe to Tanner.

While Tanner smoked with Grandfather, Amy opened the bag and pulled out sacks of flour and salt, a box of powdered milk, and a can filled with buffalo tallow. A gourd of water stood near the bag, along with a clay bowl.

A large cast-iron skillet rested near a ring of small stones just outside the door. Amy took wood from a pile near the lodge and started a fire.

Inside, Tanner and Grandfather continued to smoke.

"So, you come with a troubled mind," the old man said in Crow.

"You can tell?" Tanner said. "I thought I hid it pretty well."

"You did, but the girl didn't. What is wrong?"

"I'm working on a case where a man is killing women," Tanner said. "He's using grizzlies to do it."

"That is a bad thing," Grandfather said. "Let's go outside and walk. I don't want to talk about something like that in here. Outside, the wind will blow the words away."

"Will you be gone long?" Amy asked as they passed her.

"Hold up on the cooking," Tanner suggested. "Maybe you should plant the strawberries. I don't know when we'll be back. It could be awhile."

thirty-three

FROM THE top of the hill, Tanner could see mountains in three directions, and endless plains rolling to the darkening east. The sky was clear, except for wisps of clouds along the western horizon where the falling sun was bathing the Beartooth Wilderness in crimson.

"You have a bad life," Grandfather said as they walked. "How can things ever be good for you when all you do is chase after people who only want to kill? Kill animals, kill each other. Just kill."

"Somebody has to chase them," Tanner said. "It has to stop somewhere."

"It's like emptying the ocean with a teacup," Grandfather said. "You can never get it done."

"Would you have the earth suffer all this with no one trying to stop it?" Tanner asked. "Would it be right to let them kill all the elk for their antlers and all the bears for their gallbladders? Would you just let them go?"

"Let the Creator handle it," Grandfather said. "The earth is going to open up and swallow everyone soon, anyway. It's too late to change things. No one wants to change. So, everyone will be eaten by the earth. The earth will burp and start everything over again."

"You don't care," Tanner said. "You're too old to care."

"I care enough not to go crazy. Look at you, having bad dreams. What's going on?"

"I stayed overnight where a grizzly had killed a man and was shot. And I've been where two women were found mauled to pieces. I went into the backcountry to find the killer and he shot me full of strong drugs. I've been having some strange visions."

Grandfather pointed to a rock outcrop. "We'll sit there. You can tell me."

Tanner sat and looked across the mountains. He told about the killer who had been loose in the park and was now, he hoped, behind bars. He told of being shot with the tranquilizer gun and of his time in the hospital, the dreams of red, backward tracks and the pit where the grizzly with the man's eyes waited for him to fall in.

The old man listened attentively, nodding now and again. He lit the pipe often, sharing its contents with Tanner.

When Tanner was finished, Grandfather got up and led the way down the hill.

"Don't eat anything tonight," he told Tanner. "You can sit in the sweat lodge. At dawn, you will sweat again. Maybe you will understand some things."

"Do you know what the dreams mean?" Tanner asked.

"They are your dreams, not mine."

At the tepee, Grandfather passed Amy. "Make some fry bread for you and me. I will eat with you soon."

Tanner stood near Amy while the old man built a fire in front of the sweat lodge, singing as he placed the wood.

"What's happening?" Amy asked. "He's suddenly very serious."

"He's worried about me," Tanner said. "I told him my dreams and he wants me to sweat. It will be a good thing."

"Aren't you going to eat first?"

"I won't eat until sometime tomorrow. That's how it's done."

Tanner sat down in front of the sweat lodge. Grandfather burned dried juniper leaves in a small rock bowl and fanned the smoke toward Tanner with an eagle feather. When the ceremony was finished, Tanner stripped and entered the sweat lodge.

Grandfather, still singing, placed hot rocks in the center of the lodge with a forked stick. He sat down next to Tanner and said a prayer, then poured water over the rocks and closed the flap.

Tanner's face streamed with sweat. He was on the third round. He had lost track of time, the heat entering him and carrying him into another dimension.

He saw the strange forest with the red tracks again. From the sky came a large eagle that landed beside him and turned into an ancient warrior, with a large bow and a war shield.

The warrior's face was painted yellow and black, in the form of rings around his eyes. Along the middle of his back were two stripes, yellow and black. On the front of his shield was the image of a large bear with a humped back. The bear was also painted in yellow and black.

"The sacred bear will never die," the warrior told Tanner. "They will come and go, and they will suffer at the hands of those who do wrong, but the spirit is forever."

"What must I see?" Tanner asked.

"What you've been seeing," the warrior said. "It will come again and again until you know what it means."

Tanner found himself standing at the mouth of the pit. The grizzly with the man's eyes was glaring up at him.

The warrior, standing on the other side of the pit, tossed Tanner his shield.

"Kneel down."

"I can't do that," Tanner protested. "The bear will pull me into the pit."

"Kneel down!" the warrior commanded.

With the shield in front of him, Tanner kneeled before the pit. The bear's eyes rolled. A paw came forward but would not touch the shield.

Tanner leaned closer to the bear. It was rooted where it stood, its human eyes staring directly at him.

"You have seen those eyes, John Tanner," the warrior said. "You *know* who is inside the bear."

Tanner studied the eyes. He realized that they were very familiar to him. He had looked into those eyes before.

Grandfather poured more water over the rocks. Tanner jerked from his dream, steam rising into his face, the heat taking his breath away.

In the darkness again, Tanner thought about the eyes. They were the eyes of a man who believed he could never be stopped, who felt the wilderness was his to own and control as he saw fit.

With Grandfather praying beside him, Tanner reentered the dream. The warrior was standing next to him again. He took the shield back from Tanner.

"I think you know what to do," the warrior said. "Now go do it."

"Where do I find the man with those eyes?" Tanner asked him.

"The tracks," the warrior replied. "Your answer is in the tracks."

"What can I find in the tracks?"

"I've helped you all I can," the warrior said. "You must go on yourself from here."

The warrior drifted away, changing back again into an eagle, taking wing into the distance. As Tanner watched the bird disappear, his vision became distorted. The sky had begun to undulate, like an ocean heaving up and down.

Tanner lowered his eyes to the forest. It, too, had become distorted. He saw the red, backward tracks, painted on the trees. He saw himself following them into a dark, remote area and looking down into the pit where the bear waited, its strange human eyes staring.

The pit began to rock back and forth, bringing his stomach up into his mouth. He heaved until his insides ached, a sticky sweat pouring from every pore in his body.

When he had finished heaving, he felt his vision clearing. He realized the drugs had been fully washed from his body. He was now aware, without coming out of the dream, that more water was being poured over the rocks.

The steam rose through him, into every part of his being, cleansing as it passed. The grizzly arched its back. Its mouth opened and spewed out the figure of a man who, screaming, slid down into the darkness of the pit.

The grizzly, now appearing normal, climbed from the pit and looked back at Tanner before disappearing into the forest.

Tanner turned his eyes toward the treetops. The distorted forest became clear and normal, rising into the undulating sky, spreading itself out, entering into the vastness. All churned together in a clockwise circle, disappearing totally as a splash of cold water hit his face.

Tanner jerked awake. He wiped spittle and cold water from his face. Grandfather was singing, fanning a burning mixture of sage and sweetgrass. He took a dipper and poured more cold water over Tanner's head and shoulders.

Still singing, Grandfather rose and led Tanner out of the sweat lodge, to the spring. Tanner stood in the cool night breeze while Grandfather poured water over him from head to foot.

Tanner looked into the sky. The moon, two days from fullness, bathed the mountains in creamy white.

"Do you understand what you have seen?" Grandfather asked.

"I know," Tanner said. "I certainly know what I've seen."

"Do you know what to do?"

"I know."

"When first light comes, you will bathe again," Grandfather said. "Let's go back to the lodge. Your fine lady has prepared fry bread."

thirty-four

BEARTOOTH HIGHWAY curled upward above them, switching back and forth, rising at Beartooth Pass to over eleven thousand feet above sea level.

While Tanner drove, Amy slept, uncaring about the scenery. She was not used to spending nights in Indian tepees. Though they had gotten a late start, she couldn't keep her eyes open.

As the Jeep climbed, Tanner planned what he would do once they returned to the park. He was certain now that the killer had left markings, upside-down grizzly tracks drawn in blood.

He knew that he would find them near the locations where the women had been found. They would be on Central Plateau as well. If he found them near the Mary Mountain cabin, they would lead him to the new pit.

There was a sack of fry bread on the seat between them, along with some pemmican Grandfather had sent along. Tanner chewed, slowed down by campers and bogged traffic, anxious to get back.

Past Cooke City and Silver Gate, along the north end of

the park, through open sidehills of sage and juniper, Tanner made better time. But there was an elk jam in Lamar Canyon and another jam at Tower-Roosevelt, where a group of bighorn sheep had chosen to cross the road.

Amy had awakened. She stared out the window. "Look how the vegetation is changing," she said. "See the difference in the green shades? The plants are bleaching out. Everything will be drying up soon, getting ready for fall. I've got to get up there."

Tanner promised her he would speak to Nate Jackson. "I'll take Jim Clark and a couple of rangers with us," Tanner said. "If you can do it in a day, I think we can get the time."

"Are you sure? You weren't very positive about it before."

"They know who they're looking for now. They may have found him while we were gone. That would make it safe to go up."

Amy's smile was radiant. She began thumbing through her notebook, reviewing what data she needed to collect, making certain of her checklist.

At her apartment, she thanked Tanner and told him she would be eager to hear from him.

The administration building was in an uproar. A secretary stopped Tanner in the hall. "Nate Jackson's been trying to contact you. He's in the conference room."

Tanner walked in on a meeting: Jackson sat with Young and Grossman and the chief ranger.

"John, we've had a breakthrough," Jackson said, chewing gum furiously. "Jim Clark and the other two rangers scouting Central Plateau caught Beckle walking toward the Mary Mountain cabin less than an hour ago. He was armed with a compound bow and was carrying a sack of newspapers. They're bringing him into custody."

"That means he's the killer," Tanner said.

"I'm certain," Jackson said. "Now even Grossman, here, is starting to believe it."

Grossman shrugged. "I guess I missed some things about him. He fooled me."

Jackson put more gum into his mouth. "How's your head? Are you getting back to normal?"

"Yes, I think so," Tanner said. "I don't have headaches any longer."

"Good. I suppose you have Amy to thank for that." He grinned. The others chuckled. "Where is she?"

"In her apartment," Tanner said. "Now that Beckle is being brought in, it should be safe to take her up. She needs to finish her work right now."

"I know how important it is to her," Jackson said, "but let's wait until we have Beckle in custody—I mean, solidly behind bars and under close watch. I don't want to take any chances."

"That's a good idea," Tanner said. "Have you seen Martin Linders? He and I were going up to look for the new pit."

"He was in his office earlier," Jackson said. "He seemed pretty relieved. Maybe you two won't have to go up now."

Tanner left the conference room and crossed to the other side of the building and the Backcountry Office. Linders's desk was empty.

He found a piece of paper and left a note:

Martin—
    Guess we don't have to worry about the new pit now. Maybe all this is over.

                                        John

Tanner was careful to print the note; his handwriting often made people grimace in frustration trying to read it. He set it where Linders would be sure to see it and left.

At Amy's apartment, Tanner told her the news. She was in her bedroom, removing dried specimens from a plant press. She jumped up from her work and hugged him tightly.

"When can we leave? I mean, I'm ready. Now!"

"We'll have to wait until Beckle is safely in custody," Tanner said. "That shouldn't be long. We'll plan to go up first thing in the morning."

"I won't be able to sleep tonight."

"I'll sing you a lullaby."

"I can't believe I'm finally going to be able to go up there and finish my work," she said. "It seems almost too good to be true."

Tanner took her into his arms. "It's good to see you smiling. You look real good when you smile."

"You look pretty good yourself," she said, unbuttoning his shirt. "Real good."

Maybe it was over after all, Tanner thought. It would be good to just relax for a change and not have the case overwhelming him. Too good, actually, to believe, but he would certainly give believing it a good try. He slipped his hands under her T-shirt.

thirty-five

SENATOR HAROLD Beckle led three attorneys through the administration building and into the superintendent's conference room. As soon as the last attorney had entered, he closed the door tightly.

Leland Beckle sat near one end of the table, flanked on all sides by FBI agents and park rangers. Mark Weston, the assistant U.S. Attorney, sat at the head of the table. Jackson and Young sat opposite Beckle. Tanner sat next to Jackson, with Martin Linders next to him.

Jackson had informed Tanner early that morning that Leland Beckle had called Washington the day before, taunting Park Service authorities that his father would make fools of them all.

The chief ranger and the park superintendent, also in attendance, stared at the angry senator. Bill Young, sitting next to Weston, shared his notes with the attorney, gritting his teeth.

Senator Beckle conferred with his attorneys and announced to everyone that his son would be moving to their end of the table.

Leland Beckle got up and took a chair near his father. His eyes were pleading, his face tight, like a boy late for dinner.

"Father, I don't know what's going on here."

"Relax, Leland," the senator said in a low voice. "I'm handling this. You'll be out of here soon."

"Father, I'm sorry."

"Leland, this can wait."

Leland Beckle shrank back, like a dog sent off to bed.

The senator leaned over the table and glared at Weston. "Let's not waste any time here. I want to know the meaning of this, and I want to know it *now!*"

Weston replied cooly, "Simply put, Senator Beckle, your son is being held on suspicion of murder."

"I know that! You had better have the evidence to support it. I don't have to tell you what can happen."

"We have a lot of evidence, Senator. We—"

"You are going to be specific with me, Mr. Weston. You are going to be *very* specific."

"Listen, Senator!" Weston's voice had an edge to it, like a honed knife. "You've bullied your way around for a long time. You got your son a position in this national park. Now we've discovered a murdered woman's fingers under his desk and her blood on a pen that *you* gave him, Senator, a pen that *you* had engraved for him. We ran DNA on the blood and it matches, Senator. Now, I don't want to hear any *crap* out of you. Just listen to the facts, please."

Senator Beckle's face turned red as fire. "I'm listening."

Weston continued, the honed edge still in his voice. "There is going to be a full and detailed questioning of your son. We are going to learn from him just exactly where he was each and every minute of the day during these past months. We want to know why the fingers were under his desk and why the pen was at the scene of a crime.

"We want to know why he was carrying a sack of bloody newspapers toward Mary Mountain cabin. If you, Senator Beckle, try and stop us, we'll have you cited for obstruction of justice before you have a chance to blink. I hope you've understood what I said."

"Are you quite through?" Senator Beckle asked.

"For now," Weston said. "You have the floor."

"There is no way you are going to detain my son," the senator said. "Your evidence isn't conclusive. There is no way you can prove that the fingers or the pen left at the crime scene had anything to do with my son. You have *nothing*!"

"Can you explain the newspapers, Senator? Killers like this enjoy seeing—"

"That's no crime!" the senator yelled. "Carrying newspapers is no crime!"

"Senator, how many people do you know who carry newspapers drenched in blood, blood that matches DNA with that of the victims?"

"That doesn't mean *he* took the blood from the victims, now does it?"

Weston leaned forward. "Senator, there is evidence enough for any reasonable man to conclude he might be tied in to this."

"I'm going to decide what's *reasonable* in this case," the senator said. "There's not one piece of sustaining evidence against my son. He is going to go out of here with me today, in my custody, not yours."

"I'm afraid not, Senator," Young said.

The senator turned toward the Park Service personnel. "Let me put it this way. I'm sure you're all aware that the president is considering consolidating a number of federal agencies. It's not public knowledge yet, but there's talk of taking the best scientists from a number of agencies and forming the U.S. Biological Survey. In effect, the president is going to reduce the federal payroll significantly.

"I happen to chair the committee studying the plan. There are a lot of good scientists in this park. I'd hate to see them all get offered positions in a different agency, positions so good they can't refuse. Wouldn't you?" He looked from face to face, gloating. "I mean, there aren't enough people here as it is, and there's an awful lot of work to do."

Weston sat back in his chair, his face flushed. Tanner looked to the superintendent, who was frowning deeply.

Linders leaned over and whispered into Tanner's ear. "I think the senator is more dangerous than his son."

"You all should get back to work now and leave my son alone," the senator said. "What I'm going to do now is talk to my son in private. If you will excuse us."

Shaking, Leland Beckle rose and followed his father out of the room. The senator slammed the door behind them.

Linders leaned over to Tanner. "Do you suppose he's going to get a spanking?"

"He'll be out of here this afternoon." Tanner said. "This is liable to make us have to go up and look for the second pit."

"Oh, I got your note," Linders said. "You know, I think I know where it is."

"Where?" Tanner asked.

"The lower southeast side of the Alum Creek Burn Site."

"You were up there?"

"Not yet. I learned it from a grizzly report by some hikers. The ranger brought them to me. I asked them what they were doing back there when there were signs posted all over. They told me a friend of theirs had come across a pit with a bear in it."

"Really," Tanner said. "Did you tell Jackson?"

"Yeah, he knows. He was talking about conferring with you and the FBI, maybe going up after the meetings."

Tanner was thinking. "The lower end of the burn site? That seems like a long way from the cabin. Beckle needs that cabin."

"Why would he want to be by the cabin?" Linders asked. "I would think he'd naturally have dug the second pit a distance away this time, right about where the hiker said they found it."

"Not according to Grossman," Tanner said. "According

to the profile, Beckle needs that cabin. He needs to see his trophies, to fantasize."

"I don't know," Linders said. "I'm just going on what the hiker told me."

"Beckle should be on his way to southern Wyoming soon," Tanner said. "He'll be under surveillance in the park, and down there, I would imagine."

"You know that won't work," Linders said. "A couple of elk jams, a bison jam, he'll be loose to go where he wants. I think we ought to be waiting for him at the second pit."

"Maybe you're right," Tanner said. "When this meeting is over, I'll confer with Jackson and Young."

Linders got up. "I'll get some things done in my office, and go on ahead. I'll meet you on the old Trout Creek dump road. That's the closest way in."

"I'll see you there," Tanner said. "If we can keep track of Beckle until after the full moon has passed tonight, maybe we can save a life."

thirty-six

IN THE superintendent's office, Senator Beckle slammed his fist down on the desk. "What's this all about?"

"It's a frame-up, Father, I swear it is."

"Stand up straight, Leland. What's this about fingers, and the pen?"

"I don't know how that happened. I swear, I can't figure it. I can't."

"What were you doing in the backcountry with a sack of bloody newspapers?"

"I had a plan to try and catch the killer," Beckle said. "I could have done it."

"C'mon, Leland. This is serious."

"I *know* it's serious. Whoever's doing it is trying to set me up."

The senator began pacing. "You know, Leland, you begged and begged me to allow you to be a biologist. I always thought you were far better suited for law. But you wanted to work with bears. I got you into a good school. I got you good jobs. Now it comes to this."

"I'm sorry, Father, but it's not my fault."

"Then whose fault is it?"

Leland Beckle was close to crying. "I told you, I don't know."

"You must have some idea, if you know you're being framed."

"I've been thinking on it. Thinking hard. I can't understand it. But I'll find him. If I can get loose of these guys, I'll find who did it, who *really* did it."

"They don't have enough to keep you, son, I've looked into it." The senator's voice was low and hard. "They're going to have to let you go. When they do, I want you to promise me something."

"What, Father? I'll promise anything. What is it?"

"That you'll go home and see your mother. Visit her for a while."

"Father, she's dead. She died a number of years ago. Remember?" Beckle turned away and faced the wall.

"I *know* she's dead," the senator said. "Of course I know that. I mean, I want you to visit her grave. You haven't been there in a long time. I know you haven't."

Leland Beckle continued to face the wall, his head down. "I don't understand this. You and Mother were divorced a long time ago. Those times you took me for visits, you didn't care if I ever saw her again. What's all this?"

"I think it would be good for you, Leland. After all, she was your mother."

Leland Beckle turned to his father. "If you can get them off my back, I'll go visit her grave. Are you coming with me?"

"I'll meet you there in a couple of days. I've got some urgent business in Washington. But I'll be with you then. We'll be at the old home place. You haven't been there in a long, long time, Leland. We'll go to the grave together."

"Why?"

"Because I want some time with you, and I want to discuss the past with you. We haven't had time to do that."

"What about the present? What about now?"

"That, too. I want you to meet someone."

"Father, are you trying to set me up with a woman again? You know that doesn't work."

"Leland, you need a good wife to help you."

"Do you think I killed those women?"

"No, of course not."

"I don't believe you. I can see it in your eyes."

"Leland, for God's sake! I wouldn't think a thing like that. You're my own son."

Leland Beckle stared at his father. "I don't understand all this about Mom. Why are you pushing me to visit her grave? She was never good to me. You know that."

"Leland, I don't want to hear this."

"You know what she did to me. I tried to tell you, but you wouldn't believe me."

"That's in the past, son. You've got your future to think about. Let the past die."

"I don't want to stay at the grave long."

"We won't have to, Leland. Just a little while."

"Fifteen or twenty minutes. That's all."

"That will be enough, Leland. We'll talk then, you and I. We'll spend some time together."

"You'll get me out of this, then?"

"You're already out of it. I just have to make it official. I'll see you down home in two days. Be there."

thirty-seven

Mark Weston had decided there wasn't enough evidence to hold Leland Beckle. He had left for Bozeman, frustrated yet intent on reversing his decision should any firm evidence surface.

Young conferred with the superintendent and the chief ranger. Senator Beckle had left an hour before with his son and his attorneys. He had told the gathering that his son would be going to the family home in southern Wyoming, there to remain until the matter of the deaths in the park was cleared up.

Young had coordinated having agents stationed at various points along the route Beckle would be taking. Total surveillance would be impossible, but an effort had to be made to keep track of him. Should sufficient evidence surface for his arrest, he would then be detained.

While the others conferred, Tanner told Jackson about his talk with Linders.

"Linders told me about a second pit, with a grizzly trapped in it," he was saying. "He said that a hiker told him about it. A ranger caught them off the road and brought them to Linders. It's a good thing Jim Clark found Beckle when he did."

"Why didn't Linders tell me about this?" Jackson said. "That's important enough to interrupt the meeting."

Tanner frowned. "He said he had already told you."

"No way. I would have said something in the meeting."

"I guess you probably would have at that," Tanner said. "Linders is waiting for me on the old Trout Creek dump road. He wants to go up and stake out the pit."

"And he never told me he was planning that, either," Jackson said. "That's really not like him."

"I guess he thought I'd tell you," Tanner said.

"Maybe so, but I'm his superior, not you. We're coordinating this effort through the FBI. We don't need a lot of Lone Rangers galloping off in every direction. That's a little bit crazy. When this meeting is over, I'll radio him and get him back here."

The superintendent and chief ranger left. Young joined Jackson and Tanner, saying, "We'll hold tight. We can't do much else. The forensics people are combing every bit of evidence we have, over and over, top to bottom. Anything conclusive on Beckle and we'll have him stopped immediately. His old man has put us in a hell of a bind."

Jackson mentioned Tanner's report of a second pit.

"If you want to send some people in, go ahead," Young said. "We haven't the manpower. We're spread pretty thin right now."

Young left to coordinate with other agents on the case. Jackson and Tanner went to the dispatch center. Jackson called for Linders.

"I copy," Linders came back. "Is Tanner on his way?"

"No, we're all staying in. There are plenty of people on the case. We need you back here, Martin. Come on in. Copy?"

"Copy. I believe it's important out here. Over."

"Are you at the pit? Over."

"Negative. Waiting for Tanner. Over."

"Come on in, Martin. See me when you get here. Over and out."

Jackson handed the microphone back to the dispatcher and walked out with Tanner. "I'm going to start on that mountain of paper on my desk," he said. "Keep by your radio."

Tanner left the building and got into his Jeep. He stopped at Amy's apartment. The doorbell sounded hollow, as if ringing through empty rooms. Tanner frowned. She had been going to work in her office for a while, but she should have been back well before now.

Tanner drove back to the administration building and hurried up the steps to the Backcountry Office. A couple of summer employees were working at a computer.

"Has either of you seen Amy today?" Tanner asked.

"She took off quite a while ago," one of them said. He pointed to her desk. "She was reading a note before she left. She seemed pretty happy."

A note? Tanner walked over and picked up a piece of paper. He read:

> Amy—
>   They've decided to hold Leland Beckle. Let's go get your data. Jim Clark and another ranger are at the north end of the burn site. They'll meet you there. I've got to help with Beckle for a couple of hours. Go on up. I'll see you up there.
>
>   John

Tanner's stomach dropped. The words in the note were printed, very close to his own style. But not quite.

He walked over to Leland Beckle's desk. There was a ballpoint pen lying on a notepad, the same pad the paper had come from. He checked out the ink. It matched.

"Tell me," Tanner said to the summer employees, "have you both been in all day?" When they nodded, he asked, "Did a hiker or hikers come in here to talk with Martin Linders about a grizzly accident?"

Both employees shook their heads. One of them said, "Linders hasn't been in here since early this morning. I've been here all day."

Tanner hurried down to Jackson's office. "We don't have much time."

"What's the matter?"

"I don't suppose Martin Linders has checked in since you radioed him?"

"Come to think of it, no," Jackson said. "Why?"

Tanner handed Jackson the note. "I didn't write this. Linders did."

Jackson read the note quickly. "Jim Clark's in his office. So are the other rangers."

"And there were no hikers who reported a grizzly incident. Linders made it all up. There's no pit at the southern end. It's at the northern end of the burn. He's up there, and so is Amy."

Jackson jumped up from his chair. "Let's get Young. We've got to move fast."

thirty-eight

LELAND BECKLE was nearing the Mary Mountain patrol cabin. He had taken a different trail, by way of Nez Perce Creek, and now looked closely for anyone in the vicinity. He didn't want to be caught unawares again, as he had been by Jim Clark and the other two rangers.

He hurried through the afternoon shadows, his mind on what lay ahead. He would complete what he had set out to do, no matter what. He would show everyone who could stop this killer. He knew all along that he would be the one to do it.

He had been lucky in getting away quickly. Two agents in a brown sedan had tailed him as far as Madison Junction, where he had lost them in a bison jam. Tourists parked everywhere, all over the road, most of them moving to let him pass, then jamming the lanes again.

Then an entire herd of bison had begun crossing the road, blocking the agents. He had parked behind the Nez Perce patrol cabin, near the trailhead. The agents would certainly radio that they had lost him, but no one would find him before he had the time to catch Linders.

He neared Mary Lake, the afternoon shadows growing longer. He hurried to the cabin, his pistol drawn. No one there. He knew that he needed to reach the pit.

He had found it, the second pit, just before Jim Clark and the others had stopped him. He should have been more careful. They didn't believe him when he had told him what he was doing. "Just come in peacefully," Clark had said. "You can tell it all to the FBI."

After that, why would he tell anyone about the pit? Absolutely not. He had decided to come back up on his own—to hell with the others. He couldn't even tell his father what he was doing. He knew that his father, among everyone else, believed he was the killer.

His pistol still drawn, he passed the edge of the Alum Creek Burn Site and into Highland Hot Springs.

At the hot springs, a sound came from the trees to his right, the unmistakable sound of a grizzly's roar.

The bear had been sedated when Beckle had first found the pit. He wished he had taken his camera with him. He had gone to the cabin and had taken some of the newspapers off the wall. He had it all, everything but the killer himself, but no one had believed him.

Beckle walked slowly, his senses alert. He would show them all. He would make the headlines. Then his father would be proud of him. For once, his father would boast about him.

His picture would be everywhere—international fame! But no more thinking about reporters until he had the killer.

Beckle continued toward the pit. The roar came again.

He headed toward the bear's growls. Finally, through the timber, along a narrow trail, Beckle found them, the markings on the trees—upside-down bear tracks drawn in blood.

He had seen them before, when he had found the pit. He had known they were Native American symbols. But they were upside down, the tracks leading backward.

Beckle laughed to himself: did this killer think he was

a contrary warrior? Not a chance! This killer was no match for someone who really knew shamanism.

Beckle followed the tracks, taking his time. The killer had to be close by, preparing for the coming evening.

The growling grew louder. A little farther Beckle stopped and stared down into the pit at the huge grizzly.

The bear was tearing at the sides, pulling soil into the bottom. It roared up at him, froth drooling in a long trail down its front.

He studied the paint marks on the bear. Nicely done, meaningful. But the mission would never be completed.

Beckle stared. His mind filled with newspaper articles. Pictures! Phone interviews! TV cameras everywhere!

"You and I are going to make the news," Beckle told the grizzly. "We'll be heroes."

"Best drop the gun, Mr. Beckle."

Martin Linders's voice.

Beckle froze. He couldn't turn around. Linders had the point of an arrow in his ear. It was so sharp it was drawing blood.

"I've been expecting you, Leland, hero of the world." Linders held his bow at full draw, the arrow tip slicing Beckle's ear. "Did you hear what I said? Drop the gun."

Beckle complied. The pistol hit at his feet, bouncing to the lip of the pit.

Linders laughed and stepped back, the compound bow still drawn, his muscles bulging. "Always after the head-lines, aren't we? When are you going to learn, Beckle?"

Beckle smiled. "I always believed it was you."

"Why didn't you say something? Were you afraid it wouldn't be you who got the credit? Stupid, stupid, Leland. Now it's too late. Too bad."

"I've heard you say it before, Linders. It's never too late."

"Oh, but it is for you," Linders said.

"Are you going to push me into the pit?" Beckle asked.

Linders grunted. "I'm not going to taint this evening with the likes of you. I've got a special surprise waiting."

Beckle looked down at the grizzly, digging methodically. There was a pile of soil collecting on the far side of the pit at his feet.

"He'll be getting out before long," Beckle said.

"He'll be sleeping soon," Linders said. "Just like you."

"You can't kill another bear, Linders."

"I haven't killed any, yet."

"You've been responsible for two already."

"You're just babbling, Beckle. You've made a fool of yourself to everyone. Tell me, how did you lose your pen at Lake of the Woods?"

Beckle stared at Linders, his stomach tightening. He could see a wildness in Linders's eyes, a craziness that he had never seen in the office.

"What did you do, Beckle, pick up the fingers and then start writing with your pen? Taking silly notes?"

Beckle's fear began to turn to anger.

"What happened, silly Leland? Did you get so excited about the fingers that you lost your pen and forgot all about it? You wanted the fingers for your own little cache of evidence, didn't you? All kinds of headlines, you thought, didn't you? Silly, stupid Leland."

Beckle's jaw muscles bulged with anger.

"And what was all that with the bag of papers?" Linders continued. "And the bow? Don't you think the investigation team would have taken those things had they wanted them? They left them because they didn't want to disturb anything at the cabin. Then you come along and make a case against yourself. What kind of idiocy was that?"

"I was taking that stuff down for evidence," Beckle said. "Your fingerprints were all over that stuff."

"Are you sure, silly Leland? Maybe I wore gloves."

"You're not today."

"This is the final day, Leland. I don't need gloves, silly, stupid Leland."

Beckle lunged suddenly, knocking the bow upward; the arrow flew high into the air, becoming lost in the blue overhead.

Linders, startled at Beckle's sudden quickness, fell backward with the charge. Quickly, both men were up, their eyes on Beckle's pistol at the edge of the pit.

Both dove for the pistol at the same time. It slid off, landing at the grizzly's feet.

The grizzly turned from its digging. The two men were scrambling for position, yelling, pounding one another with their fists. Linders, with his incredible strength, quickly gained the advantage.

Beckle's head hung over the edge, Linders choking him. The grizzly came over and reached up, clawing a furrow through Beckle's scalp.

Linders pulled Beckle's head back by the hair, flipping blood everywhere. "No, no, Medicine Heart!" Linders yelled to the bear. "You cannot take this scum down there. You cannot contaminate the pit."

Still holding Beckle by the hair, Linders slammed a fist into his throat. Beckle gasped and choked.

Linders bent down into Beckle's face. "You're not falling in there! I won't let you ruin this night. You won't do it. I'll see to it!"

Beckle was still gasping for air. He lay on the ground, unable to rise. Linders tied a rope around his feet and began to drag him through the forest.

"I've got a place for you, a good place for you."

Linders pulled Beckle into the middle of Highland Hot Springs. He jerked Beckle by the head and neck to the edge of a steaming pool. "I'll bet you're thirsty after your long walk up here. How about a drink?"

Linders dunked Beckle's face in the boiling water. Beckle tried to jerk out, but Linders was too strong.

"Drink! Don't be bashful," Linders said.

Linders pulled Beckle's head up. Beckle's face was a deep red, steaming from the heat.

Beckle let out a scream, high and primal, so loud it scared birds from the trees in every direction.

"You know," Linders said, "I've heard mud is good for burns. Why don't we try that?"

Linders dragged Beckle to a bubbling mudpot and pushed his face in. Beckle tried to fight, then finally passed out.

Linders pulled Beckle's head from the mud and turned him over. His face was coated with brown, bubbling liquid. His breath was so shallow Linders thought he was dead.

"Go talk to the newspapers now," Linders said as he turned to leave. He laughed. "You should make for an interesting photo."

thirty-nine

AMY STAKED down one end of a hundred-foot rope, knotted at five-foot intervals, and laid the remainder out in a straight line. She tightened the line and staked the free end down. This would be her third transit, and she was in a hurry to get started.

She laid the Daubenmire frame down at the first knot and began listing the plant species within the 20×50-cm iron rectangle, detailing the percentage of canopy coverage for each plant. The small geraniums were everywhere.

Despite the positive progression of her work, though, Amy was becoming worried.

She had reached the north end of the burn site by midafternoon but found no Jim Clark or other rangers. She had thought perhaps they were busy elsewhere and would be along shortly. So she had begun her work. There was a lot to do and she knew she'd never finish in one afternoon.

After taking numerous photographs and running one transit, she had become totally immersed in her work. The area was filled with *Geranium bicknellii* and she had gotten a lot of samples. Her plant press was bulging with specimens. But still no rangers. And John Tanner had yet to arrive.

As she continued to read the third transit, Amy's concern grew. Something didn't feel right. She looked around her. The area was quiet, almost too quiet. She had heard birds during the afternoon. Now she heard none.

She laid the Daubenmire frame in place for her fourth plot reading. She began marking plants down on her chart, again estimating the canopy cover occupied by each species.

As she started to move the frame, a shadow appeared over her left shoulder—the shadow of a man.

Startled, Amy jumped. She turned and looked up. Martin Linders was grinning, holding a tranquilizer rifle in his right hand.

"Hello, Amy," he said. "How's your work going?"

"Mr. Linders. What are you doing here?"

"I belong up here, Amy. So do you."

Amy stood up, holding the Daubenmire frame. "I don't understand what you mean."

"I think you do, Amy." He pointed into the trees at the edge of the burn site. "We're going over there. You can get started. I'll be right behind you."

"What's this all about?" Amy asked.

"Oh, Amy, I shouldn't have to tell you." He lifted the gun. "Just walk ahead of me, please."

"There are going to be rangers here very soon," Amy said, "including John Tanner."

"No, no, my Amy. They won't know where we are. They'll be looking in the wrong place."

"I don't think so."

"Oh, yes, they will. Besides, we need to talk about your behavior with John Tanner."

"My behavior?"

"Amy, you've been bad. You'll have to pay for that. I saw you with him. Yes, you know. Up at his cabin."

"What, you were there?"

"I'm everywhere, Amy. Everywhere." He lifted the barrel toward her face. "Walk ahead of me, please. We haven't much time."

Amy started to walk, clenching her Daubenmire frame tightly. She felt faint, but she forced herself to remain calm. Her life was on the line here.

"Where are you taking me?" she asked.

"It's a special place. You will meet the Great Bear Spirit."

"I'll meet who?"

"Don't worry about it."

Amy turned quickly, swinging the Daubenmire frame toward his face. Linders was waiting. He grabbed the frame and wrenched it from her grasp, as if grabbing a toy from a child. He grinned.

"I knew you would try that, Amy. Quite predictable. I could see it in your eyes." He nudged her with the barrel. "Walk ahead, now. We're wasting time with this foolishness."

Amy walked ahead of him, through a series of bubbling, steaming geysers. Just behind, close on her heels, Linders began a strange chanting.

"Ho-ah-umm. Mmmnn-ho-ah-umm."

Amy turned suddenly. "Don't do that!"

Linders was taken aback. "What?"

"I told you to stop that," Amy said. "I don't want to have to tell you again."

Linders frowned. "Oh, don't yell. Listen, don't yell. You can't interrupt this, I'm telling you."

"I don't want you to do this," Amy said. She tried to keep her voice from quavering. "Do you understand? I don't want this."

Linders lifted the tranquilizer gun. "Oh, I'm going to have to make you sleep, I guess. I'm going to have to make you sleep. I was hoping I wouldn't, but—"

"No, you don't have to make me sleep," Amy said. "I will say no more. You can sing. That's something I wish you would do. I want you to sing."

"It's for you," Linders said. "It's for me. Go ahead, now, please."

Amy began walking. Linders began chanting again. She saw his eyes close and his head fall back, his voice raised to the sky.

Amy turned suddenly and snatched the Daubenmire frame from his grasp. She swung it as hard as she could into his crotch.

Linders partially blocked the blow with his forearm, but the corner of the frame slammed home.

Linders slumped to his knees, yelling oaths, but he wasn't hurt badly enough to stay down, and began struggling to his feet.

Amy turned and ran into the forest, as hard and as fast as she could. She knew her only chance was to get into the open, to stay in the burn area, so that someone would find her.

But she didn't know the way.

Disoriented, she turned a full circle, then another half, and resumed running. Shadows filled the endless forest. Steam rising from the geysers thickened the falling darkness, forming shapes and images that seemed to jump at her from the shadows.

Helplessly lost, she fought her way over deadfall timber, wandering through a haze of hopelessness. She fought to keep from panicking, telling herself, "I'm going to make it! I know I am!"

She had to keep going, no matter how badly her lungs hurt, for each time she stopped, she could hear his heavy breathing behind her, coming closer and closer.

Amy stopped. She saw a clearing just ahead through the trees. She was nearly to the burn area.

As she started to run, Amy caught her foot on the limb of a fallen tree and fell onto her stomach. The wind whooshed from her lungs.

She could hear him catching up to her, his boots thumping on the forest floor, cracking twigs and small branches.

She pushed herself up, seeing him stop near a tree just behind her, bringing the tranquilizer gun to his shoulder.

Amy rolled back. The dart stuck in the tree trunk, missing her by inches. She jumped to her feet and began running again.

Linders came after her, cursing. He wouldn't have time to reload another dart, not if he wanted to catch her.

He reached into his shirt pocket as he ran for her, his hand clenching a new dart tightly as he jumped a piece of deadfall timber.

"I carry more than one dart, Amy," he yelled. "I'm prepared for you."

In desperation, Amy turned and ran back toward the shadows. If she could gain some ground, she could hide. She had to do something, anything, to escape him.

Again she stumbled and fell. She jerked back in alarm.

She had fallen next to a man's feet. Leland Beckle, his face half covered with mud, was standing behind a pine, holding a large limb.

"Get out of the way," he told Amy. "Hurry! Get out of the way."

Amy scrambled aside as Linders ran past the tree. Beckle swung the limb a fraction too late, missing Linders by inches.

Surprised, Linders turned. Beckle swung the limb again. Linders raised the tranquilizer gun. The limb shattered the stock.

Cursing, Linders threw the shattered stock away and came at Beckle, blocking a blow and pulling the limb from his grasp. Beckle sank to the ground and tried to ward off the blows as Linders pounded him with the limb until it shattered.

Amy found a piece of the broken stock, but Linders had already turned toward her.

"Stay back for just a moment, please. Then I'll have time for you."

Beckle was trying to rise. Linders fell upon him and took another tranquilizer dart from his pocket. "This ought to do you," he said, ramming the needle deep into Beckle's neck.

Linders was up in a flash, rushing toward Amy. He grabbed her by the arm, a smile on his face.

"I've got one more dart left," he said. "I don't want to put it into your neck. Do you want me to?"

"No," Amy said. "Don't do it."

"Come along then," Linders said. "We have to hurry. See, over there? Look, the moon is rising!"

forty

JOHN TANNER sat in the helicopter, flying ahead of a huge full moon rising, studying the aerial photos of Mary Mountain. Nate Jackson sat beside him, chewing gum furiously.

Jim Clark and two rangers sat on the other side, awaiting orders.

They crossed the burn area, taking a second pass over the north end. Young and five FBI agents had been let out in the middle of the burn. They were covering the area, looking for signs of Amy and the new pit.

Below, Tanner spotted Amy's plant press and other items, but no Amy.

"He must have her," Tanner said. "We've got to get down there."

Jackson radioed Young; everyone would converge on the north end of the burn site.

"She'll be dead before long," Tanner said. "It's my fault. Put me down."

"It's not your fault. We'll all go in together."

"We don't have time! Nate, please, I can find her."

Jackson chewed gum as he thought. "If I let you down, you keep in radio contact. Don't do anything rash."

"I'll stay in touch," Tanner promised. He pointed. "Put me down over there."

Tanner was out of the helicopter and on the run before it had set fully down. He hurried into the timber, his pistol drawn.

Night shadows had already fallen. The sun, below the horizon, had left a broad glow of red in the west. The light wouldn't last long.

Tanner worked to settle himself. He had to be calm if he was going to feel the forest and allow himself to read the signs. Grandfather had always told him that a warrior had to be calm as well as strong. "One without the other is no good. You cannot gain honors if you don't listen to the inner voice."

Tanner took a series of deep breaths. The air was still, filled with rising steam. The forest floor was covered with pine needles and other mulch. He must walk fast but silently.

He found a trail leading toward Highland Hot Springs. A little farther, just off the trail, he found what he had been looking for.

The red, upside-down track was nearly seven feet from the ground, painted on the trunk of a large pine. Some fifteen feet on was another track on another tree. To Tanner it signaled the beginning of the trail into the second pit.

He radioed Jackson. Young and his men were closing in from the south. Jackson would take the rangers and come in through the timber on the north end.

Tanner hurried, the fear of the dream now turned to confidence. He found tracks on the trees every fifteen to twenty feet, a trail marked very clearly for one who knew what to look for.

Tanner moved very cautiously. Linders could be waiting, could have set a trap. He stopped and listened, moved forward a little, stopped and listened. This time, he vowed, he would find Linders before Linders found him.

forty-one

AMY TREMBLED while Linders tied her to a tree at the edge of the pit. She looked around the forest, where the shadows were deepening. Where was John Tanner? Didn't anyone wonder where she was?

Amy looked down into the pit, a huge grave twelve feet square by ten feet deep. One side had been raked loose. Earth had tumbled into the bottom, making a mound at least three feet high.

Lying across the mound was a huge grizzly. It was painted down the back and around the eyes in yellow and black. One paw was moving slightly.

"Sleeping, sleeping," Linders said, holding a lantern down so she could see him better. "His name is Medicine Heart, and he is dreaming. Dreaming of the spirits within him, the spirits that I will soon take from him and possess within me. Power will come to me, Amy."

Her head suddenly filled with visions of the women who had died before her. She felt she would vomit; no one could help her now.

Two ropes, one black and one yellow, hung down to the

bottom of the pit from a large limb overhead. The black rope swung free from the limb. The yellow rope was run through a block and tackle, ending in a noose that Linders placed around her neck.

Linders set the lantern down. "There are things to do before we go down, Amy, dear Amy. . . . Mother."

The area was set up for his full-moon events. He had placed a grizzly skull at the north end of the pit, with a heart-shaped rock, painted red, resting inside its mouth. There were rocks set in a line to look like arms on two sides of the pit, and rocks forming two legs at the south side of the pit.

A grizzly cape hung from the broken limb of a nearby pine.

Two video cameras were in place, tilted to film the action in the pit. A 35mm camera with flash attachment lay next to a bearskin rug, where a large rock rested. Eyes and an open mouth had been painted on one side.

Linders pointed to the rock. "My mother's head will rest there soon. She has never left me, dear Amy. It is important that you know this, for you are so much like her, yes, so very much like her. But soon you will be gone, as will dear Mother. I will have your spirit, and hers. This is the final day."

Linders took the grizzly cape from the tree limb and draped it over him. He began to chant. *"Ho-ah-umm. Mmmnn-ho-ah-umm."* He drew black and yellow lines on his face, and circles around his eyes. *"Aiee-ah-umm. Mmmnn-ho-ah-umm."*

Overhead, a helicopter sounded from somewhere nearby.

Amy looked up. Darkness was falling. She could hear the helicopter but couldn't see it.

"Help me!" she screamed. "I'm down here! Help me!"

Linders was painting his face, rocking to and fro, chanting.

"Aiee-ah-umm. Mmmnn-ho-ah-umm."

Amy stared into the heavens. "Help me! Pleeease!" *If only they would pass overhead, just once!*

Linders stopped his chanting and rose to his feet. He faced her, frowning through the paint.

"You cannot be reverent about this, can you, Mother? You were never reverent."

"It's not real, Linders!" Amy yelled. She had nothing to lose. "This is crazy!"

"You don't understand. No one understands. Look into the pit and see him. You are going to meet him, dear Mother."

Amy stared at Linders, her stomach turning to jelly. He took a yellow cloth from under the cape and gagged her, then blindfolded her with a black cloth.

"You must not speak while I prepare you," Linders said. "And you can no longer look upon me until the time is right."

Amy tried to struggle, but her bonds would not give. She could no longer see anything, could no longer talk. He laughed at her muffled cries.

"Soon Medicine Heart will have your spirit, Mother. And then I will make him sleep forever. His spirit will rise, with all the other spirits within him. I will eat his heart, and his brain. The spirits will all join with me. I will have the spirits within me then. And yours, my dear mother."

Linders released Amy from the tree and quickly tied her wrists behind her. He lengthened the noose and slid it down past her bound wrists, then secured it under her arms, tightening it in the middle of her back.

He pushed her out over the pit.

Her screams muffled, Amy swung back and forth as Linders lowered her down. She felt her feet hit the sides and then the bottom. She fell back onto the soil, gasping.

Her world was black and disoriented, but she knew that the grizzly was right beside her. She could hear its breath, heavy, in deep sleep.

Linders lowered himself on the black rope, carrying the lantern. He pulled Amy over and untied her hands.

"She has come, Medicine Heart. She will touch you. She will touch me. She will understand that we are all to join together."

Amy found she couldn't pull back, no matter how hard she tried. He took her hands, forcing her to touch the grizzly's massive head, running her fingers through the thick hair, chanting, squeezing her fingers closed around the long claws, pushing her hands into the grizzly's mouth, raking them along the heavy, exposed teeth.

Then he brought her hands to his own face and made her feel his hair, his shoulders, his stomach . . .

Linders forced her hands back to the grizzly's head. "Touch the eyes, Mother. Feel the eyes."

Amy tried to hold back. Linders pulled her forward. The eyeballs were spongy. He held her fingertips there, each finger separately, on each eye.

He moved her fingers to his own eyes, wet, spongy. She felt herself gagging.

He removed her blindfold. "Can you see, Mother? Medicine Heart is me! I am Medicine Heart! Can you see?"

Amy blinked, her sight coming back. Linders was chanting again, touching the grizzly. He tied her hands again. She made muffled sounds to him.

"No, it is not time yet for you to speak, Mother. Soon."

Linders got up and pushed Amy back against the side of the pit. The rope bit hard under her arms. He picked up the lantern. With one hand, he pulled himself out. At the top, he turned and looked down.

"I will return, Mother, dear Mother. Wait for me."

forty-two

MARTIN LINDERS, wearing the grizzly head and cape, chanted as he made his way to his special place. It was away from the cabin, away from the trail. It was secluded. It had to be away from everything.

He hadn't been to this place since the first day he had begun his mission; he couldn't come, not until the final day.

Now the final day had come. It was nearly complete: the full moon coming up over the trees, the darkness nearly total. Soon he would rejoice.

He came to the place and danced a circle around it. All was ready. He knelt down, holding grizzly claws, and began digging. Chanting, digging, stopping to look at the moon, chanting, digging. Soon it was visible—the face gray and shriveled, the eyes open and dull.

His mother's spirit dwelled here, within the head. Soon he would suck it out.

After the grizzly had killed Amy, after he had killed the grizzly, he would have the power. He would destroy his mother's spirit and send it away forever.

He continued to dig, chanting, looking at the moon, chanting. The head became looser, looser in the soil. He wedged the claws under and pulled it free.

Holding it before him, chanting, dancing, looking at the moon, he worked his way back toward the pit. So close was he to completing his mission, so close.

He stopped. Though the pit was not yet in sight, he knew something was wrong. He could hear the grizzly roaring. It had come awake! Too soon! It had come awake too soon!

Holding the head like a football, Linders broke into a run toward the pit. He must get there in time to place the head correctly.

Then he must watch. He must not miss the consumption of Amy's spirit by the grizzly. He must see it leave her. He must be there!

forty-three

THE GRIZZLY was beginning to recover, growling, tossing its head around. Amy, already in a far corner, began to strain against her bonds.

The rope attached to the block and tackle would give only a little, no matter how hard she strained. She was trapped.

Growling louder, the grizzly began to move, raking one paw through the soil, trying to pull himself up. His head lifted, fell, lifted again, fell. His head came up a fourth time, and the grizzly roared.

Amy's muffled screams reached only the grizzly. It rose up on its front legs, working to bring its back legs underneath itself.

The grizzly came to all fours, wobbled, and fell sideways.

Amy strained against the bonds with all her might. Her wrists burned like fire, hot blood running down into the palms of her hands.

The grizzly rose again, gaining all four feet. Its mouth

opened, exposing huge teeth. Amy remembered how solid they had felt to the touch.

The grizzly started toward her, wobbling slightly. He came partially up on his back legs, lost his balance, and fell forward, his mouth at Amy's feet.

The grizzly's mouth opened. Amy, trapped in the corner, couldn't move in either direction. The bear started to rise again and Amy closed her eyes.

John Tanner had heard the growling. Running headlong, his pistol out, he had expected to encounter Martin Linders.

But Linders was nowhere near.

Tanner grabbed the yellow rope. Overhead, Amy heard the sound of the block and tackle. She looked up to see who was pulling her out.

Tanner, fighting to catch his breath, strained to bring her over the edge of the pit.

The grizzly, now up on its feet, swung wildly at her as she kicked herself over the top.

Tanner pulled the gag from her mouth and cut the ropes that held her.

"John, thank God," Amy gasped. "Look out! Look out behind you!"

Linders dropped the head and flipped the grizzly cape from his back. He picked up his bow and loosed an arrow. Tanner rolled sideways with Amy, the arrow caroming off a rock and into the trunk of a pine.

Tanner was up before Linders could rearm the bow, hitting him with a flying tackle, knocking him backward, flipping the bow from his grasp. The two rolled, kicking and punching, each trying to gain advantage over the other.

In the pit, the grizzly had recovered fully, and now it reached to pull itself out of the pit, a huge paw coming up over the top. But the bear could not pull himself over and began digging again, building the mound in the bottom higher.

Tanner and Linders fought near the edge, Tanner trying to lock Linders's arms behind his back. He couldn't afford to have Linders hit him solidly with a blow to the jaw or head.

But Linders was strong, very strong. Linders pulled free of the arm lock and grabbed Tanner by the hair, jerking him to the ground.

Amy was at the pine, working to pull the arrow free, twisting, breaking the shaft. She could not break the metal head off in the trunk. She had to work carefully.

Linders swung for Tanner's throat. Tanner blocked it with a forearm and slammed an elbow into Linders's stomach. Hard as rock, Linders gave only slightly under the blow. He lifted Tanner as if he were a small boy.

In the pit, the grizzly was growling, digging, growling, pulling huge clumps of dirt from along the side, building the mound ever higher.

Linders tried to ram Tanner's head into the ground. Tanner turned before impact, taking the blow on his shoulder and back, turning, twisting, kicking Linders under the arm, and then in the middle of his solar plexus.

The air whooshed from Linders's chest. He groaned and slumped forward. Tanner, back on his feet, slammed a fist into Linders's jaw. The socket gave. Linders whined like something wild, his voice high and sustained. He rose, swinging, the blow catching Tanner along the side of the head.

Tanner staggered. His head exploded in pain. He sank to his knees. Linders was up. He swung again and Tanner pitched forward.

Amy screamed. She was so close to getting the arrow free.

Linders reached the bear cape and put it on, fitting the grizzly claws to his hands. Chanting, he started toward Tanner.

Amy pulled the arrow free and rushed toward Linders.

Behind them, the grizzly reached huge paws over the pit and struggled to pull itself up over the top.

Emerging from the perimeter, Jackson, Young and his agents, Jim Clark and the rangers, all with guns drawn, took position. No one had a clear shot.

Linders raised the claws to strike. Tanner rolled sideways. Amy drove the arrow into Linders, between the second and third ribs on the left side. Linders yelled and doubled over, then rose again, coming at Amy.

Amy saw the grizzly and started up a tree. Tanner struggled to his feet and fell away from the area as the grizzly roared and rose to all fours, facing Linders.

Linders stretched out his claw-covered hands and mimicked the grizzly's roar. He turned a circle, chanting. The grizzly dropped to all fours and charged. Bullets poured from the guns along the perimeter.

Now screaming, Linders fell under the grizzly as the bear tore chunks of flesh from his face and shoulder. Linders tried to push free, but the grizzly lifted him like a sack.

Bullets poured from the perimeter. The grizzly slumped, still tearing ferociously. Linders's neck was chewed to ribbons, his head loose, as on a swivel.

Linders slumped in death under the grizzly as the grizzly fell dead atop Linders.

Tanner came to his feet and helped Amy down from the tree. Jackson was on his radio. After the crackling radio died out, everyone stood silent for a time, the moon now fully overhead.

forty-four

PAPERBOYS FILLED the parking lot, waving copies, yelling the news. The presses had been running steadily since word had gotten out.

Tanner was tired of press conferences, tired of telling the same story, hearing the same questions over and over. Reporters had even settled around his cabin, until he had blocked off the roadway with NO TRESPASSING signs.

No relatives had stepped forward to claim Martin Linders. He had been buried quietly, in an unmarked grave, by the state of Wyoming, in a remote corner of a small-town cemetery.

Not even the city officials had known about it. No one but the FBI ever would.

Tanner and Amy Ellerman had graced the covers of *People*, *Life*, and two in-flight magazines. Additionally, Amy had found her way to *Cosmopolitan* and *Woman's World*, always with a smile, her hands filled with *Geranium bicknellii* or a Daubenmire frame.

Readers had been fascinated by her accounts of the pit and the last few hours of Martin Linders's life. Amy had expected that to be the focus of the stories, but she had still been disappointed that no one really cared about the botany.

After the initial headlines about Linders, the focus turned to Leland Beckle's disappearance. No body, nor parts of a body, had been found. No trace of him existed, beyond a set of tracks that led from Highland Hot Springs into thick lodgepole timber, there becoming hopelessly lost in the rocks along the divide.

His father had come back, roaring and yelling. Young and Jackson had taken the senator into the backcountry. The senator had searched and searched, calling his son's name at the top of his lungs. There had been no answer. He had sobbed for an entire afternoon.

Life in the park resumed a more normal pattern. Nate Jackson was able to reduce his chewing gum budget. He took to drinking herb tea and tried the Mexican eggs-and-peppers dish Tanner had offered, even admitting that he liked it.

As Amy's time in Yellowstone came to an end, she and Tanner made a trip into the backcountry. By now the hill-sides had seen heavy frost, and the bears were busy foraging for the winter.

The burn area held only small wisps of dried geraniums. Amy was glad she could look around without shuddering. She hadn't known if she could, or if she had ever wanted to see the place again.

The Mary Mountain patrol cabin stood alone and empty again, the smell of stain remover strong on the wind. They looked inside but didn't linger. The past now seemed light-years ago.

"The world keeps on turning," Tanner said, pointing out a chipmunk, its cheeks loaded with seeds. "You can't tell by looking that anything terrible ever happened up here."

"I'd just as soon forget it, myself," Amy said. "I won't, ever, but I wish I could."

"Think about it this way," Tanner suggested. "Because

of it, you've got so many job offers you don't know which one to take."

"I have to finish my thesis first," Amy said. "That's what I have to do. I won't worry about anything until that's over."

"You mean you haven't thought about where you want to work? There's a herbarium job open at Montana State University. I don't know about the pay, but you can't beat the scenery."

"I've already applied," Amy said.

Tanner smiled. "They won't want you hanging out in the geranium section, though. There are other important plants in the ecosystem."

Tanner and Amy started back down the trail, talking about the future, the certainties and the uncertainties. Meanwhile, in a patch of heavy timber just above the burn site, a lone man watched them as they walked and talked.

His face, beginning to heal from the burns, would be more scarred than before.

He had no desire to come down from the vastness, to ever be a part of society again. He had tried that once, and it hadn't worked. Now he would live in a different way.

The man sat and gazed far out across the vast wilderness toward Yellowstone Lake and remembered the night when a huge bear lumbered along the shoreline, headed for a private party. With him in charge, that night would have never happened. The bear would never have gotten free.

He thinks about this and ponders some ideas, while all around him the forest is very still and very quiet.

BESTSELLERS FROM TOR

☐ 51195-6 BREAKFAST AT WIMBLEDON $3.99
               Jack Bickham   Canada $4.99

☐ 52497-7 CRITICAL MASS $5.99
               David Hagberg   Canada $6.99

☐ 85202-9 ELVISSEY $12.95
               Jack Womack   Canada $16.95

☐ 51612-5 FALLEN IDOLS $4.99
               Ralph Arnote   Canada $5.99

☐ 51716-4 THE FOREVER KING $5.99
               Molly Cochran & Warren Murphy   Canada $6.99

☐ 50743-6 PEOPLE OF THE RIVER $5.99
               Michael Gear & Kathleen O'Neal Gear   Canada $6.99

☐ 51198-0 PREY $5.99
               Ken Goddard   Canada $6.99

☐ 50735-5 THE TRIKON DECEPTION $5.99
               Ben Bova & Bill Pogue   Canada $6.99

Buy them at your local bookstore or use this handy coupon:
Clip and mail this page with your order.

Publishers Book and Audio Mailing Service
P.O. Box 120159, Staten Island, NY 10312-0004

Please send me the book(s) I have checked above. I am enclosing $ _____
Please add $1.25 for the first book, and $.25 for each additional book to cover postage and handling.
Send check or money order only—no CODs.)

Name _____
Address _____
City _____ State/Zip _____
Please allow six weeks for delivery. Prices subject to change without notice.